BULLETS AND SILVER

BULLETS AND SILVER

NIK JAMES

THORNDIKE PRESS
A part of Gale, a Cengage Company

LIBRARY OF CONGRESS CIP DATA ON FILE.
CATALOGUING IN PUBLICATION FOR THIS BOOK
IS AVAILABLE FROM THE LIBRARY OF CONGRESS.

ISBN-13: 978-1-4328-9111-4 (hardcover alk. paper)

Published in 2022 by arrangement with Sourcebooks, LLC.

Printed in Mexico
Print Number: 01   Print Year: 2022

To Cyrus and Sam
No parent could be prouder

CHAPTER ONE

Elkhorn, Colorado, June 1878

Caleb Marlowe stepped out into the glaring
midday sun as two men, locked in battle,
rolled under some nervous horses tied
beside the wooden sidewalk.

Each man, wild-eyed and disheveled, held
a knife in one hand and the wrist of his foe
in the other. Kicking and straining for some
advantage, their ferocity was unflagging.
Dirt and filth from the street covered their
faces and torn clothes. Blood streamed from
their noses and mouths and from cuts on
arms and hands.

Between the spot where Caleb stood and
the Belle Saloon a few doors up, a small
crowd of drunken miners followed the fight.
Forming a moving line of spectators, they
shouted curses at the combatants and egged
them on. Wagers on the outcome were being exchanged.

Right then, across Elkhorn's Main Street,

a deputy emerged from the jail. He cast one look at the fight and the growing crowd of spectators, then skulked off down the street in the opposite direction. If any shooting started, he clearly didn't want to be anywhere nearby.

The fighters rolled toward the middle of the street, joined now by a barking street dog biting at booted ankles and torn woolen trousers.

Caleb was waiting for the brass band and vendors to appear with beer and apples and meat pies.

He thought about getting involved but immediately dismissed the idea. He was no longer a lawman, and he was not about to wade into a fight to the death between two fools whose battle quite possibly stemmed from something as important as a jostled elbow and a spilled drop of brandy. He'd seen it plenty of times before. He'd see it again.

The sound of a gunshot down the street drew Caleb's eye for a moment. The noon stage was leaving.

When he glanced back, the fighters were on their feet and circling warily, their knives flashing in the sun. One said something. The other nodded. The dog walked off, bored. They both lowered their hands and backed away. It was over — for now — and the crowd began to jeer disapprovingly before turning to wend its way back through wagons and horses toward the Belle.

As the drinkers went back to their bottles and the card players back to their games, Caleb's eyes were drawn to heavy clouds of black smoke rising in the distance beyond the jumbled line of buildings. There were dozens of mining claims being worked in the rugged landscape up there, but the smoke was coming from the jagged scar of a logging cut. The operation was doing its best to carve up the green spruce forest that ran up to the craggy ridges to the north. Elkhorn was growing, and it needed lumber.

The Wells Fargo stagecoach racketed past, heading east out of town toward Denver and raising dust in the bustling street. The driver cracked his whip and shouted curses at miners and drifters, riders and carters, women and children, and anyone else in his path.

Caleb was getting tired of waiting, and he ran his gaze along the street. It seemed like every time he came into Elkhorn, there were more buildings, more people, more fights, more noise. From where he stood, he counted five new buildings under construction along Main Street alone. The sounds of saws and hammering could be heard coming from the closest one — another hotel.

As he watched, two barefoot youngsters, no more than ten years old, raced across the street carrying scraps of wood they'd nicked from the building site. Shouts from the builders followed them as they weaved between wagons and carts and horses and disappeared into an alley across the way.

Caleb pulled off his wide-brimmed black hat and combed his fingers through his sandy-brown hair before putting it back on. He didn't like hanging around town. The usual restlessness was gnawing at him. It was the same feeling he got every time he spent too much time in a crowd.

Right now, he'd like nothing better than to go collect his horse, leave the congested streets behind him, and ride back to the quiet, open space of his fledgling ranch. He had a great many things to do there. He still hadn't had time to hang the damn door on the cabin he was building. He had to check on the new calves. Finish fencing off the small pasture for the bull. Build the barn. Attend to a dozen other chores.

But besides all that, Caleb didn't like waiting on anyone.

He glanced at the sign above his head. H. D. PATTERSON, JUSTICE OF THE PEACE. The very man who was keeping him here.

In smaller letters, the sign read, LAND AND MINE SALES, SIDE DOOR. Caleb had no doubt there was a line of men standing around the corner right now, waiting to hand over their money in exchange for the hope of sudden wealth in the silver-rich hills around the town.

The wooden boards beneath his feet shook in warning as the front door swung open, and Horace D. Patterson himself appeared.

"Marlowe, sorry to keep you waiting." The judge nodded to the hulking bodyguard on his heels. "Fredericks here seemed to think you'd already be halfway to your ranch. I told him that was nonsense. You agreed to share a meal with me."

At the notion of "Frissy" Fredericks thinking anything at all, Caleb had to bite back a comment. He glanced up at the small, black eyes that glittered like pieces of coal in the blotchy, white pig face. Not a friendly look.

Caleb had little choice in the matter, though. He couldn't afford to alienate the judge. His partner's release from the county jail in Denver still rested on the man's goodwill . . . and his influence with the governor.

Patterson gestured down the street, and Caleb walked beside him. Frissy stumped along behind.

"I thought we'd try out the dining room in the new hotel down on this side of Main Street," the judge said. "The cook worked in the kitchens of no less a place than the Gardner House Hotel in Chicago. And now he's right here in Elkhorn."

Caleb didn't give a hoot where the cook came from, whether it was Chicago or Timbuktu. Beef was beef, and before the year was out, he'd be the one supplying it.

Patterson broke into his thoughts. "Not that I think that would impress you, Marlowe. But it's one more thing that makes me proud of the direction Elkhorn is heading."

Two well-dressed young women approached them, and the men stood aside to let them pass.

"Good day, Judge."

"Good day to you, ladies." He tipped his hat to them.

The women — all bonnets, ruffles, and kid gloves — had their eyes on Caleb as they passed. One was wearing a plum-colored dress with black buttons the size of twenty-dollar gold pieces. The other wore pale blue trimmed with enough dark cord to truss a gaggle of geese.

As they continued along, the judge told

him, "Those two run the reception committee planning the solar eclipse events."

Caleb had been wondering how long it would be before the judge brought up the eclipse again. The event was to occur at the end of July, and Elkhorn was reported to be a prime location for seeing it.

"I have no doubt our festivities — parade, formal reception, and assembly — will outshine any show the governor puts on in Denver." Patterson paused and motioned back to where they'd come from. "I'll put the viewing stand right on the street in front of my office. Bunting and all."

As they reached the next corner, an explosive detonated beyond the western end of town. Miners. Caleb didn't think twice about it. At his ranch, he heard the blasts echoing along the ridges all the time.

Frissy, however, seizing on the chance to do his job, bulled past Caleb, leaving in his wake the smell of brandy and tobacco.

His employer waved him off. "Just some dynamiting at the mining works, Fredericks. Nothing to be alarmed about."

They crossed the street, and three pillars of the community exchanged greetings with the judge. Caleb recognized one of them as the president of the Elkhorn Bank and another as the manager of the Wells Fargo

Overland office. He didn't know the third man.

"Gentlemen," Patterson said, pausing for only a moment. "I'd like you to come to my office at four o'clock. I received a letter from the governor this morning."

Horace D. Patterson was a man of importance, and everyone knew it. He owned Elkhorn. And what he didn't care to own, he still controlled. Of medium height, he had a solid build and graying hair beneath his bowler that gave him an air of respectability. He was clean-shaven, but sported long, thick side whiskers. On the rare occasion that he stood still, he liked to slip one hand — Napoleon-like — inside the silver-gray waistcoat he wore beneath his charcoal suit. Caleb had seen a sculpture of the old tyrant in his office.

Across Main Street, a crowd was spilling out of the open doors of one of the many saloons and gathering in the street. From the center of the throng, three shots cracked in the air, accompanied by some wild whooping. A miner was celebrating some good fortune. He was staggering a little and waving a fistful of paper money in one hand and brandishing his smoking six-shooter in the other. He fired two more in the air. The last one took a chunk of wood off the mold-

14

ing at the top of the saloon's facade.

"Blast him!" Patterson exploded. "Is this the kind of behavior our visitors need to be seeing next month?"

He made a quick gesture with his hand to Frissy, who turned and whistled shrilly to a man slouched against the streetlamp at the corner. The lone surviving deputy after the recent debacle with the town's last sheriff. Getting the message, the deputy spat out the twig hanging from his lips and trotted toward the disturbance.

"This is exactly why I've been harping in your ear, Marlowe. This town needs a firm hand to guide it toward civilization. Your hand."

"You got a sheriff. Zeke will do just fine."

At Caleb's suggestion, the judge had given the badge to Zeke Vernon after the last sheriff and his rogue band came to a fitting end only ten days ago. As a miner with a nearly pinched-out claim, Zeke had already been working for Patterson when the need arose. He was no quick draw, but he was a good man. Solid as a rock and dependable as an old dog.

A curtain moved in one of the rooms above the saloon, catching Caleb's eye. As the window started to open, he instinctively unfastened the thongs over the hammers of

15

his twin Colts. A blond head emerged from the window. It was one of the women who worked the tables downstairs, looking to see what the shooting was about.

"Looks like you got everything under control, Judge." Caleb nodded toward the disturbance. The deputy had pushed to the center of the crowd, and the exuberant miner promptly holstered his pistol and pointed toward the saloon.

"Zeke Vernon is a good man, but he lacks experience," Patterson persisted. "He'll need help. Consider it a temporary position, if you must."

Watching the crowd break up and make its way back into the saloon, Caleb thought about being stuck in Elkhorn, jailing drunkards and breaking up street fights. He'd done this kind of job before, and he'd told himself, never again.

"I got a ranch to run, Judge." He tapped the elk-skin vest over his brown wool shirt. "I don't need to wear no tin star to raise cattle."

Patterson took hold of his arm and steered him along the sidewalk. He wasn't a man to take no for an answer.

"It's only six weeks until our most important visitors begin to arrive. The number of people here in Elkhorn could double or

16

even triple between now and then. The hotels will be full, and the saloons will be packed with men of all kinds. Without you to keep order, trouble could ruin our city's reputation at a critical juncture in our . . ."

The man continued to talk, but Caleb stopped listening.

He'd taken a deputy's badge for the judge last month and done what was needed. He'd left his ranch and gone up into the wilderness beyond Devil's Claw. He'd hunted down the outlaws holding up the Wells Fargo stagecoaches. He had fulfilled his end of the bargain. He didn't owe the judge a thing. It was the other way around now, and that was the way he liked it.

Like river mist on a summer morning, all sounds and thoughts of the discussion disappeared, burned off by the prickling sensation down the back of Caleb's neck. He sensed trouble, and his instincts were rarely wrong.

On the far side of an alleyway ahead of them, a boy tapping a stick on a hitching post stopped short, his eyes widening as he caught sight of something or someone around the corner of the building, just out of Caleb's line of vision.

A moment later, the gleaming muzzle of a pistol appeared. Then, the brown brim of a stovepipe hat and the eye of a gunman.

It was an ambush.

CHAPTER TWO

The gunhawk swung quickly and smoothly around the corner, the Remington in his left hand cocked and ready. Beneath the tall hat — battered and worn — his hard, dark eyes fixed on his target. The killer wore a dusty, black bandana around his neck, half-hidden by the long bush of a beard; a brown wool coat over a black-and-gray checked vest; light-brown pants tucked into worn boots. As he moved into the open, another Remington appeared in his right hand, coming up quickly.

The judge was still talking, unaware that destiny was taking deadly aim.

It was one of those times when the blood fired up and everything slowed down. The light and shadows and colors and sounds became sharp and crisp as an autumn morning.

Lightning didn't strike as fast as Caleb's draw. The twin Colts leapt into his hands, and he slammed his shoulder into the older man, sending Patterson tumbling into a line of barrels in front of the general store.

The Remington in the outlaw's left hand spit fire, and the air moved with a *thup* sound an inch from Caleb's ear. It was a bullet that would have caught the judge right between the eyes.

But the shooter's target had moved, and his gaze flicked toward the cause of the miss.

Caleb's face would be the last thing he saw in this life.

The Colts barked in rapid succession, like a drummer's roll on a battle march. The first bullet struck the man square in the chest; the second knocked his head back. As he dropped to his knees, his hand convulsed — the Remington fired a shot into the wooden sidewalk a foot in front of him. Blood trickled from the hole in the attacker's forehead. His dark eyes rolled upward, and he collapsed onto his side.

The judge had landed on a keg, where he sat with his back against the wall of the store. Frissy's Colt looked like a toy in his massive hand, and he was scowling in the direction of the dead assailant.

Caleb's eyes raked across the walkway and the street and back to where they'd come from, looking for more gunmen. In his experience, ambushers rarely worked alone.

In the street and all around him, everyone was standing still, staring, unable to make their brains comprehend what was happening.

It was like a moment from his youth.

When the war between the North and the South was still raging, a traveling troupe of players came to the place where Caleb grew up. They were going from one Indiana town to another, performing *Uncle Tom's Cabin.* All afternoon, actors in costume had been circulating, putting on bits of the play to promote the evening performance. A large hay wagon had been pulled onto the town green as a makeshift stage. Canvas backdrops hung from tall poles.

When the show began, torches and lamps illuminated everything. Then, just as Eliza, clutching her baby, was leaping to freedom in Indiana across ice flows in the Ohio River, four masked riders thundered down Front Street, reining in at the edge of the assembled crowd.

The world stood still. The actors remained frozen on the stage. When the intruders began firing their guns above the audience — mostly women and children and old folk — chaos ensued. People scattered in panic, running and screaming. The actors leapt from the stage, disappearing into the darkness.

In exactly the same way, everyone in Elkhorn's Main Street stood frozen in place. Only the agitated horses up and down the block were moving. When two more bullets cracked and thudded into the storefront behind Caleb, the street exploded with shouts and cries and people running for cover.

It took only an instant for his eyes to locate the gunman. He was the sole person not moving.

The judge saw him too. "Don't kill him!" he barked. "I want that blackguard alive!"

Caleb felt like a duck in a barrel. Too many innocent lives stood in the way, but he had to stop the man. Fredericks dove toward his employer, and his huge frame banged against Caleb, jarring him as he passed.

A few inches over six feet, Caleb was nearly two hundred pounds. He was not a man to be moved easily, but Frissy had a good sixty pounds on him. The bodyguard's momentum drove him three feet along the sidewalk, but Caleb fired as he moved, sending the pistoleer spinning into the dirt. He squirmed and then lay still.

A window next to the judge shattered.

A third killer had been trailing them, but his gunning days were nearly over. Frissy fired, and his bullet struck home. The assailant dropped his pistol and clutched the spreading circle of crimson high on his chest. With a surprised look on his face, he gasped once and went down like a felled pine, his head hitting the sidewalk boards with a resounding bang.

Three attackers. Three dead.

Caleb pouched one of his Colts and leapt down into the street. His gaze swept the crowd for more of them. He raced toward the downed man. The attacker hadn't moved, and his revolver lay far from his reach, but he wanted to make sure.

Before he could get to the man, though, two more shots rang out from somewhere across the way. They weren't done.

Without breaking stride, Caleb scanned the dozens of windows for the shooter. A pistol barked as a puff of dirt rose just to his right. He spotted where it came from. A smoking muzzle was sticking out of a second floor window above the oldest saloon in Elkhorn. Almost directly across.

He fired twice at the window, shattering the pane, and the gun disappeared. Caleb ran hard, scanning the street constantly. There was no telling if there were more of these dogs waiting for their chance.

Behind him, the judge's shouts rang out. He wanted the man alive.

When Caleb reached the far side, he vaulted up onto the walkway. The old saloon had two large windows facing the street, and they were crowded with the grizzled, wide-eyed visages of men peering out.

Damn. No way to know who was friend and who was foe.

Drawing his other Colt, Caleb burst through the saloon's open door, spinning and pointing his six-shooters at the onlookers as he backed into the center of the brandy-hole.

The bar was a shabby, smoky, dismal place, thrown up when the rest of Elkhorn consisted mainly of tents and lean-tos. A counter about eight feet long ran along the right side of the dark room. Two rows of empty tables lined up haphazardly on the left. They were filled with cards and half-empty glasses. Chairs were pushed back or tipped over.

Miners and saddle slickers at the front windows stood gaping at him.

More shots were exchanged between the street and the upstairs window.

"Drop the irons." He wasn't taking any chances. "Now!"

The men complied, hurriedly unbuckling gun belts and laying weapons on the floor.

Caleb glanced at the barman — a balding, bearded Irishman wearing an ancient, green vest over a dingy, collarless shirt. The man wiped his hands on the filthy apron tied around his waist and raised them quickly as he nodded at a set of stairs by the back wall.

"Got a gun?" Caleb barked.

The saloon keeper nodded.

"Show it."

Without taking his eyes off Caleb, he cautiously pulled a short-barreled Parker coach gun from under the counter, holding it away from his body.

"Keep them fellas covered. I don't want nobody shooting me in the back. Any one of them makes a move for their rod, blast them."

Relief showing on his face, the barman nodded and pointed the shotgun at his customers.

Caleb glanced at the stairs that led to a second floor. "Is there another way out?"

"The back door and the window at the top of the stair. It ain't a big drop off the porch there." The saloon keeper shrugged. "But we woulda heard boots above."

The sound of shooting subsided, but that

only meant the fella upstairs would be reloaded and ready for him.

Caleb moved to the bottom of the stairs and cast a quick look up. The unpainted wood wall of the hallway gave no clue as to what was waiting at the top. From where he stood, he could see the back window was open, but only a little. That meant the gunman was still there, and he had to know Caleb was coming for him.

He put himself in the man's position. The odds of escaping were getting shorter by the minute. The only thing to do was to shoot his way out. His best chance was to wait, take Caleb out as soon as he had a clear shot, then hightail it out the back way.

And the judge wanted this bushwhacker alive? That'd be a damned tall order.

At the bottom of the stairs, he reloaded his Colts. After pouching one, he started up as quietly as he could manage.

The stairway was low and narrow, and Caleb's broad shoulders filled the space. If this snake appeared at the top and started blasting, he'd have a hard time missing. When Caleb was halfway up, the sound of crunching glass reached him. He judged the gunman was still in the front room. Caleb paused on the top step with his back to the wall.

He glanced at the window, half expecting to see a shooter standing on the porch roof outside, drawing a bead on him. Nothing.

Caleb pulled off his hat and held it out beyond the corner for a second, but it drew no fire. He threw a quick look along the upstairs hallway.

Three doors opened onto the empty, dimly lit corridor. Two on the left were open. The door to the front room facing him at the end was shut.

He eased himself up the last step and moved stealthily down the hall, glancing into each room as he passed. Every nerve in his body was alert, every muscle taut. There wasn't a sound coming from the barroom below or from the street. Every soul in creation was listening.

He kept his eye on the door to the front room. The killer was in there, poised and quiet as a cougar on the hunt.

Caleb knew how quick his own reflexes were, and his aim was as deadly as anyone's. But in the split second after he opened the door, he'd need to find that knothead and somehow wing him. No matter what the judge wanted, he didn't plan to take a bullet himself.

When he reached the door to the front room, he kicked it open, splintering the wood around the latch. The smoky air reeked with the smell of sulfur.

A slug hit the jamb, burying itself in the wood with a bang.

Caleb dropped down on one knee, leaned forward, and fired twice into the room before quickly pulling back.

He caught only a partial glimpse of the assassin. Over by the window, he was barricaded behind a chest of drawers with a mattress thrown over the top.

That brief look was enough for the gunman, though.

"Damn me," the man chirped. "It *is* you, ain't it?"

It wasn't a question.

"Caleb," came the voice again. "Caleb Starr!"

Damn it to hell.

CHAPTER THREE

"Caleb Starr! This damn world gets smaller all the time."

Caleb peered into the room, and his stomach clenched.

Bat Davis. The name leapt from the past.

The faces of some folks never changed. Bat Davis had the same whitish cast in one eye and the same ears that stuck out like sails on a river scow. It had been thirteen years since he'd looked at that face, and it was one he had no desire to see now.

"Caleb, I *never* thought I'd see you again."

Bat was standing up, his six-shooter pointed not at Caleb but only in the general direction of the door. He had a grin pasted across his stupid face, and he looked like he was genuinely happy to find Caleb here.

"Damn me, but I heard you run clear to Mexico to get free of the law. What you doing here?"

Caleb was a few years older than him, but

this ghost from the past knew the truth that he'd worked hard to keep buried since he ran off. Bat knew everything about the first decade and half of his life. He knew about the crime that drove Caleb to the anonymity of the open road and the frontier.

For thirteen years, Caleb had been telling folks that he was born under a rock and raised by wolves, but that was no good now. Cold sweat beaded up along his spine.

Since the last time he saw Bat, a lot of hard miles had separated him from Indiana. For three years, Caleb drifted along a road filled with more trouble than he'd ever expected. It was a time of dark deeds, dark companions, and a savage fight to survive every day. It was a journey that nearly killed him.

Nearly.

Then, one winter day over a decade ago, Jacob Bell — mountain man, trapper, wilderness guide, legend — found a half-frozen nineteen-year-old on the snowy bank of the Keya Paha River up in the Dakota Territory. Beaten, robbed, and left for dead, Caleb had reached the end of the line.

But he didn't die on that riverbank. The old man picked him up, thawed him out, and tucked him under his wing. Old Jake showed him how to make a man of himself.

In the six years that followed, the two of them crossed the frontier from the Missouri to the Wind River, and from the Bighorn Mountains to the Calabasas.

And when he finally told the old scout the truth about his past — of what he'd done — it had been Jake's suggestion that Caleb Starr become Caleb Marlowe.

"Don't matter what I'm doing here," he said coolly. "Why don't you put that gun down nice and easy? Then we'll talk."

"So, you're on the side of the law now? After what you done?" Bat scoffed, still waving his pistol in Caleb's direction. "Don't recall hearing nothing about you paying your dues, as the man likes to say."

What did Bat Davis know about the dues he'd paid?

Caleb had spent years serving what folks back East thought of as civilization. Alongside Old Jake, he'd made a name for himself exploring and opening the frontier to homesteaders pushing ever westward. He'd blazed trails to the Montana gold fields. Even the army sought him out, conscripting him for his skills as a scout to take Indian lands for use by white settlers. When he was through with that, he'd somehow found himself wearing a badge up north.

Caleb had paid plenty of dues — all for a

crime he felt not one twinge of guilt about committing. Hell, he'd do it again.

And for all these years, not once had he come close to being found out . . . until today.

"Lay your iron down now."

"Shit, man," Bat wheedled, acting like he hadn't heard. "I can't see you settling here, pretending you're part of this. Don't try to tell me you done opened up a shop along this street. I won't believe it. Even when you was a kid, you never fit into no *follow the rules, go quietly along* thing. I know that. I looked up to you."

He was not about to admit it to this knothead, but there was a lot of truth in what Bat was saying.

For his whole life, Caleb had felt . . . apart from things. On the fringes of "decent" folks. Looking on, crouched in the shadows beyond the light and warmth of the fire. Never getting more than a whiff of the shared meal simmering in the pot.

He was a loner by choice. After leaving Indiana, he'd chosen his path. Towns and cities were not for him. He was drawn to the open spaces of the frontier. It was out in the wilderness, beyond the corrupt laws of corrupt men, that Caleb could follow his own code of right and wrong.

32

And now, here he was, holding a gun on a man from his past, a fella who could put a noose around his neck.

"I can't let you do no more shooting, Bat. Too many innocent folk on the street could get hurt."

"I got to admit, I came here intending for *somebody* to get hurt." He glanced out the window beside him. "But it wasn't nobody innocent. And it wasn't you neither."

Bat stretched his shoulders and moved his gun to his free hand. He tugged down on the black wool vest he wore over a checked brown-and-white shirt. He'd shed a light-colored duster that lay in the corner with a dusty blue derby. His brown hair was slicked down, and he looked like he spent more time drinking at card tables than he did in the saddle.

His attitude was as breezy as if they were standing around jawing about the price of beans in China, but Caleb wasn't about to be gulled. Bat still had the same eye and acted like the same jughead, but he was far different from the young fella Caleb remembered.

The boy he'd known had grown up to be a killer. The Remington in his hand could spit fire at any moment. And Caleb had no intention of getting hurt.

He kept an eye on the weapon. He didn't particularly want to kill this ghost from his childhood, but Bat Davis presented a serious problem.

This was a new kind of life for Caleb. When his friend Henry Jordan suggested buying land for a ranch, Elkhorn was still so new that a man could make a life that was his own. It felt right in many ways: putting down roots, building a cabin, raising cattle, maybe even scratching some silver out of the hills. It was a stable kind of life he'd never known.

Now, he stood to lose it. Not just for himself, but for Henry too.

Caleb shifted uneasily in the doorway, feeling the knot tightening around his throat, not liking it one damned bit.

"You know, when I took this job, Caleb, I had no idea I'd be running into an old friend."

Friend? The way he remembered it, Bat had been more of a thorn in his side. His boyish hero worship never really seemed to be real, considering how he was constantly telling on Caleb and getting him into trouble. He was an annoying brat who never failed to snitch for any misdeed. And then he'd stand by and watch with obvious enjoyment while Caleb took a beating from his father.

They were definitely not friends. But this was not a point he wanted to bring up right now.

"It's mighty quiet out there in the street. Your Judge Patterson must put a lot of faith in you."

Caleb shook his head. "He ain't my Judge Patterson."

"Well, that's just fine, then." Bat cocked his head. " 'Cuz if that's the case, why don't you let me walk right out that door so I can finish the job I was sent here to do?"

"That ain't about to happen. Them fellas you're riding with are all dead. You're the last one."

"So you're a hired gun backing the law now?"

"Never mind what I do."

The muzzle of the Remington floated a little closer toward Caleb, but Bat's finger was relaxed on the trigger.

"You was always smart as a whip, Caleb, so you must know that shady sonovabitch of a judge deserves to die." He took another quick look toward the window.

Every time he turned his head, it was another chance to finish him. Caleb felt his finger tightening on the trigger.

A bullet between the eyes would solve a

lot of problems. For him. For Henry and the future of the ranch. Regardless of what the judge said about keeping this one alive, he'd still owe Caleb for saving his life.

Damn, he cursed inwardly. A man had the right to protect himself, but how far did that right go? He was no murderer.

"I'll make a deal with you," Caleb said. "The judge will wanna know who hired you to take him out. You tell me who sent you, and I'll let you go right out the back way."

"Who sent me?" Bat laughed out loud. He waved his pistol toward the window. "Never mind what this damn judge wants to know. Brother, I'd think *you* would wanna know who sent me."

"Why would I care who — ?"

Before he could finish, a shot rang out. Bat's body lurched sideways, and he hit the floor like a bag of rocks.

"Damn."

Caleb holstered his pistol and moved quickly to the window. Zeke Vernon stood in the middle of Main Street, looking like a hairy, gray boar in a stovepipe hat. His smoking Winchester was still pressed to his shoulder.

Caleb waved the man off and then crouched next to Bat, who was lying on his side and shivering.

The bullet had struck him in the back, a few inches below the left shoulder blade. It had traveled upward at a sharp angle and ripped a good-sized hole where it exited by his right collarbone. The blood was pumping from the wound onto the floor, and the crimson pool was spreading.

He rolled the man onto his back, knowing there wasn't much Doc Burnett or anyone else could do for him.

"Caleb," Bat gasped. "Feels like a hot poker run through me."

"Save your breath."

"Ain't it funny . . ." His face clenched with pain.

He coughed up blood, and flecks of it fell on his lips and chin. His left hand clutched at Caleb, taking hold of his vest. He was trying to say something, but his time was running out.

"Never believed him . . ."

"Never believed who?"

Bat's face twitched once and then relaxed. The light faded in his eyes. As he breathed out one last time, blood pulsed from the corner of his mouth and tracked across his cheek.

The sound of boots thundering up the stairs preceded the appearance of the deputy who'd steered the celebrating miner back into the saloon earlier.

"Dead?" he asked, breathing heavily.

Caleb nodded.

The deputy frowned and holstered his pistol.

"I would have wagered a week's pay old Zeke couldn't make that shot," the man said, going to the window and looking down at the street.

Caleb rose to his feet, gazing down at the fella he'd known forever. Maybe not the way he should have died, but men often choose the way they die by the way they live.

"The judge is waiting to talk to you. One of them gunslicks down there is alive. They already sent for Doc."

As Caleb started for the door, he thought about Bat's last words: *Never believed him . . .*

Believed who? What was he talking about?

Stepping out, he wondered if the wounded man in the street might also be someone from his past.

CHAPTER FOUR

South of Bonedale, Colorado

Elijah Starr reined in his horse on the rise overlooking the Caswell farmhouse. Off to his right, the Roaring River shimmered like some heathen snake god in the midday light. Stretching off into the narrow valley to the east sat the curving brown furrows of the fields, no doubt newly planted with potatoes and corn the farmer took such inordinate pride in growing. The damp smell of the freshly turned fields hung in the warming air.

Here in the higher elevations of Colorado, the seasons ran later than they did back in Indiana. Back there, the clods who worked the fields would be finished with the first haying. And in the cornfields, green shoots would already stand more than a foot high, waiting for the plague of locusts to destroy everything.

Elijah couldn't understand why Cain's

descendants took such great pride in their farming. Things didn't turn out too well for him.

And they wouldn't for Caswell either.

It was God's plan that the white man should serve as the rightful steward of His creation. To do that, the railroads needed to open this pagan land. *I am the voice of one calling in the wilderness, 'Make straight the way for the Lord.'* Only a sinner would stand in the way of His plan. And Elijah, as his servant, would strike down those sinners.

He wouldn't admit it to his men, but he'd looked forward to coming down here himself. This was the last property the company needed to complete the branch line from the mining region around Aspen northward to the Blue River. There it would join the main line that would eventually stretch from the terminal in Denver all the way through Salt Lake City to Reno. The railroad was going to be built. And this fool Caswell had pushed Elijah's patience to the bitter end.

There was no sign of the farmer in the fields. Smoke curled from the chimney of the gray wood-frame house. A number of aspens clustered around one corner of the building, and a mature orchard of fruit trees extended out beyond a chicken coop. It was the very picture of domestic bliss. Elijah envisioned Caswell sitting right now at the kitchen table, his wife serving up the noon meal, a child riding on her hip.

Enjoy that meal, he thought, for the contented, prideful life you're enjoying at my expense is about to change.

The sun was growing warmer, and he removed a glove and ran a finger under the edge of the patch he wore over his right eye. Or rather, what had been his eye before a rebel ball had taken it. There was a time when the patch annoyed him, but not so much now. He removed his stovepipe hat.

As he wiped the beads of sweat from his face, Elijah's fingers skimmed over the mass of scarred flesh that marked the left cheekbone all the way to the ear. That other remnant of his past still caused his blood to rise. Because of it, he couldn't grow the full beard favored by his employer and by the other men of business in the East.

It was his cross to bear, but *vengeance is mine, sayeth the Lord.* Someday.

Shaking off the thought, he jammed his hat back on and looked at the large barn and the sheds and outbuildings that formed the heart of the farm. His tracks would run directly through the house, take out the corner of the barn, and continue on to the

41

railbeds that had already been laid to the south.

Elijah turned in his saddle. His prune-faced secretary and the half dozen men he'd brought along were a pack of hounds awaiting their master's command. The guns holstered at their waists and the rifles in the scabbards lent them an air of real and imminent menace.

Beyond them, Elijah could see smoke from the construction camp rising above the line of ridges and hills. As he often did, he'd ridden out from his base office in Bonedale and inspected the work. Not two miles north of here, his crews were ready to push onto Caswell's land. From this point, the terrain was flat enough to complete the rail into the gold fields ahead of schedule.

They'd made good time with this project, and if the director deigned to come through on his planned trip West, he'd surely be pleased. Elijah had given his word that the entire line would be operational by the first of September. He was going to make it. And no potato farmer was going to stop him.

With a gesture to the men, he dug his heels into the sides of his chestnut stallion.

They were not halfway across the field when the farmer emerged from his house and strode toward them. He was hatless and carrying a shotgun. As they drew closer, Elijah realized he'd never seen the man in the flesh. But he was exactly as he pictured him. A dirt farmer who wasn't worth the worn-out boots on his feet.

"That's far enough," Caswell barked, raising the barrel of the gun. "Who are you?"

Elijah had no time for lies or pleasantries. His people had done enough talking with this pissant. He reined in about fifteen feet from the farmer, and the others formed a line to his right and left. "Your last chance."

"Told them before. Git."

"You're not hearing me. You're selling."

Caswell peered up at him. "I don't know who you think you are, but you ain't telling me what to do on my own land."

"I *am* telling you. You're leaving."

Caswell's wife appeared on the porch of the farmhouse a hundred yards away. Two boys, one taller than the other, clung to each side of her apron. She carried a third one in her arms.

"Who in tarnation are you?" the farmer asked.

"I'm Elijah Starr."

"Don't give a damn about a name. Say your business."

"I am putting the rail line through here."

"Well, you're not." The fool was running

the muzzle of that shotgun up and down the line of men like he thought it was a Gatling gun. "I seen that sour-faced clerk enough, and there ain't nothing more to talk about. You done all the jabbering and threatening and lawing that I can stand. So turn around and get off my land. I ain't selling."

"We're done talking."

"This is my family's land. My grandpappy bought this land from Chief Ouray hisself," Caswell continued, wound up and foaming at the mouth. "And no two-bit four-flusher with a dang patch over his eye is gonna drive me off. So you git. This is yer last warning."

A breeze had begun to pick up out of the west, and the scent of sage wafted in. It was quiet out here, except for the low murmur of the distant river.

"Do you know the Bible, Caswell?"

The man frowned. "What's that got to do with my land?"

"Proverbs. 'Pride goeth before destruction, and a haughty spirit before a fall.'"

Elijah drew his Remington from his holster and took aim for the center of the farmer's chest. Caswell had no chance. The bullet struck home, and he dropped to his knees before falling flat on his face. There was a ragged, bloody hole the size of a fist on the back of his shirt, between the straps of his worn suspenders. His shotgun lay in the dirt beneath his body. He twitched only once.

The wife screamed like a banshee from the porch. Still clutching her child, she left the older two and stumbled toward them, wailing as she ran.

For a moment, Elijah considered dealing with the woman himself. He frowned and decided against it. He had more important things to do.

Holstering his pistol, he turned to his secretary. "Take her back to the house. Explain to her that her husband threatened to kill me. Give her five hundred dollars, and have her sign the bill of sale. If she hesitates at all, shoot the older boy. She doesn't sign, kill the other two. Go."

The secretary and one of the other riders rode forward to head the woman off before she reached the body.

Elijah Starr yanked the head of his horse around and rode back across the field. He'd give his construction foreman orders to proceed immediately. Tomorrow, they would pull down that house and barn. A very satisfactory transaction.

And the way was made straight.

He looked out at the Roaring River as he

cantered along. He'd be back in Bonedale in time for an early dinner.

CHAPTER FIVE

"What happened up there?"

Zeke Vernon met Caleb at the bottom of the stairs. Built like a battery mortar with whiskers, the former miner was short, solid, and as wide as he was tall. He was also as explosive as the old artillery gun. He wore gray wool — jacket, waistcoat, and pants. Since becoming sheriff, he'd acquired a new pair of black boots that shone even in the murky light of the saloon. They went with his new stovepipe hat. He was holding his Winchester in one hand.

"He's dead."

"When I saw you come to the window, I figured as much."

"You didn't have to shoot. I could have handled it."

"I know that," Zeke blurted. He leaned his rifle against the wall and wiped his hands on his coat and pants. "Ain't no doubt in my mind that you could handle everything.

There's no better gun in Elkhorn."

The saloon customers had mostly returned to their tables. The room was quiet as a Quaker meeting but with more glasses of brandy scattered around. A few men leaned against the serving counter. They'd retrieved their gun belts, and the proprietor had stowed his shotgun.

And every eye and ear in the place was on Caleb and the sheriff.

The deputy thumped down the stairs and stopped at the bottom, drawing a glare from Zeke.

"Don't you be lollygagging here," the sheriff snapped, scowling fiercely beneath the thick bush of beard, moustache, and eyebrows that obscured most of his flushed face. "Go tell the undertaker to come fetch this one too."

The deputy slouched out, muttering under his breath.

"Let's go," Caleb said, steering Zeke toward the door.

"Don't let nobody go up there till they come for him," the sheriff barked at the barman.

As they went out, a number of patrons clapped them on the back and congratulated them. Zeke nodded, but Caleb ignored the attention. He was still feeling the cold chill down his back that came on the moment he laid eyes on the gunman. Bat Davis was dead, but the unsettled feeling continued to linger.

When they reached the street, it was obvious Zeke was still a bit rattled. "There weren't no way to tell if you was in that room or not. All I saw was him yapping and waving his pistol around."

Caleb nodded, reminding himself that being sheriff wasn't an easy job.

Zeke gestured toward the retreating back of the deputy. "Right after I done it, this mangy dog come dancing up, telling me the judge don't want the man dead."

"A little late."

"And how was I to know?" The former miner was rolling. "I come in after the shooting in the street was over, and there was no saying that the gunman didn't have a hostage up in that room."

Caleb scanned the street. Wagons and men on horseback moved past them. The thoroughfare had returned to its usual bustle of activity. The three shooters had already been carried away. Spilled blood still marked the places where they'd fallen, but people were ignoring it and going about their business. It was as if there'd been no shooting only minutes ago. As if no men had died.

"Your deputy said one of them survived."

"So far. But he ain't in good shape."

Caleb wanted to see Bat Davis's partner in the ambush. "Did they take him over to the jail?"

"The judge told them to carry him straight to Doc Burnett's house."

Like Caleb, Bat hadn't any brothers that might have come out West with him. But it was still possible that he was traveling with someone else from their town. From the man's dying words, Caleb couldn't help but think that he wasn't done running from the past.

He needed to get a good look at the wounded bushwhacker's face. He had to make sure it wasn't someone he knew. Someone who could pull the rug out from under him here.

"Frissy says they was after the judge," Zeke said. "And I ain't surprised. Patterson puts men away and loops a rope around the neck of others."

It was easy to see someone like the judge having enemies.

Zeke continued, "He wants to see us back at his office."

"You go and talk to the judge. I'm going over to Doc's."

"You do that, and I'll just be coming after

50

you. You know he thinks of me as a glorified message runner. 'Tell Marlowe this, or tell Marlowe that. Get Marlowe. Send for Marlowe. Where is Marlowe?' " Zeke tapped the star on his chest. "It ain't no secret that he wants *you* wearing this tin star."

"This town got the right man."

"I don't know. I'm thinking that taking this job was a mistake. I never should have let you talk me into it."

"You *are* the right man."

They started down the street. Judge Patterson's office was on the way to Doc's house.

"That was the first fella I've killed since the war." Zeke took a handkerchief out of his pocket and mopped his face. "Was he ready to throw his gun down? Did I shoot too fast?"

"No."

"Say anything worth hearing before he died, at least?"

That depended on who was listening. "Nothing. None of it made much sense."

"Tell you his name?"

"No." That was the truth. There was no need.

"Why didn't you shoot him as soon as you went up there?"

"Patterson was barking at me as soon as

they came after him. As your deputy told you, he wanted him alive."

"Well, I wasn't there for it when the trouble started," Zeke growled defensively. "He can chew me out all he wants — I didn't know nothing about it."

"You said that."

"Damn, Caleb." He touched the star on his chest again. "I don't reckon I'm cut out for this."

"You're doing fine."

"It's only been ten days. It feels like ten *years*."

It had taken some persuading on Caleb's part to convince Judge Patterson to trust the miner with the job. Caleb's intentions had been reasonable. A month ago, Grat Horner was the sheriff of Elkhorn, but that miserable snake was a thief who happily gunned down men from behind. After Caleb and Horner finally had it out up in the mountains beyond Devil's Claw, Caleb thought the people of this town deserved to have an honest lawman for a change. But seeing how troubled the older man beside him was, Caleb wondered if maybe he shouldn't have gotten involved.

When they reached the building with the judge's name over the door, Zeke pulled off his new hat, mopped his forehead with his handkerchief, then jammed the stovepipe back on.

The lobby was wide enough to house at least three railroad cars, side by side. Even before the door closed out the noise and dust of Main Street, two clerks were staring at them from high desks behind a railing on the right. Caleb had seen the pair of them plenty of times before, and they always looked like they'd just bitten into an unripe apple, only to find a worm. They were about the sourest fellas he'd ever seen. They must have heard about the shooting, though, because they were more goggle-eyed than usual.

On the left side of the lobby, behind a closed door, was Patterson's courtroom. When he first saw it, Caleb had been appropriately impressed by the judge's high bench and the imposing pictures of three presidents — one alive, one fairly recently deceased, and one long dead.

He and Zeke went up the wide stairs at the far end of the lobby.

At the landing at the top, Frissy Fredericks stood in front of the judge's office. Since the shooting on the street, he had yet to brush the shards of glass off his coat sleeve.

When he saw Caleb, the judge's body-

53

guard spat in the general direction of a spittoon on the floor nearby.

"Don't need you doing my job, Marlowe," he said in his unexpectedly squeaky voice.

"Don't want your job, Frissy."

Fredericks was holding a short-barreled shotgun like it was a six-shooter. Because of the attack, Caleb figured. The front of his coat was pushed back, displaying a brace of short-barreled Colts in cross-draw holsters, ready in case the coach gun didn't do enough damage.

"I coulda took out all of them rats without no help."

"I reckon you could have handled the three in the street," Caleb replied coolly. "But climbing that one flight of stairs across the way would have killed you for sure."

While Fredericks tried to decide if he was being insulted, Caleb and the sheriff started to move past him. He held out a massive arm, blocking the way.

"Judge wants to see us, Frissy," Zeke said. "You know that."

The bodyguard turned and knocked once. A muffled voice answered. He opened the door and stepped aside.

The judge's personal secretary, a balding, pasty-faced man, was standing by an open inner door. He too was looking wide-eyed at Caleb. He shot a quick glance at the pistols on Caleb's hips and the rifle in Zeke's hand. Without a word, he ushered them in.

The judge's office was a regal affair. Entirely paneled with dark wood, it was at least as large as the barn Caleb had laid out to build at the ranch. A long, heavy table and chairs of carved oak sat at one end of the room beneath a brass and crystal chandelier that was rumored to have been stolen from some Southern governor's mansion at the end of the war. Heavy drapes, the color of blood, were held open with golden ropes. The carpets covering the floor were decorated with colorfully organized flower gardens unlike any Caleb had ever seen.

He doubted that the office occupied by the late Commodore Vanderbilt could compare. But that was surely Patterson's intention.

The judge didn't acknowledge them as they entered. Zeke shot Caleb a look as the nervous secretary escaped, closing the door quietly but firmly.

Every time Caleb had been here before, Patterson had used the arrangement of the office in the same way that he used his courtroom. Sitting like a king in a throne-like chair behind the huge desk, he handed down tasks the way he handed down decisions during a trial. This was the absolute seat of power in this part of the Rockies, and he wielded his authority like a restrained but wrathful god.

The scene unfolding before Caleb was far different from usual. A bronze Napoleon holding down a cowering British lion watched solemnly as the older man moved across the far end of the room at a furious pace before turning sharply at the window and storming back. The gun belt with a Remington in the holster was something Caleb had never seen on Patterson before. The ambush had apparently brought out the fight in him.

When Zeke pulled off his hat and cleared his throat, Patterson sent a sharp glance in their direction. He waved them in but didn't tell them to sit. That suited Caleb fine. He had no interest in prolonging this meeting.

"Gentlemen, is that gunman still alive?"

"Don't know, Judge," Zeke replied. "Last we heard —"

"He'd better be."

Patterson's bark was sharp enough that Caleb expected to see lightning start flashing from his eyes.

"We was about to go to Doc's house to check on him," the sheriff continued.

The judge stalked in silence to the unlit fireplace, kicked at a log, and came back to them.

"You did well, Marlowe. I'd be a dead man right now if it weren't for you. Those sons of bitches meant business."

When the attack came, Caleb hadn't thought about anything except stopping them. A man acted or he died. There was no hesitating. It was when a gunslinger felt the keenest edge of his precarious existence.

"I didn't see that first gunman coming," the judge continued. "When you drove me into the wall, I thought you'd lost your mind. That bullet would have done me, for sure. But you cut him down like the dog he was."

Once a fight was over, it was over. There was no need to drag through it again. The only thing still bothering Caleb was Bat Davis.

Patterson stopped and slipped a hand into his waistcoat. "One of them is alive. That's enough for my purposes."

There was no telling if the wounded man was still alive, but Caleb decided to let that hang a bit.

The day was bleeding away, but the judge seemed to be cranking up. He stood before Caleb, a head shorter, but rocked back on his heels and looked him straight in the eye.

"How much more evidence do you need, Marlowe? I'm telling you, this is just a sample of what is to come. Today wasn't the first time assassins have attacked me, and it won't be the last. Think of what the next two months will bring." The judge ticked them off with his fingers. "The population swelling daily. A crowd of luminaries will be here to view the eclipse. The governor's people coming to measure the progress we've made. Investors who want to see stability."

Patterson spread his hands out as if he were addressing a crowd of thousands.

"*This* is the Elkhorn we want to show them? Drunken miners firing off guns at will in the streets? Gunmen sent to town to kill a judge, a leader in the community?"

Caleb felt the weight of Zeke's gaze. All it would take was one word from Patterson. The miner-turned-sheriff was ready to drop his badge and run for the Belle Saloon.

"Is this the town we want them to see? A lawless place filled with brigands and guns for hire? How can we convince them . . . convince anyone . . . that Elkhorn has a future?"

Caleb had heard all of this before.

"You may not think the growth and prosperity of this town holds any importance for you. You've told me enough times that you wish to raise your cattle. But I don't need to remind you that your partner, Henry Jordan, remains in jail."

Now he was getting him pissed off. Henry's release was still pending.

"I've done my part, Marlowe. I've communicated with the governor. But imagine how much stronger our case would be for freeing Jordan if his business partner was also the sheriff of Elkhorn. Think how much a situation like that would ease the governor's mind."

Caleb fought down the anger rising inside him. Not an hour ago, he saved the man's life, and now the judge was tightening the damn screws on him.

"I'm willing to rely on you keeping your word," Caleb said coolly.

"But as you know —"

"And I've told you," he continued, interrupting the older man, "that I'm willing to help Zeke out. That should be good enough."

Patterson shook his head in disappointment and walked away.

"I've stated my position strongly here. I admit my feelings are running high after today's assassination attempt. But that doesn't change the passion I harbor in my heart for Elkhorn. And it doesn't change the fact that I need your help. I need both of you."

Hallelujah! It was about time Patterson acknowledged Zeke.

"I *know* who wants to undermine all that we're doing here. I know, without a shadow of doubt, who is behind that cowardly, failed attack on my person."

CHAPTER SIX

"Eric Goulden."

Caleb knew the name well. Eric Goulden was one of the most powerful moneymen in the country. Seen by some as a pioneer in transportation, buying and building railroads all over the West, he was seen by others as a ruthless robber baron who crushed anyone and anything that stood between him and a dollar.

Over the past few years, the newspapers had been full of stories about him, and even the editors who respected the man didn't like him much. He was a man to be feared.

"Eric Goulden is the one behind this attempt to kill me," Patterson repeated as he once again resumed his pacing. "He's made it clear he wants me dead."

Zeke scratched his head. "This fella got a bone to pick with you, Judge?"

Caleb had personally seen Goulden's way of doing things. It was during the time he'd been wearing the tin star up in Greeley. Surveyors were working the area, laying out lines for the Colorado Central to put in their rails.

Goulden was trying to gain control of every rail route and spur between St. Louis and San Francisco. Because a local family owned the Colorado Central, Goulden had been paying men to delay the railroad line from going in until he wrested away ownership of the company.

His methods were well known to the men working with the surveyors, as well. Several of them had worked for him before, and they had plenty of stories about how Goulden's minions abused their underpaid employees. Anyone who complained or tried to organize for decent wages was dealt with swiftly. Those rail lines, they told Caleb, were paved with the bodies of men shot or beaten to death and buried along the route.

The robber baron's agents were everywhere, and they were merciless. Tents and equipment burned. Shots fired in the night. Horses poisoned. Provisions stolen.

Those hired men were tough, efficient, and slippery as river snakes.

In the end, it had taken a contingent of armed guards to safeguard the lives of the surveying team.

"Goulden controls four major railroads in the west. He wants them all, large or small," Patterson said to the sheriff before turning to Caleb. "Do you know who he is?"

"I know he ain't a fella to be trifled with."

"Trifled with?" The judge snorted. "Goulden lives on the blood of his victims. He started from nothing, but he's made a fortune for himself through shrewd speculations, fraudulent stock issues, and outrageous financial manipulations. He and his partners were directly responsible for the Black Friday financial collapse back in '69. They care about nothing but putting more gold in their pockets."

A glance at Zeke told Caleb that the sheriff was foundering. As far as Caleb knew, the man standing beside him didn't know a thing about land speculations or financial crises. He didn't give a fiddler's damn about the affairs of the rich and powerful.

Caleb liked Zeke. Doc had introduced them at the bar in the Belle Saloon not long after Caleb arrived in Elkhorn. Like so many others out here, Zeke had fought and watched friends die during the war between the North and South. After the fighting was over, he came west, hoping to leave those memories behind. He had a silver claim up in the hills and had been at it for years. But he was getting tired of digging and was never going to strike it rich.

"Goulden is as corrupt a man as ever lived. He buys the law," Patterson continued. "Politicians eat out of his hand like lapdogs. He does anything he wants. He gets away with murder."

"So, what's this fella have against you, Judge?" Zeke asked again.

"I wouldn't play into his hand."

Caleb stood and listened, waiting for Patterson to finish laying out all the chess pieces. Between the sheriff asking questions and the judge talking, almost everything he needed to know was being answered. Almost.

But Bat Davis's words kept echoing in his head.

Never mind what this damn judge wants to know. Brother, I'd think you *would wanna know who sent me.*

Caleb wondered if Patterson was mistaken. Maybe it wasn't this railroad magnate at all. At the end of the day, how would a kid from Indiana end up working as a hired gun for someone like Goulden? And Bat said that *Caleb* would want to know. Why?

"I'm surely missing something, Judge, 'cuz I still don't see why he's coming after you,"

Zeke pressed. "He sent four gunhawks to shoot you dead in your own town. What did you say no to?"

Patterson waved a hand impatiently at the window. "I said no to selling Elkhorn to him. He wants the town. And he wants every piece of land suitable for a rail line."

The judge stalked back and stood in front of Caleb, as if he were the only one who'd be interested in hearing this news.

"He wants to run his railroad right through us. Take down everything in its way. And to run his rail south toward Santa Fe, he'll take your ranch too."

"What happens if folks don't want to sell?" Zeke asked.

Patterson turned to the sheriff. "He'll send his hired guns to take care of you, like he tried to do to me today."

Caleb pondered that threat and decided he didn't want to get involved. If it came down to blood being shed, the judge had the sheriff, the townspeople, and plenty of miners he could call on to stand up to the robber baron. Patterson had the law and his political clout in Denver to back him too.

Still, men like Goulden didn't usually go into a fight they didn't figure to win. And even if the battle got nasty, they never got hurt personally. They were too protected.

Fighting them was like clearing a briar patch with a paring knife. A man could cut away at the branches all day and never get near to the center. And the cost was always high.

Caleb could protect his own land, but it wasn't up to just him. Once Henry got out of jail, the two of them could decide if fighting for a patch of dirt three miles south of Elkhorn was worth the trouble.

"Marlowe, I need you to help me here. To help the sheriff. To help the people of Elkhorn. We won't be able to stop Goulden without you."

The judge had played this tune before. A month ago, he'd used the same approach to convince Caleb to go after the Wells Fargo stagecoach robbers. No one could do the job but him, he'd said. There were no scouts as skillful as him. And on he went. At the time, he'd also dangled the release of Caleb's partner from the jail in Denver as more bait.

They were still waiting for Henry's release.

"I've said it before, and I'll say it again, Judge. I ain't gonna wear the badge."

"And I'm not giving up until I have the very best people on my side."

"Zeke knows where to find me if —"

"That's good enough . . . for now. As long as we can call on you," the judge interrupted with a curt nod. He looked a little too satisfied for Caleb's liking. "That gunman, the one taken to Doc Burnett's house, we need him talking. I want you two to go over there and question him. Make him tell you the name of the person who sent him. He has to come out and say he works for Goulden. Then I can use his words as leverage in Denver."

"What if he *don't* work for the man?" Caleb had to ask.

"He does. I'm certain of it." Patterson stalked back to his desk. "Make him admit it."

Zeke broke in and pointed out the biggest possible flaw in the judge's plan. "That fella might already be dead by the time we get there."

"He can't be. Doc cannot allow that to happen. By God, Marlowe, I want him to stay alive long enough to confess before witnesses."

Caleb knew it was pointless to remind the judge, but he wasn't much of a churchgoing man. What he had to offer — tracking and shooting — weren't the most useful skills when it came to negotiating with the Almighty. Hell, he'd have a better chance making a deal with the devil. And he had a good idea the judge had a running account

67

down there already.

It didn't matter, though. Caleb wanted to get a look at the face of the wounded shooter, so he was going to Doc's anyway.

Frissy ignored them when they left the judge's office. That suited Caleb just fine. He was in no mood for a scrap with the bodyguard right now. His trip to Elkhorn had already run much longer than he'd planned.

Caleb and Zeke descended the steps, crossed the huge lobby under the watchful gazes of the two vinegar-pussed clerks, and went out onto the busy street.

They turned in the direction of Doc's. He didn't live far. His house was on the last street before the edge of town.

As they passed the Belle Saloon, the sounds of men laughing and shouting over cards and drinks reached the street. The sheriff cast a hopeful look in the open door.

"Marlowe, think we got time for a quick one in here?"

Since leaving the judge's office, the nervousness was quickly melting off Zeke. He never used to be so tense. But wearing the badge and reporting to Patterson had definitely been hard on the miner.

"No, I don't. But I hear talk that you ain't paid for a drink since coming back from

Devil's Claw."

Zeke chuckled. "That's a fact. Riding back into town with Doc Burnett and all that Wells Fargo loot made me sort of a local hero, thanks to you."

"It ain't 'cuz of that star on your chest that you're getting free liquor?"

"Hell, no." The sheriff's bushy eyebrows bunched up, and he tried to look offended, but he couldn't hold back the grin. "Truth is, between showing off that monster of a cougar skin and telling the tale of you taking him on with only one bare hand and your teeth, fellas are always offering to buy the drinks."

"And that ain't stretching the truth at all?" Caleb scoffed. "I believe there was a hunting knife involved."

"That's what we scholars call *poetic license.*"

"So it ain't like regular lying, then?"

"Not at all," Zeke retorted. "In fact, I think there's something in the Bible about it."

"You don't say. We'll have to ask Preacher next time we see him."

The sheriff shook his head. "You'll have to take my word on it. That old goat already took his mule and headed back up into the mountains. We won't see him for years, I reckon."

"Good thing for you."

It had been a close call for the itinerant minister on the trail up by Devil's Claw pass. That mountain lion had decided Preacher's ancient mule would make a fine breakfast, and the old man had gotten in the way of the big cat. He'd gotten chewed and scratched up some, but it was fortunate for everyone and everything — except the cougar — that Caleb had been nearby.

He looked down at the tough old boar walking beside him. It was good to have the old Zeke back.

The sheriff's steps dragged a little as they left the saloon behind. "Listen, Marlowe. Let me give you this tin star right now and save us both a pack of trouble."

"Not you too. Let it go."

"Believe me, there'd be no hard feeling between us, old man."

"That ain't about to happen."

"Why you so dead set against it? It'd sure make the judge happy, and that ain't a bad thing."

Caleb sent him a sidelong look. "You've been here in Elkhorn, mining and making a living, for how long?"

Zeke scratched his beard. "About two hundred years, I reckon."

"Well, I been here only five months. I'm not tied to Elkhorn the way you are. If Henry Jordan don't get released soon, I'm saddling up and moving on."

"Well, you know that is a cartload of horseshit, pure and simple," Zeke grumbled. "You ain't going nowhere."

"And what would make you think that?"

Before the sheriff could answer, two boys no more than ten years old came tearing along the sidewalk behind them. Their bare feet thumped along the wood planks. Caleb moved to the side, but the first one still banged into Zeke and tumbled off into the street. He rolled and sat up and brushed off his hands and elbows, cursing like an army mule driver.

"What d'you mean, cussing like that?" Zeke barked.

The boy's young companion circled around behind him. The one on the ground hopped to his feet.

From their spiky blond hair and buckteeth, Caleb figured them for brothers. They were both dressed in filthy sack-like shirts and brown woolen pants that ended in a ragged fray just below the knees. The boys were now competing for who could direct the more scornful looks at them.

71

"And what in tarnation are you looking at?"

"Two old men blocking the damn way," the first one chirped back at him. "What else would we be looking at?"

"Why, you brassy-mouthed little varmint. What this old man ought to do is come down there and give you a good thrashing."

"You and who else, you hairy polecat?" the other boy taunted.

"Hairy polecat!" Zeke pointed at his badge, "Don't you know who you're talking to, you mangy street urchin? I'm the sheriff of this here town. I'll lock you up and throw away the key."

The first boy only snorted derisively.

"And this here is the fastest gun and the bestest scout west of the Mississippi."

The boys' eyes darted toward Caleb and focused on the twin Colts hanging by his hips.

"We seen him. He gunned down them shooters in the street afore."

"Is he really Caleb Marlowe?"

"The very same," Zeke replied.

"Is it true that you kilt a cougar with your bare hands?"

"That's a fact, or so I hear," Caleb said, trying to hold back the smile.

Their eyes rounded, and they stepped back.

"And he's skinned fellers bigger and tougher than you," Zeke added. "And roasted them too."

They edged away from them, jaws hanging.

"So . . . git!" The sheriff took a step toward them.

The boys turned and raced up the street.

"You and your yarns, Zeke."

"Just relating the deeds of a legend." He glanced at Caleb and chuckled as they started walking. "Them little devils was surely the spitting image of me and my brother when we was about their age. Damn, but the trouble we got into . . . and the lickings we took! You got a brother?"

"No."

He thought of Bat Davis. There were a handful of boys back in Indiana who followed Caleb around. Son of the headmaster. But Caleb wasn't allowed to have friends. He got in plenty of trouble, but the only one that took the lickings was him. He didn't want to even remember those years. He'd buried them, along with the name Starr.

"Sisters? Any kin?"

"Not a one."

They walked in silence until they turned the corner onto Doc's street. The sheriff cocked an eyebrow and pointed at the Burnett house, which was now in view. "That house is a fine thing, ain't it?"

Caleb was relieved there were no more questions about his past. People who knew him at all learned not to ask. Zeke was learning too.

"The house," the burly little man repeated.

Caleb shot a questioning look at it. "Indeed, it is."

Doc's house was the only one on the street with a porch, and Caleb's friend made good use of it on warm evenings. He had a couple of rockers out there. There was also a table big enough for a chess board, used when Caleb was in town and the weather was fair. At the end of the porch, he even had a comfortable bench with a woven seat and back. Doc found it in a catalog and had it shipped out from the Shakers back in Ohio.

"It's more of a home, I reckon, now that he's got his daughter living there."

"If you say so."

"Would you say that color he's painted it looks more the shade of a yellow warbler or a goldfinch?"

"What the devil are you talking about?"

74

"Just thinking that if *I* was ten years younger, I'd be thinking about building myself a house just like that one."

"Painted the same color?"

"Tell the truth, Marlowe, I've always been sorta partial to a white house, but that don't matter none. What matters is what's inside. A good woman, a few mop-headed children, a yellow dog."

"I got a yellow dog. Can't beat a yellow dog."

"Damn it. I ain't talking about no dogs. A man needs family, Marlowe."

Zeke was an old bachelor.

"Like you have?" Caleb asked.

"A fella would be a mule-headed fool if he thought I got things right."

"I'm fine enough as I am."

"Who do you think you're fooling? Tell me there ain't something between you and that pretty daughter of Doc's."

"All that time you spent digging silver has affected your brain, Zeke. There's nothing going on there."

"Pshaw! Do you deny that when you come down from Devil's Claw, you two didn't go riding off to that miner's cabin to inform the widow, all cozy-like?"

"Hell, no!"

"I coulda swore you was holding hands

75

afore you even got around the bend."

"There was no hand-holding. Did somebody drag you away from a bottle this morning when the shooting started?"

"All I'm saying is that gal was fluttering her eyes at you so hard, I thought her pretty head was gonna lift clear off her shoulders."

"You have gone plum crazy."

"And one of them fellers with us thought he heard wedding bells coming all the way from Elkhorn."

Caleb snorted, but it didn't sound convincing, even in his own ears. He shook his head and glanced toward Doc's house, wondering if Sheila was at home now.

He'd sure as hell not admit it to this old coot, but Caleb had been trying to ignore the jumble of feelings Sheila Burnett stirred up in him. He couldn't quite fit her into any type of woman he knew.

When she arrived, no one knew it, but her father was being held by outlaws in the mountainous wilderness out beyond Devil's Claw pass. Right off, Caleb took her for an impulsive, high-strung city girl of questionable intelligence. He didn't think she'd last a week in the rough Colorado mining town, considering she'd followed a bunch of rustlers onto his ranch in the dark of night. She'd shown no understanding of the tough and violent ways of the frontier. She'd also taken exception to the fact of life that a man had to protect his property, often with his gun in hand.

Sheila had showed more spunk than he expected, however, when she too had been dragged off into the mountains by the men who had Doc. Left alone on foot in the middle of nowhere with almost nothing for protection against both wild animals and murderous road agents, she'd shown good sense and a lot of strength. She'd survived that ordeal and even helped free her father.

But she was an ornery thing. As waspish as she was pretty. And that was going some.

Whatever or whoever she was, however, Sheila deserved more than him.

"Ain't that third rocker up there new?" Zeke asked.

"I believe it is."

"There you have it." He slapped Caleb on the arm. "It's the prospective son-in-law's chair. Is that a *C* she's carved on the back?"

The sheriff looked off innocently into the distance, and Caleb seriously considered taking that rifle away from him and giving him a beating with it.

But he was right about the new chair, at least. The last time Caleb dropped by, there had only been two rockers out on that porch. Doc acquired the third one only since Sheila arrived unannounced from back East.

Since their adventure with them outlaws up in the mountains, Doc had confided in him that she'd left New York to escape a marriage arranged for her by her grandfather. It was, apparently, an effort to secure family fortunes. But Sheila had a fire in her belly and rebellion in her soul. She was not about to be traded away like a prime breeding filly, and definitely not to a much older man, Doc told him. His headstrong daughter had no intention of going back East.

If Caleb's life were different, and if he had any desire to settle — really settle — Sheila Burnett held charms that he couldn't deny. But he had no such plans.

And he kept telling himself that.

He and Zeke scraped the street from their boots and climbed the steps onto the porch. Before they could knock, the door swung open, and the young woman herself was standing in front of them. And damn, she was fine-looking.

"Good day to you, Miss Burnett," Zeke said, yanking his stovepipe off his head. Caleb thought for a second that the hairy little sheriff was about to bow to her.

If Doc's daughter had been caught up in

the fashions of the day back in New York, she'd decided on a different style out here. Gone were the frills and the bows, the long-waisted, form-fitting dresses, and the ridiculous little hats with silk flowers.

While Zeke was clucking at her like a mother hen, Caleb ran his eye over her. She wore her golden-brown hair in a long, thick braid down her back. Over a white, open-necked blouse, she wore a woolen vest of the same deep blue color of her eyes. Beneath the black skirt, she was wearing black house slippers embroidered with blue and white flowers that Caleb couldn't identify. Maybe no one could. He'd noticed that when she went out, she covered her head with either a black, wide-brimmed hat or a floppy cloth thing like the Scotch wore.

His gaze settled on her face. Though she was paying attention to Zeke, Caleb could tell she was watching him out of the corner of her eye. Finally, she looked straight at him.

"Miss Burnett," he said, touching the brim of his hat.

"Mr. Marlowe," she replied. "Won't you gentlemen come in? My father was expecting an official visit."

"Yes, miss," Zeke replied, going past her. "The judge sent us."

As Caleb approached her, he lowered his voice. "Still here, I see. Doc ain't shipped you back."

"I'm still here," she replied, eyeing him coolly. "And I see you're still doing what you do best. How many men have you killed today, Marlowe?"

CHAPTER SEVEN

"I took the bullet out and stitched him up."

Doc Burnett, still wearing a bloodied butcher's apron, gestured to the patient lying unconscious on the sturdy leather-covered table he used for operating. His surgical tools were scattered on a smaller table that held clean linens and a porcelain bowl filled with water. He was making a production of cleaning each of his instruments before putting them away.

Caleb was looking on, far enough away that Doc wouldn't feel crowded. Zeke stood in the doorway.

"The bullet was lodged very close to the heart, so I don't honestly know if the man is going to live or not. Then again, it may not matter much, considering where he'll be going once he's well enough for the judge's men to drag him out of here."

Doc sent a quick look in Zeke's direction and stopped whatever else he was going to say. He gathered up bloody linens from the floor and deposited them in a basket.

Caleb met John Burnett the first week he arrived in Elkhorn, and they hit it off immediately. Since then, the two of them got together regularly for a game of chess and dinner or for an occasional drink over at the Belle Saloon. There were other, nicer establishments to drink in, but the Belle was the closest, and they were both comfortable in the familiar surroundings.

It occurred to Caleb that there was some truth behind Zeke's teasing. After the arrival of Doc's daughter from New York last month, the nature of the visits had changed somewhat. The dinners were a bit fancier, and Caleb had begun to make a habit of getting a bath and a shave before coming to the house. The chess games continued, but they hadn't been doing much drinking at the Belle. And there was definitely far less cursing over the chess battles.

If Caleb were pressed to name a friend in these parts, Doc would be the one. For an educated man, he was a straight-talker, and he wasn't one to hide his feelings. And though Doc never carried a pistol, Caleb had never seen him show any fear. The man willingly went out at all hours of the day or night to parts unknown to care for some injured miner or wounded cowpuncher or even, last month, a woman in an outlaw hideaway. Doc told Caleb once that he'd spent the war working in battlefield medical tents and had seen too much death to be threatened by it.

And knowing Doc as well as he did, Caleb realized that his friend was in a particularly sour mood right now. It was a rarity since Sheila's arrival. As complicated as it was having a city-bred daughter living in the wild frontier town, the man was genuinely happy to have her in Elkhorn with him.

Sheila came to the door with the offer of some sandwiches. Caleb declined. He wanted to finish his business here and get back to his ranch.

The sheriff immediately accepted but then hesitated. "Let me know if this varmint stirs, will you?"

"That won't be anytime soon," Doc replied.

"Well, in that case, I'm much obliged to you for the offer, Miss Burnett. I'd be happy to join you for a bite to eat."

With the sheriff out of the room, Caleb moved closer to the bed to take a good look at the gunman.

The man was a decade, if not more, older than Bat Davis, and he'd clearly seen his share of the tougher side of life. Half of his right ear was missing. A jagged scar — still healing — ran from the corner of his left eye down across his stubble-covered cheek to his chin. He'd taken that knife wound to his face not too long ago.

Happily, that face belonged to a stranger. Caleb was sure he'd never laid eyes on him.

"Know him?" Doc asked, moving to stand next to Caleb.

"Nope. Never seen him before."

"It appears he's quite used to being shot and cut." Doc lifted the sheet covering the patient's chest and pointed to the scarred torso. "Before your bullet, he's had this hole in the arm, then there's this other one he took in the stomach. I'm surprised it didn't kill him. Look at this stab wound. And this scar from a knife across his chest is a good eight inches long. The one ear was shot off. An inch this way and the bullet would have taken out half of his skull. And that's just what I can see above the belt."

Doc was right. There wasn't enough unmarked hide on him to make a good tobacco pouch.

Caleb looked back into the man's face, and a feeling of relief washed through him. Running into Bat Davis was a freak incident. Maybe this was really the end of it. Maybe his past was truly behind him.

"I wouldn't doubt it if there were a reward on his head." Doc covered his patient again with the sheet.

"Probably."

"But regardless of if he's wanted or where, Patterson will hang him in front of his office on Main Street, as sure as we're standing here."

"Likely so. But I won't be there to watch."

"Are you against hanging?"

Caleb was never partial to hangings. He'd never willingly attended one — not since he was a boy — not even during the two years that he wore a badge in Greeley.

"Some fellas deserve it, I suppose," Caleb said. "Only way to get their full attention. But it's a fearsome way to go. You?"

"I agree." Doc ran a finger inside the collar of his shirt. "It's better than skinning alive or boiling in oil or burning at the stake. Drawing and quartering had to be messy, but it sent a message. The French hold that their guillotine is the cleanest and most humane way to do the job. But yes, I'd have to agree with you about hanging. It's fearsome and unnatural. But almost none of us have a say in how or when we meet our Maker."

Caleb looked away as his mind flooded

with the long-buried image of a battered woman, lying dead in her own blood. *She* had no say. The knot growing in his throat was suddenly big enough to choke him.

"It's not your fault that they're going to hang him. You had nothing to do with it. He is the one responsible for his actions."

Caleb shook his head, realizing Doc misunderstood his silence. "I got no regret about him. Or the others, neither. I did what I had to do."

And that'd been the way with Caleb for all of his life. He refused to keep count of how many men he'd killed. Each of them deserved to die.

"If I work it right, maybe a fever will take him first."

Caleb knew Doc didn't mean what he said. Criminal or a saint, the physician treated them the same. He'd do anything to keep his patients alive.

"But I know the judge wants him alive." Doc wiped his hand with a rag. "He *always* wants them alive. No entertainment value in hanging a dead man."

Crowds sure enjoyed a good hanging, Caleb thought somberly.

"At times like this, I get so sick of it," Doc continued. "If there were going to be a fair trial, with the honest application of law and

86

justice, then I'd have no problem. I'd patch them up. But there never is . . . not in this town."

"This knothead *did* shoot at the judge, Doc. I saw him, and he had killing in mind."

"I know. I know." Doc threw the rag on the table. He went to the other side of the room and poured two glasses of the bourbon that he liked to go to when something was eating away at him. "Maybe he really is a bad apple. But I've been here too long, and I've seen too much. There have been too many hangings in this town over the years. I have the right to be cynical."

He held out one of the glasses. Caleb walked over and took it.

His curiosity was piqued. He was still green here in Elkhorn, and he only met the judge about a month ago.

"You say he has a lot of hangings?"

"I've lost count how many. Rarely does a month go by that the gallows doesn't go up on Main Street. About a year ago, there was serious talk of leaving it up."

That was one way to build a name for yourself and your town. A hanging judge's reputation got out pretty quick. Maybe it persuaded trouble to bypass a place, Caleb couldn't really say. But then he thought about the man Patterson hired before Zeke became sheriff. Grat Horner was a crooked, low-down snake. He made most gunslicks and cold-blooded killers look like fresh-faced schoolboys.

"I've had to patch men up well enough to walk on their own two feet over to his courtroom. Those trials are quick, and they're followed by a short trip up the steps to where the hangman is waiting."

"Well, I don't work for him, Doc. And I don't reckon I'll be staying around to see what he does to this fella."

"Maybe. But you're still here. He wants a confession out of this fool. And if none of us hears the man say the words, Patterson will lean on us until we actually think we *may* have heard it. That's the way he does things. And he always gets what he wants."

"Don't sound like you care too much for the man."

Doc poured himself more bourbon. "Another one?"

Caleb raised the glass, still untasted.

"Did I mention to you that I've been here too long?"

"You did."

"He's not what he appears to be."

"I figured that much already."

"And I know what he wants." The physician motioned to his patient with the glass.

88

"This one is supposed to wake up and tell us Eric Goulden sent him."

"How did you know that? You talked to Patterson already?"

"A week ago."

His words startled Caleb. "You're saying that he told you, a week ago, Goulden would be sending gunhawks here to kill him?"

"He told me that the man would be looking for a way to get to him. The judge was defying Goulden. There are plans in the works that Patterson believes encroach on territory that he sees as his own. The two of them want the same thing."

Goulden might be sniffing around the judge's boneyard, but the railroad magnate struck Caleb as more of a sneaking backbiter than a look-a-man-in-the-eye fighter. It would take real brass to send men to gun down a man of Patterson's importance in his own town.

Besides, if the judge had stretched as many necks as Doc said, Caleb reckoned there'd be more than a few folks out there waiting for their chance to strike him down.

He mentioned his thinking to his friend.

"Patterson has plenty of enemies, to be sure, and not all of them are big shots from Denver or from back East," Doc continued.

"But he's shrewd and quick. It doesn't matter if this man works for Goulden or not. It only matters that we say he did."

For about the hundredth time, Caleb was glad he wasn't the sheriff. In fact, now that he'd seen that the gunner was no one who knew him, there was no reason for sticking around.

Doc wiped out his glass and set it down. "Patterson is as ruthless and ferocious as a wolf. He gets what he wants. So whatever he told you about Goulden, don't just accept it as gospel truth. With the judge, there's always more to the story."

CHAPTER EIGHT

Caleb's helpers were late.

But what else was he to expect from a twelve- and fourteen-year-old? By the time Gabriel and Paddy arrived to help him raise the barn, the day was half gone, and they were carrying two strings of good-sized trout and a pair of fishing poles.

"Look what we caught." Paddy, the younger boy, held his catch up proudly. "Good-looking fish, don't you think, Mr. Marlowe?"

Caleb nodded appreciatively. "Where'd you catch them rainbows?"

"Gabe knew a good spot on a creek up that away."

"Up this side of the ridge. There's a good creek runs through a gulch."

Standing, Caleb turned his gaze toward the rising woodland in the direction Gabe pointed.

Located about three miles south of town,

the ranch he and Henry owned largely consisted of the grass-covered valley between two parallel ridgelines running north and south. It was about eight miles long and maybe three miles wide, as the crow flies.

The land deed listed the western boundary as the Denver road, which ran through Elkhorn before turning south toward Santa Fe in the New Mexico Territory. The eastern boundary was the top of a pine-covered ridge. Beyond that point, his neighbor was a fellow by the name of Frank Stubbs. The boys had come from that direction.

He'd only seen Stubbs at a distance. According to Zeke, the man had a profitable silver mining concern over there, but he had few friends in town. The bastard was well known as a mean drunk. Every dollar Stubbs took out of the ground, he spent in the saloons, often abusing the women who worked there.

It was better not crossing paths with some people, and Stubbs was one of them.

When Caleb and Henry were purchasing the ranch land, there had been some talk that there could be mineral deposits on this side of the ridge and an old lost mine up there somewhere as well. He had very little interest in digging for silver, though his partner's sentiments differed. Henry believed silver would be the making of them. Caleb had done enough prospecting for gold with Old Jake out in Montana to know that he was not cut out to be a dedicated miner.

It was the meadowland and the pines and the groves of cottonwood along the river that appealed to Caleb. There was game in the forests and fish in the river and streams. Raising cattle, their plan was to supply the ever-increasing number of miners and townsfolk that needed to be fed in and around Elkhorn.

Caleb's thoughts turned to how he'd felt about the whole thing after seeing Bat Davis. This was the first piece of ground he had ever owned. Regardless of how good he had it here, yesterday he'd been ready to leave it all behind. The mountains and deserts and open ranges to the west offered enough elbow room for any man who tried to hide.

"We would have caught more," Paddy said. "But some miserable old man started hollering and shaking a stick at us from way up atop a bluff."

Caleb turned to Gabe. Most of the time, the older boy worked for his father, Malachi Rogers — a former buffalo soldier — who owned one of the two stables in Elkhorn. "Recognize him?"

"Sure I did. Mr. Frank Stubbs. He does business with the other livery in Elkhorn." Gabe grimaced. "What's wrong with him anyhow? Anytime I've seen him, he's angry."

"Can't say. Never spoke to him."

Bear was circling Paddy, his tongue hanging. The scent of the fresh-caught fish was almost too much of a temptation for the dog.

"Better hang them rainbows on the wall of the cabin," Caleb told them. "High enough where Bear won't be helping himself to them. And hurry back."

The boys ran off — the dog in pursuit — to do as they were told.

Caleb watched them poking and trying to trip each other. Their mouths were running the entire time.

They were both good boys, to be sure, even if they were easily distracted from working. Gabriel, tall and strong for his fourteen years, was the more responsible of the two.

Paddy, two years younger, lived with the Rogers family, though he was a new addition. Gabe's father and mother had been kind enough to take the orphan in only a few weeks ago.

It was a true kindness, for the boy had made an impressive entrance showing up at the livery stable one day with a loaded Colt Dragoon in hand, bent on revenge for the killing of his brother.

And that meant gunning Caleb.

The night before, Paddy's brother — along with five buffle-headed friends — had made the ill-advised decision to rustle cattle from the ranch. After opening fire, the brother and the others achieved an early demise, each with a .44-.40 bullet from Caleb's rifle embedded in their vitals.

Helping Paddy understand that his brother had died as a consequence of doing wrong was far easier than figuring out what to do with the boy. Even though no one would blame Caleb if he turned his back and left the lad to make his own way in the world, he couldn't avoid feeling some responsibility for him. Paddy had no one and nowhere to go.

Matters were complicated by the fact that Caleb had been on his way out to Devil's Claw and the mountainous wilderness beyond in pursuit of the road agents who'd taken Doc. That's when Gabe's father stepped in.

On his return, Caleb had been able to strike a bargain with the livery owner regarding room and board for the boy. It had nearly been a knock-down, drag-out fight getting Malachi to take anything, but the men had eventually worked it out. Since then, the two boys came out to the ranch to help — more or less — when it was needed.

"Sorry we're late getting here." Gabe was the first one back from the cabin.

Caleb picked out some tools for the boys. "We got a barn to put up. I know it's only June, but I'd like to get the thing built before the snow flies."

"Whaddya want us to do?" Paddy stopped next to Gabe, his ginger-colored locks bobbing in the wind.

Caleb gave each of them a job to do and showed them what he wanted done. Gabe was tasked with squaring off logs with a small axe. Meanwhile, Paddy would work on chiseling out notches at the ends. While they did that, Caleb would haul more logs for the barn walls into position using the team of draught horses he'd gotten from Gabe's father.

They dove in, applying themselves to their jobs. They were good at following directions.

"You're always working on the ranch, Mr. Marlowe. Where is your partner, anyways? Why don't he carry his weight?" Gabe asked a little while later, when they paused to take a drink from a bucket of water Caleb had brought up.

"Henry Jordan will do his share when he gets here."

"When would that be?" Paddy asked.

"End of summer, maybe sooner." Caleb hoped.

"Why so late? You're building now."

"Where is he?" Paddy seemed to think talking was a sign of quitting. He dropped his chisel and mallet and sat down next to Bear, petting the beast.

Caleb could have made something up, but he knew from Doc that rumors had already been circulating in Elkhorn. And it was best if they knew the truth.

"He's in jail in Denver."

Both boys' eyes rounded. Bear was momentarily forgotten.

"What's he done?" Gabe wanted to know.

Caleb tried to decide how much to say. He himself had nobody he could consider a good role model when he was their age. That only came later, when he'd spent six years following Jacob Bell around the frontier. And the old scout believed that a man's life was about learning from mistakes and changing and learning again. If he survived the mistakes, that is.

"When he sees something that's wrong, Henry Jordan has a hair-trigger temper. He flares up hot as a prairie fire. So his fists sometimes get him into trouble. He got into a fight in a Denver saloon. That's why he's in jail."

"What do you mean, something wrong?" Gabe was curious.

"Suppose you see Bear getting kicked. What would you do?"

"Stop it."

"That's Henry." Caleb put a booted foot up on a log. "He is as fine a man as I know."

Gabe's face was creased in a thoughtful frown. "You ever been in jail?"

Caleb decided he wasn't asking about the occasional times in his youth after some heavy drinking. Nor was he talking about the night the last snake of a sheriff had put him in a cell just to be a sonovabitch. "Never after going in front of a judge."

Luck had some role in keeping him out of jail. But Caleb wasn't about to go into that with these boys.

"How do you know Henry Jordan? You kin?" Paddy asked before going back to stirring up the dog. Wrestling with Bear was a favorite pastime for him. And that yellow monster didn't seem to mind at all.

"Not kin." Caleb didn't like talking about

his past, but now that Henry's name was out, he felt he needed to say more. "We met up north in Lakota territory. He was in a unit I was scouting for."

Nearly as tall and broad-shouldered as Caleb, Henry liked to say he had three true loves — poker, whiskey, and women — and "I'll be faithful to all of them, or the devil take me."

Caleb believed that would probably be the case, either way. But he also knew Henry could always be counted on in a tight spot.

"We became good friends up there."

"We're good friends, ain't we, Gabe?" The twelve-year-old's eyes were bright as he looked up.

"You are such a chucklehead." The older boy cuffed the other on the head. "Come on. We got to get to work."

Paddy reluctantly pushed the dog away and collected his tools. "Is your partner a gunhawk too?"

"He was a sergeant in the cavalry," Caleb answered. "So he knows one end of a weapon from the other."

"We heard the shooting in town yesterday. But by the time we got down to Main Street, it was all over."

"Except for the sheriff taking out the fella through the window," Gabe corrected.

Paddy nodded, eyeing Caleb's six-shooters, which were draped over the end of a nearby log. "When was it you started slinging your Colts, Mr. Marlowe?"

"When I had to."

"When was that?"

Persistent little cuss, Caleb thought. He knew what lay at the bottom of the lad's interest. He'd lost his brother in a shooting. In addition, though, every frontier town had its stories of gunfights and the men who fought them. He heard that back East, magazines and even novels were now being printed that were filled with tales of courage and cowardice, heroes and villains, all taking place out here.

When Caleb was a boy, he'd read the myths and legends of King Arthur's knights, Ivanhoe, Jason and the Argonauts, and Odysseus, the three musketeers, and the pirate-fighting lads of Coral Island. Those stories nowadays gave way to make-believe tales of the Wild West, where a man's worth was often determined by the steadiness of his nerve and the speed of his draw, and where the hero always won the day.

"I never shot a gun till I was sixteen," he answered.

"Did you practice lots to get so good?"

Caleb shrugged. "Some."

100

"When was the first time you killed a man?"

"Don't recall."

He was sixteen. The tightness in Caleb's chest was old, painful, and too damn familiar. But it wasn't the man he killed that caused it. It was the battered face of his mother that still burned a hole in his heart and in his brain.

"Stop asking questions," Gabe ordered his friend. He was looking intently at Caleb's face. "Let's go, Paddy. We got work to do."

But the red-haired boy wasn't giving up. "Ever sorry about killing a man?"

"I done plenty of things that I ain't proud of. But I don't kill for no reason."

"Yesterday, your dead aim and quick draw saved the judge's life. You had reason."

"Them fellas were guns for hire. They came to kill. But I was lucky too."

"I wanna sling a gun when I get older," Paddy said solemnly. "But not like no stone-cold killer or road agent or . . . or rustler. I wanna be like you."

Caleb knew what the boy was referring to. He was talking about his dead brother.

"I'm a rancher, Paddy. I only fire my gun when I need to. Too many fellas make the mistake of keeping an iron strapped to their hip. It's easy to think you're tougher and smarter than the next man. But there's always someone a little faster . . . and looking to prove it. And it ain't much of a life always looking over your shoulder."

CHAPTER NINE

The day went better than Caleb had hoped. The three of them levered a number of logs up the sloping supports and into position. The walls of the barn were beginning to rise.

Working with Gabe and Paddy was all well and good, but it would take Henry's return to really put the ranch in order. Every time Caleb thought about what they'd need, the list kept growing. Finishing the barn and the corrals, putting up a chicken house, and — after the summer rains — digging a well. And that didn't include all he needed to be doing with the livestock.

Everything in its season, Caleb told himself as he watched the youngsters. Right now, he was satisfied to have his helpers here where they could earn a wage and a feeling of accomplishing something. The ranch was a safe place for them. Better than the streets and alleys of the town. And he was glad they were trustworthy enough to watch over the herd and the dog whenever Caleb had to go away.

He stretched his tired shoulder muscles and looked across the rock-studded meadow at a loosely organized regiment of thunderheads marching ominously across the sky to the southwest. The sun was still shining, but he wondered for how long.

At that very moment, Bear put his massive paws on Paddy's chest and knocked him right onto his butt. The dog clearly thought these two only came here to keep him entertained.

After casting his tools aside, Paddy rolled in the dirt with the furry beast. They were close to the same weight, even the same height. In their playfulness, they were very much the same, except that Bear was rougher.

After a few rolls in the dirt, Paddy stopped, pushed the dog away, and sat up.

"Lordy, Bear! I swear, your breath smells like week-old fish."

Gabriel laid down the axe and wandered over to where his friend was wiping his cheeks on his sleeve. "And now you're gonna smell like it too . . . though it might be an improvement."

"How come this dog just loves putting my face in his dang mouth?"

"Maybe he's trying to figure if he can swallow you whole," Gabe suggested.

"I reckon that's *exactly* what he's doing." The twelve-year-old scratched his head, leaving the reddish hair spiked up at odd angles.

Gabe bent down and scratched behind Bear's ears. "They say a rattler can unhinge his jaw and swallow a whole jackrabbit."

"That true? Swear and spit."

"I heard a fella tell Pa about seeing a rattler up in Montana swallow a full-grown steer. Said that creature looked more like a diamond-backed whale than a snake. Couldn't hardly move for a month."

The younger boy's eyes opened wide, and then he scoffed, realizing Gabe was joking.

This was another reason why Caleb liked having these two here. He was helping a friendship get a good foundation. At their age, Caleb hadn't been allowed to have boys over to the house, nor could he rattle around with them anywhere else. He was the schoolmaster's son, and his father made sure he was always working. He was watched constantly. And if anything went wrong, he felt the lash as an example to everyone else.

Bear went to the pile of pegs Caleb had fashioned and, after selecting one, began gnawing away at it like the thing was a well-

105

aged elk rib. That dog always knew how to distract him from the darkness of the past.

"You are a troublemaker," Paddy declared. "Don't you be chewing up work Mr. Marlowe already done. He needs them pegs."

The boy went to the nearby stack of kindling and pulled out a sizeable stick. Showing it to the dog, he tossed it into the field.

"Fetch it, boy," he commanded. "Get it, Bear."

The animal lifted his head and looked at Caleb and Gabe before turning his brown eyes to Paddy. The two stared at each other for a full minute. Finally, Bear went back to chewing on the peg. He had no intention of fetching anything.

"Ornery. That's you, Bear."

The dog ground away at his found treasure harder.

"Half mule, I reckon," Gabe added affectionately.

Bear lifted an eyebrow at them, his powerful jaws continuing to reduce the peg to splinters.

"He can have the one," Caleb suggested. "Let's clean up before them storm clouds close in."

Paddy gathered the loose pegs that had rolled off the pile and tossed them back where they belonged. Suddenly Bear was interested. Pushing to his feet, he raced over, grabbed the pieces, and returned with them.

"He *is* a retrieving dog."

Bear had plans that didn't include fetching, however, and he began reducing the new peg to splinters.

"Give me that," Paddy ordered.

The dog ignored him.

Lunging, the boy grabbed hold of the piece of wood the dog had firmly in his teeth. Bear pulled back, yanking him off-balance. A moment later, Caleb watched Paddy being dragged across the ground by the growling creature.

Gabe dove into the fray, grabbing for the dog's tail and then getting an arm around the animal's legs. Bear dropped the peg, and Caleb shook his head as they all wrestled around like a litter of wolf pups. Even when a forearm or shoulder ended up in the animal's jaws, Bear never bit down but continued to growl and snarl with mock ferociousness.

Someone had to clean up, and Caleb was the only one doing it. He unhitched the team, removed the harnesses, and led the horses out into the meadow to graze. He had more logs ready to go up into place another day.

When he returned, the wrestling had subsided. The boys were working diligently, cleaning up. Bear was lying on his side in the sun, making no such effort to look industrious. The splintered peg lay between his massive paws.

Caleb glanced off across the rolling meadows, where his cattle were grazing contentedly in the midday warmth. Some were standing in the shallow water at the edge of the river, and some were lying on the ground. For as far as he could see, from the line of cottonwoods below the western bluffs to the pine-forested ridges in the east, the long grass was bending in waves as the breeze moved across the valley floor.

A sense of belonging stirred in his chest. He was part owner of a ranch. He had a home. A place where he could put down roots if he wanted to. Zeke's teasing words about Sheila came back to him. How quickly he was getting tamed and settled. And how fast the bubble burst when he crossed paths with Bat Davis.

If the man had lived, Caleb's life would already be in shambles. He doubted that anything other than that bullet would have stopped Bat from telling anyone who'd lend an ear about how Caleb Starr was a runaway. An outlaw and a runaway.

He ran a hand down his face. But Bat Davis was a hired gunslick, and he was dead. Caleb could put that worry behind him. He had to focus on now, what was his, what he could control.

Caleb glanced at the cottonwood logs he'd cut and hauled up for the building. What he wanted to do over the next few days was get the walls up for the barn, which would consist of two large stables with a wide, roofed space connecting them. A few days ago, he'd finished putting up a privy, which would be damn handy when the snows came. And before the boys arrived this morning, he finally hung the door on his cabin.

His helpers were finishing up their chores just as a rumble of thunder rolled along the distant ridges.

"Where'd you get Bear?" Paddy crouched down beside the animal and petted him. "I want a dog."

"Don't know if Mr. Rogers would take kindly to having you *and* a dog."

"Pa don't hold with keeping dogs." Gabe sat down on a log he'd been working on before. "He only tolerates cats in the barn to keep the mice and rats from eating the grain."

Paddy sighed. "So, where'd you get Bear from, anyways?"

"He got *me,* actually," Caleb replied.

"Dogs don't get people. People get dogs."

Caleb shrugged. "He's smarter than most dogs."

"Will you tell us the story?" Gabe asked.

"And then tell us how you took down the cougar. The sheriff tells it different every time."

"Give the man a chance to talk, Paddy."

Caleb was not much of a storyteller, but they were done working. Bear also lifted his head and stared at him, as if to say, *Tell it right, 'cuz I'm listening.*

He sat on the log next to Gabe. Some memories were easier to share than others.

"It was the same day I made the purchase of the ranch at the land office in town."

"When was that?" Paddy asked.

"Five months ago," Gabe replied to his friend.

"That's exactly right. You remember when I first came to Elkhorn?"

The boy shrugged, but a smile tugged at the corner of his mouth. "There was still snow on the ground."

Caleb nodded. "And it was cold as a turtle's tit."

He recalled stopping at the livery and having a long conversation with Malachi Rogers about Elkhorn. They stood in the little office area, and he'd warmed himself by the stove. Gabe had been there as well while they talked.

"After I left the land office, I come riding my horse out here. It was quiet, except for the wind sighing through the trees. Then, I caught something out of the corner of my eye. An animal moving through the pines off to the left of the road."

"Was it Bear?" Paddy chirped.

"At first, I thought it might be a cougar stalking me —"

"Like the one you kilt up by Devil's Claw," the younger boy added.

"Right. But there was something about how he moved that made me rule that out. I thought, maybe a hungry wolf or a coyote."

"Good thing you didn't shoot it." Paddy petted the dog.

"I wouldn't. Not unless it attacked me first. Also, I saw nothing more of it till I reached that place over yonder where the valley opened up onto a meadow."

Caleb remembered how the brown grass and gray boulders poked up through the thick snow. The sky was the deepest blue, with wisps of clouds far off to the east. Ice formed a glistening fringe all the way down the river as far as he could see. The air was so cold, Pirate's breaths looked like smoke from a locomotive.

"As I turned to ford the river at a shallow place, that yellow dog come right out of the trees, the biggest, fattest rabbit this side of Denver dangling loose from his jaws."

Bear lifted his head, eyeing them. Caleb was sure he understood they were talking about him.

He'd immediately been struck by the dog's thick, healthy coat. Lighter-color fur, almost white, spread across his chest and legs. His muzzle and ears had splashes of black. From the long legs and loose-limbed gait, he was young too, Caleb had judged.

"He followed me across the river and over the meadow till I finally reached this rise where I'd decided to build. When I climbed down off Pirate, that dog come up within eight feet of me, dropped his catch, and lay right down."

"What did you do?" Gabe asked.

"I went over and picked up the rabbit. The critter was fresh and didn't have a mark on it. I reckoned the dog must have scared him to death. So I asked him, 'What's this, a peace offering? Or are you the welcoming committee?' "

"Did he answer?" Paddy wanted to know.

"No. He was being bashful. So I built a fire, skinned and roasted the rabbit, and the two of us ate our first meal together."

For the next couple of days, the dog came and went, always returning with something from his hunts. Pheasant. Turkey. More rabbit. And he was good company, alert and focused on Caleb, though still reserved. A strange sense of kinship began to grow between the two of them. The dog started sleeping at the edge of the camp, right at the point where the campfire gave way to darkness.

"That was it? You cooked him a rabbit, and he became your dog?" Paddy asked.

"No. That ain't all." Caleb had more appreciation for Zeke's storytelling skills now that he was trying to weave a tale himself. "One night, not long after, I woke up with Pirate all restless and worried. There was no moon, and the fire had burned down low. That dog was standing not a foot from me. His yellow hackles were standing up like a porcupine, and he was staring off into the dark, growling low but fierce."

Both boys growled in fun, and Bear cocked an eye at them.

When a man had the hard earth for a bed and the night for a blanket, danger lurked out in the darkness. The weather had begun to warm with a January thaw. That night, the heavy thump of large approaching feet had Caleb reaching for his rifle.

"As I was looking out to see what he was growling at, a grizzly walked right up to the edge of the camp, drawn by the smell of fish or horseflesh, maybe. From the look of his shaggy coat, that bear had been hibernating. He was moving in that groggy, hungry way they get when they start to wake up."

"How big was he?" Gabe asked.

"I reckoned that monster would run to four hundred pounds, once he started eating regular again."

But he wasn't going to start his spring feeding on Caleb's horse or on him either.

"Where was your gun?" Paddy asked.

"Under my bearskin bedding. Real slow, I eased that Winchester '73 out. But before I could cock it to fire, there was a flash of yellow fur. He charged right after the grizzly, barking and growling and sounding like a true hound from hell."

"You rescued him." Both boys spoke their praise at once, and the dog was showered with affectionate petting.

The beast rolled on his side, watching Marlowe.

"What happened next?" Paddy exclaimed.

"The griz was up on his back legs in a

114

wink, ten feet tall at least, roaring and waving them long claws of his. But this dog wasn't impressed. He was moving like lightning, darting in and out, side to side, barking and snapping at the legs and haunches. That bear was not thinking about food no more. He was only thinking about saving his hide."

Caleb thought about that battle and gazed at the dog, who seemed to be smiling at him.

"The last I saw of that bear was his big rear end disappearing into the darkness with a yellow blur nipping at him and hurrying him along." He brushed off his pants. "I listened to the barking and roaring and growling till I couldn't hear nothing."

That night, after adding a couple of logs to the fire, Caleb made sure Pirate was settled and then sat against his saddle, looking out into the black meadow, his rifle cradled on his lap. He was worried about the dog, but he couldn't go after him in the dark.

"Did he come back right away?"

"He did. A few minutes later, he trotted back into camp, proud as punch. Then the damnedest thing happened."

"What?" Paddy asked.

"He lay himself down right next to me. It was the closest he'd come. And when I put a hand out to pet him — like you're doing now — he didn't move away."

"Like you said, he picked you."

"He did."

"He's a natural-born bear hunter," Gabe said.

"That's exactly what I thought." Caleb nodded. "So I decided to call him Bear."

"What a good dog!"

Paddy tried to pet Bear again, but the animal was done with all the affection. Standing up, he shook the wood splinters out of his fur, stretched, and trotted off in the direction of the river.

"Where is he going?"

"Probably hunting."

"See if you can find a good-sized turkey," Gabe called after the dog.

"How about if we throw one of them rainbows in a skillet and make up some biscuits?" Caleb asked them.

Suddenly they were starving, moaning and complaining like they hadn't eaten for days. They were both on their feet, racing in the direction of the cabin, boasting about how much each of them could eat.

Caleb shook his head and started after them.

The familiar prickling sensation on the back of his neck had Caleb pause and look around. A movement caught his eye on the eastern edge of the meadow. He stopped as a rider burst from the line of trees.

He wondered who the visitor could be. He was expecting no one. Since buying the place, Caleb hadn't had anyone — except Doc and Sheila and Zeke — stop by for what might be considered a social call. And from the way this one yanked the reins and dug his spurs into the flanks of his horse, it didn't look like this was going to be friendly either.

The man was sitting bolt upright in the saddle, though he appeared to be leaning a little as he came. Elbows out wide. Shoulders bunched up like he was trying to keep his head straight. He was pushing the sturdy chestnut mount at a full gallop.

He was halfway across the meadow before Caleb recognized him.

Frank Stubbs.

Caleb felt his hackles rise. His neighbor had no business here, but he was barreling toward him like a man on fire. He had a rifle in a saddle holster but didn't appear to be packing a six-gun.

Stubbs looked like a man bringing trouble.

CHAPTER TEN

Frank Stubbs was coming hard, and as the man drew nearer, Caleb saw the sour look. His neighbor was angry, but about what, he only had a suspicion.

The boys. They said earlier that Stubbs had been hollering at them while they were fishing. But that still didn't explain the visit or the stormy look on his face.

Caleb took a quick glance toward the cabin. Gabe and Paddy were standing only a dozen steps behind him and to the right, watching Stubbs approach. If he really did mean to start trouble, Caleb figured he could handle it. He considered himself a man of reason first. It was better to talk a problem through before bullets were needed to settle things.

A couple of yards away, Caleb's gun belt was slung over a log. He could get to his Colts quickly if he had to.

Stubbs galloped up and reined in hard.

The sides of the chestnut gelding were heaving.

Caleb nodded at him. "So, neighbor, we finally meet."

Without returning the greeting, Stubbs glared in the direction of the two lads as he climbed down from his horse. He was tall, nearly Caleb's height, with a long, horse face and the gaunt, drawn features of a hard-living man. His cheek, bulging with chaw, and his lantern jaw were covered with a week's growth of dusty stubble. A heavy, brown mustache framed a thin-lipped slash of a mouth and hung to the jawline. His small, dark eyes were set close together on either side of a hooked and battered nose. A scar an inch long split his left eyebrow, giving his face a fierce and unbalanced look. It was the face of a man who had taken, and probably given, his share of hard knocks.

"You're Frank Stubbs, ain't you? My neighbor over the ridge?"

"It ain't you I come to see, Marlowe. This ain't no social call."

He had a voice like gravel in a prospecting pan. Caleb heard the shuffle of steps behind him. The boys were moving closer to him.

Stubbs had to be nearly forty, but he looked as tough as a Mississippi longshoreman. His worn work coat of dark-brown

119

wool covered a black waistcoat. From a button on the vest pocket, a silver ribbon disappeared into a watch pocket. Long, greasy hair hung nearly to his shoulders. A brown bowler sat low on his forehead, giving him the attitude of a man leaning into the wind.

"Then why are you here?"

He jerked his head at Gabe and Paddy. "It's them two I come for."

"Too bad. 'Cuz they're working for me, and they ain't taking visitors."

Without taking his stony eyes off them, Stubbs yanked a cane from the scabbard that also held a Henry rifle. He started toward the boys with a white-knuckle grip on the stick and clear intentions.

Caleb put himself directly in the man's path. "Maybe you didn't hear me."

"Outta my way."

"That ain't going to happen."

As Stubbs drew closer, he brought with him the smell of brandy mingled with the sour odor of old sweat and urine.

Caleb held up one hand, angling his body slightly to the right. In his boot, he carried the long hunting knife Old Jake gave him when the man went to live out his years on his farm in Missouri.

"You'll stop right there if you know what's good for you."

Stubbs hesitated, stopped, and slapped the cane into the callused palm of his big left hand. "I said my business got nothing to do with you."

The stick was about an inch and a half thick. It had a worn silver nob on the end, and from the marks on it, his neighbor clearly knew how to use it.

Caleb figured the brandy might slow him down a bit, depending on how much he'd put away, but Stubbs appeared to be a man who was well practiced at holding his liquor. Caleb judged him to be the kind of drinker who got meaner and meaner but lost little of his edge until he was well into his cups.

"You need to climb back up on that fine horse of yours and go on home."

Stubbs glowered at him. "I s'pose you think you can just waltz right into Elkhorn, all high and mighty with your fancy six-guns and your four-flusher ways. Well, that don't mean shit to me. We have our ways here. So move outta my way."

If he had a dollar for every time some knothead said that to him. "I ain't wearing no iron, and I ain't dancing with you. But this is my land, and you already wore out your welcome."

"And maybe you ain't half the man without them pistols."

Stubbs slapped the cane into his hand again. He was obviously not accustomed to anyone standing in his way.

"Maybe I am, and maybe I ain't. But you got no good reason to find out, far as I can tell. Best thing for everyone is if you hop right back up there and go to wherever you came from."

"You ain't telling me what to do. Them two was on my land, and they're getting a beating. And you ain't stopping me."

Caleb heard a low whimper of apology from Paddy behind him. The boy's fear hung in the air like camp smoke in the rain. He had a good idea that if he let Stubbs have his way, this wouldn't be the first stick to mark that young hide.

Stubbs tried to step around him.

Caleb moved as well, cutting him off again. "When I was scouting up north, I ran into scum like you. Blackguards not fit to sleep with hogs. Fellas who thought big talk was all it took to get their way."

Stubbs's eyes narrowed. Caleb could see the rusty wheels turning in his brain.

"I got property and —"

"Like I said," Caleb interrupted. "You don't need to do this. When you're back drinking with your pals in the saloon . . . if you got any pals . . . you can tell them that

122

you and me met real neighborly, and we're gonna be fast friends."

"I'd rather be friends with a mangy, three-legged coyote. Now I'm telling you, get outta my way. And that's twice I warned you."

"Three times. But maybe counting ain't your strong suit, neighbor."

Stubbs lifted the cane and rested it lightly on his shoulder. It would take only a snap of the arm and wrist to put it into action and lay open Caleb's skull.

"I'm done talking. Them boys got a lesson to learn about property," Stubbs said, his fingers flexing and tightening on the shaft of the stick. "I'm gonna learn them."

Caleb had seen men do real damage with a cane like that. His own father was famous for giving a thrashing. As headmaster at a training school in Indiana, Elijah Starr found plenty of opportunity to perfect his cruel skill. And he took advantage of every damn chance he got. Unfortunately for some, he didn't limit his practice to students.

"This is my ranch." Caleb spoke low and clear. He'd been trying hard to keep the sparks of anger inside of him from flaring up. He'd given this dolt every opportunity to go. But his patience was growing thin.

"You ain't coming onto my land to teach nobody about property."

"Told you afore. This business —"

"Well, I'm telling you now, if you got business with them, you got business with me."

"They owe me."

"Tell me. Maybe I can settle it."

Stubbs's eyes spit fire at him from beneath the brim of his hat. "I done warned that little Black bastard afore about coming onto my land and stealing from me. And now he found some scrawny, ginger street rat to help him."

This was what it came down to. Here was the answer to Gabe's question about why Stubbs was always angry at him. He said that the miner didn't do business at their livery stable. He was one of them bone-headed fellas who couldn't see past the color of a man's skin. He wasn't the only one around Elkhorn, to be sure.

"Go to hell. These boys ain't thieves."

"I'm telling you," he rasped, the pitch of his gravelly voice rising. "They was trespassing on my land. I found them up sniffing around my mines."

"That ain't so," Gabe replied, his first words since the man appeared.

Stubbs cleared his throat and spat angrily to the side. Using his free hand to smooth his moustache, he sent a fierce glare past Caleb.

"I say, it *is,*" he countered, speaking directly to Caleb. "And this ain't the first time I seen him on my place. Not by a long shot. And I ain't about to stand for that."

There was a change in the man's tone, in the dead, quiet look in his eyes. It was subtle, but the menace was unmistakable. It was the sly, stealthy look that came just before some fool reached for his iron.

"You ain't going nowhere near them boys."

Stubbs turned slightly, and Caleb saw that he was measuring him up. He'd seen it in a hundred fights in a hundred towns and camps.

"I could have shot the two of them dead and been within my rights. I should have. A man got to protect what's his. They was on my land. Next, they'll be carrying off silver, right outta my mines."

"We wasn't stealing nothing," Paddy squeaked.

"We didn't go nowhere near any mines," Gabe said again.

"I know where I saw you!" he barked. "Don't try to say no different."

"I swear, Mr. Marlowe. And the only times I ever went near his old land was when I went fishing, like this morning, on the creek up this side of the ridge."

"Liar!" Stubbs took a threatening step forward, interrupting Gabe. The stick lifted an inch off his shoulder.

Distant lightning flashed in the darkening sky to the south. A low rumble rolled up the valley.

"Back off," Caleb snapped. Hot blood coursed through his veins, but the words slid out cold as mountain ice. "The land this side of the ridge belongs to me."

"You gonna believe this Black sonovabitch over me?" Flecks of brown spittle had appeared on the man's moustache.

"I don't know you from a pile of buffalo shit, Stubbs. But I know them. And I'd believe them over a low-down dog like you every time."

The man's eyes opened a fraction wider, and his right shoulder jerked back. Caleb knew what was coming. He once saw a gambler knock a card player's pistol out of his hand with one motion — breaking the man's wrist in the process — and then crease the side of his face with the backhand blow. No rattler ever struck with that speed.

Caleb had two choices.

The first was that he step away and move out of the reach of the moving cane.

126

If he backed up, several things would happen in an instant. Stubbs's shoulder would swing forward, and the twist of his body would add debilitating force to the intended blow. At the same time, his elbow would snap downward, and his wrist would complete the whiplike action of the arm. The combined speed and muscle would deliver devastating power to the head of that cane.

If Caleb misjudged the distance he needed to go by even an inch, the stick would find a mark, crushing skull or bone or — at the very least — paralyzing muscle and flesh. Trying to catch the flashing cane would surely break his hand and render it useless. And then more blows would fall.

But Caleb had never been one to back away, and that was his second choice.

As the attack came, he stepped forward quickly. He fired his left hand up to deflect Stubbs's wrist with his forearm. The jarring impact caused a puff of foul air to burst from his opponent's lungs along with a sharp grunt of pain. The cane came loose, hit the ground behind Caleb, and bounced away.

He was nearly nose to nose with Stubbs, and he wasn't about to lose his advantage. A sharp, quick right hook to his foe's jaw snapped his head to the side, sending the brown bowler sailing along with a wad of tobacco. As Stubbs's head swiveled back, Caleb dropped his left shoulder and came up with a shot to the chin, staggering Stubbs backward.

As the man's eyes refocused, Caleb saw how tough his foe was. Stubbs roared like a wounded bear as he launched forward. Pure animal fury was driving him now.

Caleb had no desire to prolong this. Dropping his chin, he planted his right heel, turned his hips, and drove his right fist deep into the soft section formed by the V beneath the man's ribs, exactly in the center of his vest, to the left of the watch pocket.

The blow stopped Stubbs in his tracks and lifted him onto his toes. His chin hit Caleb's shoulder, and then his legs crumpled. He folded like a Barlow knife before dropping onto his knees and falling forward. As he collapsed onto his side, he immediately began to throw up. The stench of liquor and bile filled the air as he coughed and gagged and tried desperately to draw breath.

Caleb crouched over him, keeping him from rolling onto his back until the vomiting subsided. The brown coat had ridden up, and he saw Stubbs had tucked a holstered ivory-handled derringer into the waistline at the back of his pants. He yanked it free and tossed it into the grass.

"Think . . . think you busted something," Stubbs gasped.

"Wouldn't be surprised."

"Can't see straight."

"You ain't dead," Caleb said in a low voice. "But you ever try to lift a hand against these boys again, you'll wish you were."

Grabbing Stubbs's wrist, Caleb hauled him to his feet and jammed the man's bowler back on his head. His legs were wobbling, but Caleb half dragged, half carried him to his horse. Propping Stubbs up against the flank of the animal, he then pulled the Henry rifle from its scabbard and dropped it on the ground. He didn't want this knothead doing anything else foolish today.

Caleb lifted Stubbs's booted foot into the stirrup and hoisted him up into the saddle. His vanquished foe sat slumped forward over the horn, face white as a ghost, eyes glassy.

"Do I need to tie you up there, or can you make it home?"

"I'll make it," Stubbs answered raggedly. "What about my things?"

Caleb shook his head. "You can get your guns from the jail tomorrow. I'll leave them with the sheriff. But I might just burn that damn stick."

Stubbs took up the reins in his hand, but Caleb grabbed the bridle before the man could ride off.

"Don't forget what I said about them boys. If anything happens to either one — and I don't care if it's a wagon brushing past one or a mad dog nipping at the other — I'm coming after you. And don't you forget it."

CHAPTER ELEVEN

Caleb pushed aside the curtain in Doc Burnett's front parlor window and peered out into the approaching night. The thunderstorms that threatened earlier had come in hard, bringing a gloomy twilight, rain, and wind that beat against the house. In the dim light beyond the porch, he could see the streets had been reduced to muck and mire.

It would be a long, slow trek back to the ranch tonight, but it couldn't be helped. Hell, it wasn't the first time he and Pirate had gotten muddy and wet.

On the porch, one of Zeke's men sat on a rocker with a Parker shotgun across his lap. The hat was tipped forward over his eyes, his duster pulled tight against the wet and the chill. His chin rested on his chest, which was rising and falling with the regularity of a man fast asleep.

He was the same no-account deputy who

used to work for Sheriff Horner. Caleb rapped on the window, causing him to sit forward, look around slowly, and then settle back into his previous position.

Caleb shook his head and crossed the room, going through an open archway into the back parlor. In the alcove to the right, Doc sat at a table with the chessboard in front of him. Three brass wall sconces held oil lamps, illuminating the game being laid out.

"Is he the only one that's been out there these past two days?"

Doc shook his head and paused, the knight in his hand. "No, the sheriff had a couple of his new deputies taking turns out there. And he stops in himself several times a day to check on the condition of my patient."

"You mean, his prisoner."

"That's right," Doc scoffed. "I stand corrected."

The gunman Caleb shot in the street during the attack on the judge had survived, thanks to the doctor's skill.

As soon as he'd arrived at the house, Caleb went to check on the wounded man. He was relieved to see the gunman's chest and wrists and ankles were strapped to the bed. Caleb motioned with his head toward the surgery, where the hired gun was being kept.

"When I looked in on him before, he was out cold."

"He comes to, now and again."

Doc finished arranging the chess pieces on the board. A fierce blast of wind-driven rain slapped against a nearby window, rattling it. The storm and the early darkness had pushed their game inside tonight. A chair for Caleb sat facing his friend. A third one had been pulled near, in case Sheila decided to join them later.

She'd disappeared into the kitchen after their supper, and even here he could hear her banging pots and pans around. He wondered what she was doing. Mrs. Lewis, Doc's housekeeper, had cleaned up and gone after serving them dinner.

Caleb sat across the table from his friend. "So this fella ain't said nothing to you?"

"Nothing at all." Doc shook his head. "Other than he's much obliged that I dug the bullet out of him."

"As he ought to be."

"He's not too happy about being restrained."

"Then he ain't gonna be too happy about the restraints Judge Patterson has in mind for that scrawny neck of his either." Caleb picked up a pawn and turned it around in his hand. The carved wood piece was smooth and cool.

"What drives a man to kill for a living?"

"Money."

"Of course. But there has to be something else." Doc's forehead had two creases in it so deep, he could hide a silver dollar in each one.

"For some fellas, it's just a job," Caleb replied. "No different in their eyes than clerking in a store or panning for gold or turning tricks in a saloon or being president of the United States."

"Maybe," Doc said, obviously not convinced.

"These gunhawks all probably figured they were damn good at what they were doing. Till they ran into some bad luck."

"It was bad luck for them that you happened to be walking beside the judge."

"Sometimes a hand don't play out like you think it will."

Caleb hadn't thought about it, but Elkhorn would be a different place tonight if it had only been Frissy Fredericks trailing along with Patterson. Like him or not, trust him or not, the judge was the bull in these parts. If he'd been gunned down, the rest of the herd would be easy pickings for wolves like Eric Goulden or whoever was behind the attack.

"You'd think a man could find some positive use for his God-given talents," Doc said.

"What if he's got none? Life don't always throw much more than scraps at a man. He's got to survive."

Doc had seen his share of killing, and Caleb knew he didn't support it in general. But there was a time and a place for everything.

"Maybe that's so, but to *choose* killing as a profession. I don't understand it."

"Some fellas ain't the best at making good choices, Doc. I'd wager that patient of yours could be rethinking some of his, right now."

Both men stared at the chess board as if some answers to their questions lay hidden amid the opposing lines of tan and brown warriors.

Caleb shook off his thoughts and looked across at his friend. "We playing this game or setting and jawing all night? 'Cuz if you're afraid . . ."

"Ha! Lay on, Macduff."

From the smells beginning to drift in from the kitchen, it appeared that Sheila Burnett was doing more than just punishing pots and pans.

Doc won first move and pushed a pawn two spaces ahead on his king's side. It wasn't his customary opening, so Caleb paused for a moment and considered his next couple of moves before playing.

"You reading a new book on chess, Doc?" he asked.

"I don't know what you're talking about, old man."

When it came to chess, the two men were fairly matched in ability, but they had completely different philosophies regarding strategy.

In contrast to his gruff but peace-loving personality, Doc always attacked like a mad dog, drawing blood in every direction and at every opportunity. He would willingly and wildly sacrifice his own pieces to take out one of Caleb's. He loved to strike unexpectedly, but as some old poet said, there was a method to his madness.

Caleb was a more of a thoughtful strategist. Lay back, set the trap, and then reap the rewards. He liked to plan ahead, try to see every possible response. He considered everything from the movement of the first pawn to the formation of a mating net to finish off his opponent. He had come to sense that his friend's chuckles and occasional shouts of triumph at some violent move were intended to interrupt his thoughts, but Caleb wasn't about to let on about it.

The sound of a plate clacking on a counter reached him from the back of the house. Having Sheila in the house was a definite distraction, and Caleb's game had suffered for it since she arrived.

The door to Doc's surgery was down the wide central hall near the back of the house, beyond the stairway leading to the upper floors. The surgery entrance was situated near the back door and the kitchen. Caleb wondered if Doc had warned his daughter against feeding or going near the gunman by herself. Of course, she was more likely to do the exact opposite of what she was told.

Better to stay out of it, he reminded himself.

"Your patient. Did he tell you his name?"

Doc scoffed, not looking up from the board. "He's not quite ready to trust me with that kind of information."

"Do you feel safe keeping him here in the house?"

Doc moved a chess piece. "Safe enough. What makes you ask?"

"If he's mending, it might be a good time to move him on down to the jail."

"Are you concerned because I'm living here, Mr. Marlowe?" Sheila asked as she swept into the room, graceful as a hawk in flight. She carried a tray and stopped beside the table. "You know better than anyone that I can protect myself. No?"

Both men came to their feet, and Sheila set the tray down on a nearby table.

"I ain't worried about you protecting yourself, Miss Burnett," he lied.

Actually, he *was* worried about that hired gun being in the house while she was here. But he'd sooner stir up a nest of rattlers than get her going on that subject.

After the events following the robbery of the Wells Fargo stagecoach last month, she'd become more confident about what she could handle and how suitable she was for frontier life. Too confident.

Sheila poured coffee for the two men. When she handed Caleb a cup, his fingers accidentally brushed against hers. He looked into her blue eyes and nodded his thanks.

"What is it, then?" she asked.

"The thing is, we don't know who that shooter in there is or where he's from. But men like that tend to have friends."

"True. They always have friends," Doc repeated, never lifting his eyes off the game.

"If they decided to bust him out of here, I wouldn't want to rely on the deputy sleeping out there on your front step to handle any trouble."

Doc took a cup from his daughter. "I see your point, Marlowe. So far, my patient hasn't been well enough to move, but I think we can safely do it now. I'll have a chat with Zeke when he comes in tomorrow. I can look in on the man at the jailhouse."

Caleb glanced toward the front window. The storm wasn't easing up. He'd be happier if the gunman were down in that jail tonight, but there wasn't much chance of that happening.

"There you go, Mr. Marlowe," Sheila said. "No need to worry. Now you'll be able to sleep soundly."

"I haven't slept soundly since . . ." He cut his words short.

"Since when?"

Since she'd showed up at his ranch in the middle of night. But he wasn't going to admit that her pretty smiles and blue eyes robbed him of shut-eye.

"I started that wrong. I sleep like the dead."

"You? Never."

"How would you know that?"

"Because you're here and there and everywhere at all hours of the day and night." She scoffed. "The judge needs you, and the sheriff needs you, my father needs you —"

139

Doc made a motion to leave him out of this.

"I don't know that's true."

"For all I know, the man who lights the streetlamps in town probably needs you too."

"Think you might be stretching things a little, Miss Burnett?"

"And," she said coyly, "I suppose I ask your opinion occasionally. But I believe you enjoy the meddling, Mr. Marlowe."

"That so?"

"All I know is, for a man who gives the impression that he'd rather be riding the range with his dog and his cattle, you're about the busiest man in Elkhorn."

Caleb grumbled and stared at the chess board, suddenly feeling like she'd tied a knot in his tongue.

Her teasing hit home. He had a tough time saying no when people needed help, but that was not meddling. Sheila Burnett was different than everyone else. In a thousand years, he wouldn't say it, but he *did* care what happened to her. He worried about how ill-prepared she was to carry on in Elkhorn. And he had no damn right to be thinking about it at all. She was Doc's daughter. She was no responsibility of his. Never would be.

140

Caleb realized she was holding out a plate of cookies in his direction like a peace offering. He didn't hesitate and took two, stuffing one in his mouth.

Sugar cookie. Damned if that wasn't his favorite. And there was some other flavor to it that he recognized.

He had to fight back a groan of pleasure. "Don't recall Mrs. Lewis ever baking these before."

"She didn't. I baked them." Sheila's smug smile was enough of an answer.

"What's that spice in them?"

"Cinnamon."

"That's right," Caleb said, remembering an apple pie a neighbor used to make when he was a boy.

"You're becoming quite accomplished in the kitchen, Sheila," Doc said. "Your move, Marlowe."

She held out the plate to him again. "I made a batch yesterday, but I gave them to Imala. By the way, she sends her regards to you."

Caleb moved a piece and looked up at her. "You went all the way out there . . . alone?"

"Is there something wrong with me visiting her?"

Imala was an Arapaho woman who'd been married to a miner name Smith. She lived in a cabin on their claim, about two hours outside of town.

"That Denver road ain't exactly safe. You could meet up with all kinds of rogues and blackguards out there."

So much for minding his own business.

"He's right, Sheila. You need to be careful, my love," Doc put in. "Your move, Marlowe."

Imala's husband was killed by the same road agents who'd taken Doc last month. There were too many lowlife dogs out there who would be only too happy to come upon a woman like Sheila Burnett.

"I like and respect Imala greatly. And she likes me. We enjoy each other's company. She's teaching me so many important skills about frontier life." She looked at Caleb. "I'm very careful."

"As careful as you were when we met the first time?"

Her eyes spit fire at him. They'd made an agreement not to mention that incident in front of her father. "More careful."

Her back was straight, her hands fisted in her lap.

"Why do you need to go out there?" Caleb was having a hard time keeping a muzzle on.

"With Imala, I'm doing things that I was

142

never allowed to try back in New York. I'm clearing fields, planting, hunting . . ."

He stole a glance at Doc, who gestured impatiently at the board. Caleb moved a piece that his friend immediately pounced on.

Doc seemed perfectly fine with his daughter talking about doing manual labor. Years ago, after his wife's death, Sheila had been left behind with Doc's rich in-laws. She'd been educated and pampered, but things had changed since she arrived in Elkhorn.

There was nothing wrong with a woman doing the chores and working, but this one? Sheila was a high-society, city-bred girl who, in her past life, probably changed her kid gloves ten times a day.

"Last week, she showed me how to skin a beaver. I did quite well too, if I do say so myself." Her face disappeared into her coffee cup.

It was a little bit surprising to Caleb how quickly Imala had accepted Sheila as an acquaintance. Before marrying Smith, she'd survived the extreme brutality of white men against her people. Befriending a young East Coast woman raised in opulence and comfort seemed more than unlikely. He'd have thought the two would have nothing in common and any kind of bond between them would be out of the question.

One more reminder of how little he knew about women.

"Next week, we're making beaded leather bags for carrying tobacco." She smiled. "Mr. Wilson at the general store has agreed to buy twenty of them from her. All the smokers in Elkhorn will be clamoring for them, I'm sure."

"Your move, Marlowe."

While the conversation continued, Doc was busily cutting a bloody swath across the chessboard. Caleb could already see that his game was in trouble. He moved a piece, and his opponent's rook immediately knocked it clear off the table.

"You already know that I'm a good rider, Mr. Marlowe," she persisted. "And a competent shot as well. I'm quite prepared to handle any situation —"

"No one is prepared to handle the killers you could run into out there." He stared at the board. In two moves, Doc's queen and knight would have Caleb's king in check. Right now, much as he hated it, all he could do was run. Delay the inevitable. Hope he could lure Doc into making a mistake. "All I'm saying is that you shouldn't go out there alone. You could at least get Gabe to ride with you or —"

"And endanger a fourteen-year-old for my sake?" she exclaimed. "What if something happened to him? I'd never forgive myself."

Doc showed no mercy and took down Caleb's queen.

"So you admit there's danger." He stared into her face. She was the orneriest woman he'd ever met. "Ask Mr. Lewis at the hardware store. He has a trustworthy fella who sometimes delivers supplies out to the claims. Maybe not that far, but you could ask him."

"Your move, Marlowe."

"All I'm saying," he repeated, "is that you shouldn't ride alone."

Caleb had to put his bishop in the path of Doc's assault. It was a quick death.

"I've met the man Mr. Lewis employs. He's about a hundred years old, deaf as a stone, and blind in one eye. I'd be protecting *him*."

"Your turn."

The father and daughter were after him. Caleb realized they were working together.

"The man is my age," Caleb replied, knowing that wasn't the truth. But Lewis's helper was probably not much older than fifty. Or sixty.

Her eyes rounded. "Just how old are you, Mr. Marlowe?"

"Twenty-nine."

"Your move," Doc nudged.

She held out the plate of cookies. "Why, that's not old. We're closer in age than I thought. Unless you're saying that *I'm* old."

She pulled back the cookies before he could take one.

"I said no such thing."

"I believe you did. But I don't mind. After all, it just adds to my argument that there's very little to worry about me going out there. Who would bother an old spinster?"

Spinster. Sheila Burnett.

She was probably the prettiest woman in Elkhorn, Denver, and everywhere in between. And she was making it her mission to rile him and distract him. He had an idea she was also fishing for compliments at the moment.

No way was he playing into that hand. There was no way he was gonna make a play for this woman or any other. Not one who was looking for a husband and partner to set by the fire and grow old with anyway. No, a woman like Sheila Burnett deserved better than him, and sniffing around here was only asking for trouble. Damn it, he couldn't even believe he was wasting his breath arguing with her. He didn't need the trouble.

He turned his focus back to the board and shook his head. Besides all that, he was certain Sheila was in cahoots with her father. He had eight measly pieces left of the army he'd begun the damn game with. Thankfully, they'd made no wager on to-night's game.

"Check."

Doc's knight, queen, and bishop were keeping Caleb on the run. His choices were limited, but he wasn't going down without a fight. He moved and took a sip of his cool-ing coffee.

"My father has no opinion on it, but what would you think if I started wearing a vest and trousers?"

Caleb's gaze was drawn momentarily to the fitted dress and the curves of her hips. He quickly looked away, picturing her long legs in pants and boots. He put his coffee cup down before he could spill it.

"Why would you do that?"

"So I can wear a six-shooter."

"Of course, why didn't I think of that?"

"I'm so glad, Marlowe. I knew you'd agree."

She leaned over and patted her father on the arm. "I told you he'd think it was a good idea."

"Check," Doc responded sharply before

nodding vaguely in his daughter's direction.

"And I plan to cut my hair too."

"Your hair?"

"To look more like a man. That way, even when I ride to Imala's, everyone can stop fussing and worrying about me."

"And by *everyone* you mean . . . ?"

"My father and . . . and whoever is worried."

Their eyes locked. She was doing her best to distract him. The chess game was a mess. One more move by Doc would have Caleb's king in checkmate.

She smiled at him. "I do think I could use a lesson or two in using a revolver, though. Will you be willing to spend an hour or two with me?"

"Checkmate," Doc exclaimed triumphantly as he knocked over Caleb's king with his queen. He sat back happily in his chair, studying the chessboard. "I don't think I've ever beaten you in so few moves, my friend. What's wrong with you tonight?"

They had him. The two of them. Caleb eyed the plate of cookies. There was one left. As Doc reached for it, Caleb snatched it first.

"I won that cookie, Marlowe. To the victor go the spoils."

"The hell you say." Caleb frowned at

Sheila. "I was outnumbered."

She immediately pushed to her feet, not really trying to hide her grin. "There are plenty more in the kitchen. Even a few for sore losers. I'll get them."

As soon as she left the room, Doc leaned toward him, his voice low. "Just so you know, she doesn't ride alone to Imala's cabin. She's gone twice, and I went with her. I used the excuse that I needed to check on a few miners who have claims out there. And today, the two women had arranged to go to the general store together."

"And skinning a beaver?"

Doc shrugged and smiled. "Who knows? Maybe she did. Maybe she didn't. I couldn't tell you. But one thing I do know . . . she does enjoy seeing you squirm."

"There was no squirming."

"You looked like a wax worm on a hook, friend."

"If she brings back a dozen cookies, Doc, I'm eating them all. Just so *you* know."

The older man laughed. "It's all good-natured fun. She enjoys teasing you."

And she was getting pretty damn good at it.

Caleb harrumphed and finished the cookie. Rising to his feet, he looked at the rain beating on the glass. It was still falling in sheets, though the wind seemed to be easing up.

Doc started putting the chess pieces into a dark-green velvet bag. The sound of dishes getting moved around drifted in from the kitchen. Caleb wandered into the front parlor to the window facing the porch and the street.

There was more than Sheila's teasing that was playing on Caleb's mind. He'd be a fool not to see she liked him. And it would be a fat lie for him to deny that he felt something for her.

It didn't matter, though. He wasn't going to do anything about it. He was a loner with an ugly and twisted past.

Looking out the window, his gaze fixed on the deputy. He was no longer sitting and sleeping in the rocker. He was lying on the porch. Caleb pushed the curtain back to get a better look. In the light spilling out the window, he could see the pool of blood around the man's head.

A dish broke somewhere toward the back of the house.

He whirled, snatched one of his Colts from the gun belt he'd left on a table by the door, and raced toward the sound. Doc looked up in alarm as Caleb went past him.

"Someone's in the house."

CHAPTER TWELVE

Caleb moved quietly into the wide central hallway. No one had come in through the front door. The only other door to the outside was by the kitchen, where Sheila had gone. It had been latched when he checked earlier.

The open stairway to the second floor was ahead of him and to the right. The steps turned at a landing and formed an arch over the downstairs hallway. Beyond the arch, at the end of the narrower passageway, he could see the back door. It was closed. The kitchen entrance was to the right. The surgery was to the left.

He listened for any sound of dishes or footsteps from the back of the house. There was nothing. He cursed himself for letting his guard down. While he was playing a game, a deputy had been murdered. And Sheila could be hurt as well.

His boots moved noiselessly across the

floorboards. Alert for any movement, Caleb passed under the arch and headed down the passageway. He spotted jagged pieces of a broken plate and sugar cookies on the floor at the entrance to the kitchen.

Concern quickened Caleb's steps. There were no sounds coming from either room. He feared someone had her.

He went past the broken plate and side-stepped as he entered the kitchen, his six-shooter at the ready. His eyes swept the room, illuminated only by the flickering light from the stove's banked embers.

Caleb saw her, standing with her back to a cabinet, a butcher knife in one hand and an iron skillet in the other. Eyes wide, she was positioned like a practiced street fighter, ready to take on whoever came through the door. Recognizing him, she rushed forward.

Relief washed through Caleb, and he closed the distance between them in a heartbeat.

"I heard a noise." Her gaze flickered toward the door. "The surgery. I went to look in."

When faced with the possibility of danger, some people backed away or stood frozen, unable to process the threat. A few moved toward and challenged it. Sheila Burnett was one of those.

She pointed with her knife. "He was going toward the patient but stopped when I dropped the plate."

Caleb had known someone could break into the house, but he'd done nothing about it. Livid with himself, he turned on his heel and strode out of the kitchen. Doc was coming down the hall from the front of the house, carrying a shotgun.

"What is it?" he asked.

Caleb didn't pause to answer. He raised his Colt and moved to the surgery door.

On the far side of the room, a window facing the empty side lot was open, and a shadowy figure was disappearing through it. Whoever he was, he was quick and agile and gone in an instant.

Caleb bolted across the floor, glancing toward the recuperating gunman as he ran. He expected the bed to be empty. It wasn't. The patient was still strapped down, though there was no longer any need for restraints.

He was staring at the ceiling, his throat cut from ear to ear. Blood was on the floor, on the bed, on the bed linens.

The judge's warnings about Goulden sprang into his head. An assassin had been sent to kill the man to keep him from talking. More important than Patterson's troubles, Sheila had come close to having her throat slit.

He was not about to let this snake get away. Caleb climbed through the window and immediately spotted him. He didn't have much of a head start.

The street in front of the house was the last one before the edge of Elkhorn. Beyond Doc's house, the road made a long, rising bend to the right before becoming what was little more than a trail leading up to dozens of mining claims and logging cuts in the heavily forested hills to the north of town.

The rain began to fall even harder. The ground was soft and slick. Caleb's boots sank into the mud, making it difficult to run. Two long flashes of lightning lit the darkness, and he saw the man slip but get back on his feet quickly. Caleb bore down on him.

The open lot next to the house was no more than a hundred yards wide. Groves of young cottonwood and scrub pine formed the far border, though they were lost now in the darkness and the storm.

Caleb figured the fleeing assassin had his horse tied there. It was possible he had a partner or two waiting as well. He'd take care of that problem when he came to it.

The killer had gone through that window with the agility of a cat. The man was small

154

and lean, but even with his short legs, he was having no easier time finding his footing in the mud than Caleb was.

Caleb still had his iron in his hand, and he thought about using it. He could easily shoot him down right now, but he wanted the assassin alive and talking.

The injured gunhawk was dead. This one murdered him. He'd cut the throat of a man who was strapped down and unable to defend himself. From his time as a sheriff, Caleb knew members of a gang each had a purpose. Four men were now dead. What was this one's role?

Caleb guessed he was here to make sure no one was left behind to incriminate whoever was paying them.

He stuck his pistol in his vest and sprinted.

He had a personal vendetta in going after him too. Caleb wanted to get his hands on the throat of this villain who'd had the brass to enter Doc's house. He'd brought the threat of violence into the home of people he cared about.

The assassin slipped and went down on one knee, but he was up again in an instant. As he came up, Caleb was surprised when he spun around.

He had barely an instant to react. They were close, and his footing was bad. Caleb skidded to a stop as the knife flew toward him, whirling end over end, the blade a deadly blur.

The weapon hit him in the chest as he managed to twist his body. The knife made a deadened metallic sound and stuck in his vest. By sheer luck, the gun Caleb had slipped into his garment had diverted the point.

The rogue didn't wait to see the results of his action. He was running again.

Caleb yanked the knife from his vest, dropped it, and flew after him.

They hadn't gone ten steps when he caught up and dove at the weasel. He sent him sprawling into the mud, but they were both on their feet in an instant.

The man's eyes glared from a pinched, feline face. He made a move to run again.

As he turned, Caleb grabbed the shoulder of his coat and yanked him off-balance. There was no way this blackguard was going to escape him.

His foe was quick to find his footing on the slick ground. He twisted around, batting at the arm holding him in an effort to free himself.

Still clutching a handful of the duster, Caleb drew back the other hand. He focused on the point of the bearded chin, his fist poised and ready to finish this.

The killer was startlingly fast, and he was neither frantic nor panicked. He simply had other plans.

Before Caleb could even unleash his punch, he caught sight of the long, thin blade in his foe's hand. It darted through the darkness from below. The enemy was spinning toward him to add power and speed to the upward thrust. The point of the knife was aimed directly at his heart.

Caleb arched his body sideways to evade the lethal assault. It wasn't enough. The blade punched into his side.

The fiery pain was sharp, exploding upward through his midsection and chest into his brain with unexpected ferocity.

The man drew his arm back in a flash, ready to strike again. But Caleb — still holding the assassin's coat — jumped away, slinging the cutthroat to the ground. The attacker was on his feet in a single motion.

The blade had pierced his vest, but it hadn't found his heart.

Caleb was still alive and blind with fury.

As the weasel turned to run, Caleb shoved him again, sending him flying. The assassin faced him while trying to spring to his feet, and Caleb's boot connected with his shoulder, driving him up and over onto his back.

He rolled and lay flat, crying out in pain.

The rain battered them, and distant lightning flashed. Caleb moved closer. The dark handle of a knife protruded from high on the man's chest. In his fall, he'd landed on his own blade. He squirmed and cried out again.

Caleb was hardly in the mood for sympathy. He'd given this viper two chances. He wouldn't get another. Caleb could feel his own blood pulsing from the wound in his side. Dropping onto one knee, he twisted the knife in the assassin and then yanked it out, eliciting a sharp cry.

Caleb held the blade where the man could see it. "Talk."

"Go to hell."

The rogue lay panting in the mud, looking up. His face hardened as Caleb pulled two more knives from the man's boots and tossed them away. He carried no concealed pistol. He was a blade man.

"You first." Caleb pressed the point of the knife under the man's chin. "Who sent you?"

His pinched face squeezed shut, and his lips pressed into a tight thin line.

"Talk, or I gut you right here."

"Go ahead. Do it."

The image of Sheila's pale face in the

kitchen flashed before Caleb's eyes. This man would have killed her with no more thought than brushing a spot of lint from his coat.

Caleb grabbed a fistful of coat, lifted the blackguard six inches, and slammed him back to the ground.

"Damn you to hell. Kill me. Be done with it."

"Not until you've suffered enough."

Lightning, closer now, lit the sky, and the crash of thunder rolled over them.

"Or I can you let you go."

His eyes cleared for a brief moment, and then he smirked. "You wouldn't."

"Give me a name."

He scoffed. "Nobody sent me."

Caleb had been right in his thinking. This one was smart enough to be put in charge and tough enough to hold his tongue. Caleb shoved a hand inside the rogue's coat, looking for a purse, letters, or anything that might give a clue as to who he was.

Nothing. If he was carrying anything, it wasn't in his coat.

Another bolt ripped the sky, reflecting off the blade. Caleb stared as the cold light of recognition flooded his brain.

The knife.

As he held it up, lightning continued to

strike the hills to the south. The insignia was there. Strips of silver inlaid into the handle.

A six-pointed star with an *E* in the center. "Where did you get this?"

"Go to hell." The assassin shut his eyes.

Caleb grabbed the man's collar again, lifted him, and hammered him into the ground. His eyes opened, and hatred — cold and deadly — shone in their depths.

"Where did you *get* this?"

"It was a gift."

"Who gave it to you?"

"Go to the devil. I ain't *never* saying."

Caleb knew the insignia. He knew the knife. He'd seen it a hundred times before. And if he dared to even touch it when he was growing up, the punishment was swift and sure.

"This knife belonged to Elijah Starr."

CHAPTER THIRTEEN

The man's eyes widened for only an instant. The look was unmistakable, though, confirming what Caleb knew. And it passed as quickly as it came.

"He'd never part with it," he hissed into the man's face. "You stole it."

"I don't give a shit what you think."

Caleb held the weapon up. "Starr. This knife. Bat Davis. They came from the same corner of Indiana."

"How would you know that?"

"Bat and I were friends."

Suspicion clouded the features of the blackguard. "Good for you."

He wasn't giving any information freely.

"We grew up in the same town. We . . . we both knew Elijah Starr."

"Didn't stop you from killing Bat."

"I didn't kill him. I was as surprised as him when we faced off. I was ready to let him walk. He was gunned from the street by the sheriff."

Caleb heard some commotion and more shouting coming from the front of the house. People from Main Street were answering Doc's calls for help.

They'd only have a few minutes before they'd be swarmed by townspeople. Whatever answer he got had to come before everyone else reached them.

"If you're such good old friends, why ain't you working for us?"

Caleb motioned with his head toward the house. " 'Cuz falling short costs a man."

The killer scoffed. "No sinners in heaven; no forgiveness in hell."

The words were sharper than his blade and cut Caleb deeper.

No sinners in heaven; no forgiveness in hell!

Those words. They'd haunted him every day of his life. As a child, he'd heard them often, usually as the rod striped his flesh.

No sinners in heaven. And the blows fell. The cane. The punch. The kick. *No forgiveness in hell!* The hard, unbending hickory on his shoulders and back. The huge fist to his face. The boot driven into his stomach, robbing him of breath, leaving Caleb a bloody and gasping lump as his mother cried, unable to stop the beating, often taking the abuse herself to save him, her only child.

Elijah Starr was fond of the words, used them, believed them.

In the eyes of Caleb's father, sin was branded on people's souls. Everyone except himself. He was one of the elite, one of the chosen few. He was the self-ordained hand of some twisted god, sent to punish human frailty, to lay the lash and the cane across on the backs of the weak and the fallen.

The pain of the past drove its pointed end straight into Caleb's brain.

He let go of the man's coat and staggered to his feet. He'd stood over his father's dead body.

Caleb pressed a hand to his side where blood continued to pulse from the wound.

The man tried to roll and get himself up, but he fell back, clutching his shoulder.

The downpour had eased, and a steady rain now fell, spattering in pools between clumps of grass. To the south and the east, bolts of lightning continued to flash, and distant thunder rumbled along the huddled ridges and blackened escarpments.

Could it be that he'd left that bloody kitchen too soon? Had Elijah Starr actually survived?

A chill, cold as the grave, washed down

his back, and Caleb wiped rain from his eyes.

Doc's voice drew his attention toward the front of the house. He was shouting directions. ". . .and tell the sheriff his deputy is dead. We need him here right now."

Caleb ran his thumb across the insignia on the handle. Thirteen years ago, after finding his mother dead at the house, he beat his father to death with his bare hands. And then he ran away with nothing but the bloody shirt on his back.

He had no money. He had no destination. Caleb carried nothing but his swollen fists to remind him of where he'd been and what he'd done. As well as a soul scarred with memories that would never fade.

He glared at the man lying at his feet. The blackguard was breathing hard and squirming from the pain. Caleb thought of what Bat said only a moment before dying: *I'd think* you *would wanna know who sent me.*

How could this cutthroat know his father?

His face did not belong to one of the Shawnee or Kickapoo children taken from their people and transported to the training institute. There were also people who worked on the Indiana farm where Elijah Starr had set up his school. Laborers like Bat Davis's father and uncle. Many came and went. Caleb didn't remember all of the faces, and he didn't recall this one.

Once again, the image of his father, lifeless on the kitchen floor, flooded his brain. How could this outlaw come to possess his knife?

Sudden, sharp, white-hot pain raked through Caleb's side. He bore down on it as a brilliant flash stretched jagged fingers across the sky to the north. A deafening crack accompanied it immediately.

"Help me get out of here." The wounded man's voice was strained.

Caleb leaned over him again. "You ain't in no shape to ride."

"I can make it."

"Too risky."

"I can pay. Some now. More later."

Caleb could see no horse nearby, but the man no doubt had a mount waiting somewhere beyond the line of the trees. "You ain't got time. But maybe your people can get you out later. Where can I send word?"

He thought for a moment that the weasel was going to tell him. But the man's eyes fixed on his face, and he scoffed. "My mama raised no fool. And even if you was telling the truth, he'd kill me if I spilled anything."

"You mean Elijah Starr."

The rogue said nothing but winced as he

turned his pinched face toward the sound of voices coming from the direction of the house.

Caleb saw a muddled line of dark shapes approaching. Light from swinging lamps gleamed off ruddy faces and gun barrels.

In all the years he'd been on the road, Caleb had never gone back to Indiana. Never sought out information. He'd wanted to sever all ties to that past. If his true identity were revealed, if the connection were made between him and the dead schoolmaster, a noose would fit snugly around his neck. But what if his father was still alive?

"Caleb."

Sheila's voice came from behind him. He turned to her and squinted through the rain. She'd come from the back of the house, and he didn't know how long she'd been standing here, what she'd heard and seen.

Her clothes were soaked. Her hair, dark and wet, lay plastered to her head. The water ran down her face and dripped from her chin. She still carried the knife she'd been holding in the kitchen.

"What are you doing out here?"

"I was worried. I came after you."

A hard thought ran through his head. What if he hadn't bested this scoundrel? She could have been hurt or killed at the house or here. Still, she'd come after him alone. Prepared to fight.

"What would you have done if I was already dead?"

"I'd go after him," she whispered fiercely. "I'd make him suffer."

She had no fear. Like his mother, her instinct was to protect regardless of any danger to herself. The emotion running through him was raw. What if his mother's death was never avenged?

He took a step toward her and opened his arms. Suddenly, she was wrapped around him, and it felt right to hold her. His arms tightened around Sheila. Her hair smelled like lavender in summer. She was shivering badly.

Sheila touched the side of his shirt. "This is warm. It's blood."

She pulled away, staring at his side. He again pressed his hand against the wound.

"Just a scratch."

"He stabbed you?"

"It ain't nothing some catgut and a knot or two can't fix."

"Let me see," she said, trying to pull his hand away.

He slipped the knife into his boot and motioned to the man lying at their feet. "See to him first. We gotta keep him alive."

167

Caleb wasn't done with him. There was plenty more the sonovabitch needed to say.

"What do I care about him?" She kicked angrily at the cutthroat's feet. "He can die in the mud. Let the lightning and the devil take him."

Why he'd ever thought she wasn't tough enough to make it in these parts was beyond him. She had a backbone of steel and a fire in her veins.

"That's a lot of blood. I have to get you back to the house."

She didn't need to take him anywhere. Doc and his party of miners and townspeople arrived, forming a circle around them.

"Marlowe's bleeding," she immediately announced.

The doctor didn't ask permission, simply held up a lamp and peered and poked at Caleb's side. "The wound looks bad. We have to get you inside."

"I'm alive."

"Damn right," Doc said. "And we're making sure that you stay that way. Can you walk?"

"To Denver, if I have to."

More folks appeared, coming from every direction. Neighbors and customers fresh from drinking in the Belle Saloon running, slogging through the mud. They must have heard the call for the sheriff.

"I need two men to haul a dead body out of my surgery," Doc ordered the men around him. "Put him on the front porch with the deputy. You fellows, help me carry this one in."

As the hired assassin moaned with pain, Doc motioned to Sheila.

"Make sure Marlowe comes in."

The injured man was lifted and carried, none too gently, toward the house. As they moved off, he cursed and bellyached with every step.

Caleb began to trudge after them. He was already calculating what needed to be done. Getting more out of this rogue was at the top of the list, but he'd only be able to get so far with him anytime soon.

A better option for him right now was to go and see Patterson. The judge was connected in many circles outside of Elkhorn. He might be able to provide him with more information about Elijah Starr. But there was no way Caleb was going to reveal his own connection to the man.

Sheila walked alongside, not giving up her position at his elbow. "You're dragging."

"I'm fine."

"Can you make it on your own, or should I have some of these men help you?" she persisted.

"I can walk," he told her.

"Well, I'm going to make sure my father tends to you before that outlaw," she said staunchly.

"First, I'm gonna go see the judge."

She yanked at his elbow, causing a hot dagger of pain to cut through his midsection. "You're not going anywhere until you have that wound taken care of."

"Doc's got his hands full. I'll be back."

She stepped directly in his path and faced him, her fists on her hips. Even in the darkness, he could see her eyes spitting fire.

"You're not going anywhere but inside that house."

"Got things I need to do."

"They can wait."

Caleb looked toward the road, trying to decide if he could show up at Patterson's house unannounced. He knew approximately where the judge lived.

"You're not paying attention, are you?"

"I promise to come back."

"Don't make me hurt you." Her tone was deep and sharp.

"More than I am, you mean."

"Much more."

He glanced down at the knife she was pointing at him, obviously in jest. He held his hand out, and she gave it to him.

"There're better ways of convincing me to do something."

Her tone softened. "Please come in, Marlowe."

There was no fighting with this woman once she set her mind to something.

His thumb brushed away the wetness from her cheek. She was soaked to the skin. So was he. "All right. Have it your way."

She took hold of his elbow again, not giving him any chance of escaping.

It probably was a good idea to see Doc first. With every step he took, Caleb felt like he was being stabbed. While his fighting blood had been up, he'd barely noticed the wound, but it ran through him like the blazes now.

The rain was easing up. Far to the east, sullen flashes marked the retreating storm. To the west, there were breaks of starry sky through the clouds.

Near the house, two young fellows were standing barefoot in the mud, gawking at the proceedings. He was quite close before he recognized them as the bucktooth brothers who'd knocked into Zeke on the sidewalk the other day.

Caleb stopped and beckoned to them. "Need you to do some scouting for me."

They glanced at each other and then nodded enthusiastically.

"This weasel that they're carrying rode in on something. I'm guessing he left his horse over there." Caleb pointed at the line of trees. "Bring it back here and tie it in front of Doc's house." He frowned as a thought occurred to him. "But I need you to go quiet as a pair of Arapaho hunters. Stay in the shadows, and don't let nobody see you. If there's anyone waiting over there, come back and tell me. Got it?"

Without a word, the young recruits ran off, quickly disappearing in the darkness.

Caleb wondered what that blade had managed to slice up inside of him. He was sure he'd lost a good deal of blood because he was starting to feel a coldness set into the left side of his body.

"Are you *always* right?" There was an edge in Sheila's voice, but it sounded more like worry than pique.

"Don't know what you mean, exactly. But I like the way that sounds."

"I think you know." She cast a quick glance at his side.

Caleb realized she was trying to distract him. "Go ahead and tell me. I like hearing you apologize."

"Apologize?" Her temper flared. "For

what? Why would I?"

"For not believing me."

She scoffed.

"I believe I told you that patient in the surgery would have friends who'd come calling."

"Some kind of friend," she said with disgust. She was quiet for a few steps. "Who is Elijah Starr?"

Caleb was right. Sheila *had* overheard him talking with the cutthroat.

"Might be the man who sent this blackguard. I ain't sure yet."

"But you recognized that the knife belonged to him?"

"I recognized the markings on it."

"You've seen it before?"

"Some marks you never forget."

They reached the front of the house. The rain stopped, with only a residual mist in the air. There was a small crowd milling around a wagon.

Caleb realized that it belonged to the undertaker. He'd certainly gotten here quick enough. Zeke was supervising as four men carried the deputy's body down the porch stairs. The dead outlaw had already been brought out from the surgery and deposited in the wagon.

Sheila stood next to Caleb. She was making sure he went in and had Doc tend to the wound. Before they could go up the steps, Zeke joined them, tipping his hat to Sheila. He took a handkerchief from his pocket and wiped the rain off his beard.

"Damn it . . . pardon my language, miss . . . but I'm tired of this, Marlowe. I'm packing my gear and heading out. Montana, maybe."

"You ain't going nowhere."

"That mangy hound cut two throats. Just a good thing he didn't do the same to Doc. And to you too, Miss Sheila."

"He couldn't," she replied, sparking with anger. "I would have flattened his head with a skillet and gutted him with my knife."

"I'm sure you woulda given him what he deserved, ma'am."

They heard Doc calling to his daughter from inside the house. She went up onto the porch to answer him. "I'll be right in with Marlowe."

The sheriff's eyes fell on Caleb's vest. "He got you too?"

"He's quick and tough."

"Should've used a skillet on him."

"I heard that, Sheriff." Sheila glared and beckoned to Caleb from the top step. "Let's get you patched up, Marlowe."

He started up the steps but stopped and

turned to Zeke. "I need to talk to the judge tonight. Can you go and let him know?"

"I imagine he's home now," the sheriff said. "Can't wait till morning?"

"No."

"I'll tell him. But I ain't promising nothing."

As Caleb made his way slowly up the steps, the sheriff barked more orders at the throng and stomped off, gray and surly, into the darkness.

In the wide central hallway, men filed by, touching the brims of their hats as they passed Sheila on their way out.

Her shoulders were tense. By the added light inside, Caleb could see she was pale as a ghost. He realized from her worried looks that she was more nervous about his wound than he was.

"Looks like there's as much mud in here as there is outside," Caleb said, glancing at the floor.

"Nothing new there. It goes with the territory."

When they reached the back of the house, Doc was waiting for them. He gestured into the kitchen, where the wounded outlaw was propped up in a chair with a deputy and another man watching him. They looked like a pair of street dogs guarding a bone.

The killer was clutching his shoulder. He shot a quick glance at Caleb then turned his pinched face away.

"Come into the surgery, Marlowe," Doc said.

He led them in, and Caleb climbed onto the table. The window where he and the assailant had climbed out was closed now. The floor was still wet and shiny from a quick mopping. A nearby basket was filled with cleaning cloths, and the coppery scent of blood lingered in the air.

Doc eyed the wound and went to collect the instruments he'd need. "Take off your vest and shirt and lie back."

Caleb pulled his Colt from the vest and handed it to Sheila. He watched her put it on a smaller table close by. After unbuttoning his vest, he took it off and laid it next to him. Sheila moved it beside the six-gun. The shirt was a bloody mess, and he struggled to pull it over his head. She was right beside him, helping. The feel of her soft, cool fingers on his fevered skin was a welcome distraction from the pain.

He glanced up and found Sheila staring at his naked chest. He had a half dozen battle scars of various sizes and varieties. Knife wounds. Bullet holes. Even a nasty-looking thing from a hatchet. She was reading the personal history of his life on the frontier.

Suddenly, her eyes flicked to his face, and she blushed crimson, realizing she'd been caught.

"Help Marlowe lie back." Doc poured out a liquid into a bowl.

She helped Caleb stretch out. "The wound is worse than he's letting on."

"I know. I saw it. But since you've decided that you're a doctor now, you can assist me. I'm certain he won't mind."

"I'm lying right here," Caleb commented. "I ain't passed out yet."

"Ignore him," Doc ordered. "Adjust that lamp. I want more light on him."

Having gathered what he needed and laid it all out within reach, the doctor began cleaning and examining the wound. The liquid on the cloth stung like a swarm of wasps, but Caleb steeled himself against the pain.

"How long was the knife blade?" Doc asked.

"Six inches, give or take."

"It angled upward upon entry?"

"Some. He was aiming for my heart," Caleb replied, forcing a grin. "But he couldn't find it."

"If the blade had entered an inch or two to the front, my friend, you might not be joking about it."

"I told you it's worse than he's admitting." She twisted a wet cloth in the bowl and put it within Doc's reach.

"You're lucky to be alive. Do you want something strong before I start stitching you up?"

"No. I got work to do tonight. None of that laudanum stuff."

"How about a knock on the head?" she suggested. "I've still got that skillet handy."

Both men looked at Sheila. Her blue eyes rounded, and for the first time, a smile touched the corner of her lips.

"You'd hit a man when he's down, Miss Burnett?"

"Only a stubborn one."

"If you two are finished chatting each other up . . ." Doc shook his head with amusement and picked up his needle. "On second thought, keep it up, Sheila. You do fine work distracting him. Do what you have to do. Soon as I'm done, we can bring that chess board in here."

Caleb grimaced as his friend wiped oozing blood away. "I knew it was two against one."

"Roll onto your side." The doctor poured some of the liquid from the bowl directly into the wound. Caleb held his breath and

178

gritted his teeth, thinking he was about to explode clear out of his own hide.

"Don't tell us that actually hurt, Marlowe," Sheila said innocently.

Caleb glanced at her and let out his breath. "I'm about ready for that skillet to the head, Doc."

The feel of the needle piercing his flesh hurt like hell. But he refused to complain.

He tried to focus on what he needed to do. He thought about his father. If Elijah Starr were truly alive — and Caleb was beginning to believe it — then the two of them had unfinished business.

When he was done, Doc straightened his back and admired his handiwork. "Sheila, go up and get one of my clean shirts. Might be a little tight on you, Marlowe, but it'll have to do."

"I'll return it to you, soon as I can."

Sheila went out and came back with the shirt while her father was finishing up bandaging Caleb.

"You don't need to come to Elkhorn," Doc said. "I can come and see you. You should rest this wound."

"I am a fast healer."

She muttered something under her breath that Caleb couldn't hear clearly, but he was certain it had to be a jab at him.

"I'm going to have them bring that villain in here from the kitchen," Doc told them as he started for the door. He paused and turned around. "I don't want you in here, Sheila. I don't want you anywhere near him."

"All right," she replied, helping Caleb dress.

Doc was correct. The shirt was tight, but it would have to do since he was heading over to talk to Judge Patterson right after leaving here. The buttons were a struggle, but she came closer to help.

"As my father said, you need to take it easy for a few days, Marlowe. No fooling."

The sound of heavy boots in the hallway saved Caleb from having to answer. Zeke came into the surgery.

"The judge will see you tonight, Marlowe."

Caleb nodded and stood up.

Sheila helped him into his vest and handed him the pistol. "If you're not going to take it slow tonight, at least see if you can avoid getting shot or stabbed again."

"I'll do my best."

CHAPTER FOURTEEN

The storm had passed, but far-off lightning continued to sporadically brighten the sky to the east and south as Caleb and Zeke walked from Doc's house across town.

Main Street was a mire a foot deep where the two men crossed it, but neither that nor the storm did anything to subdue the night-life in town. Raucous laughter, tinny piano music, and off-key singing came from the Belle Saloon. Farther down Main Street, light and noise from the other saloons spilled out onto the wooden sidewalks, along with drunken miners, cowboys, and migrating homesteaders.

"I told him everything I knew about what happened at Doc's house," Zeke said as the two men approached the side street leading to the judge's house. "He was about as happy as a long-tailed cat in room full of rocking chairs."

Outside a brothel a few doors down from

the jail, three men covered with mud from head to toe were staggering about in the street, slipping and sliding and putting on a display of the most ineffective fighting Elkhorn had surely ever seen. A dozen fellows crowded the edge of the sidewalks, shouting taunts and encouragement.

Zeke did his best to ignore the whole affair.

With every step Caleb took, shooting pains fired inward from the stab wound, and a dull ache had spread into the rest of his body. His face felt flushed and hot. Even so, the tangle of thoughts in his mind would not allow him to rest, in spite of Doc's threats. He had to see Patterson. He needed answers, and meeting with the judge was as good a starting place as any.

"You don't mind me coming along, do you?" Zeke asked.

" 'Course not."

"Wait till you see where His Majesty lives."

Two blocks south of Main Street, Judge Patterson's house sat on a huge, elevated lot. A wrought iron fence bordered the entire property as far as Caleb could see. The other houses around it, all in darkness now because of the hour, were large and ornate, but they were dwarfed in size and architectural style by the judge's residence.

It was by far the largest and fanciest home in Elkhorn with its three stories, wrap-around verandas, scores of windows, steep slate roofs, cone-topped turrets, and a tower that probably offered a view all the way to Washington, DC.

"For a widower with no children that anyone knows of, that's a whole passel of rooms, I reckon," Zeke commented, eyeing the residence. "Don't know what a man would do with himself in a place that big."

Caleb said nothing, but he knew from seeing Patterson's office on Main Street that the man valued size. The bigger and richer in appearance, the better.

As they began to cross the street, the hackles on Caleb's neck rose. He slipped the thongs from his twin Colts.

Before he and Zeke reached the other side, two men carrying shotguns emerged from the shadows. One came from the large stone pillars flanking the front gate, and the other from behind a mature cottonwood tree near the corner. Caleb scanned the darkness and sensed more than saw several more human shapes guarding the property.

The one by the front gate leveled his shotgun at them as they approached, but Zeke called out to him. Recognizing the sheriff, the gunman touched a hand to his brim, followed them to the gate, and resumed his watch.

"Looks like the judge is feeling a little nervous," Caleb commented.

"Bunch of them hired on yesterday." Zeke motioned to the departing guard. "His own little army."

Their boots made loud clacking noises on the slate walkway between the front gate and a gravel drive that ran from the street to the stately entrance. Stone columns supported the wide veranda roof, and lit lamps hung on the ones on either side of the stairs. Lights appeared from quite a few windows.

When they mounted the steps, Caleb noted the presence of another guard with a coach gun lurking in the shadows of the veranda.

The amount of precaution was impressive, but whatever Patterson did or didn't do to keep safe was none of Caleb's concern. It didn't involve him at all.

Before they reached the massive, oak double doors, one of them swung open. Framed by the light of an entrance foyer, the hulking form of Patterson's personal bodyguard appeared, blocking their way.

"I told you I'd be right back," Zeke said as they scraped the mud from their boots. "Judge still in the library?"

Fredericks ignored him and smirked at Caleb.

"Heard you run into some knife trouble, Marlowe," he squeaked. "Need some help cutting your meat at dinner?"

"Looks like the judge got an entire infantry regiment to help you do your job, Frissy. Got the cavalry waiting around back?"

The giant sneered. Caleb glared back.

"Frissy, the judge is waiting for us," Zeke interjected.

The bodyguard grunted and backed into the foyer. "One day, Marlowe," he muttered as Caleb went past him. "You and me."

"Looking forward to it, little fella."

The entrance hall was wide and about a hundred feet high. Panels of gleaming wood bordered huge, woven tapestries covered with lords and ladies, hunting dogs, horses, dragons, and several deer clearly taking their final breaths.

One of them had a mounted knight putting his lance into a giant snake, which didn't look too happy to be giving up the fair-haired lady it had tied to a tree. Caleb wondered how that armless serpent was able to manage the tying-up part but reckoned that wasn't really the point.

A very stiff-looking Limey butler eyed them with disdain he could barely conceal, took their hats and coats, and turned the garments over to a young Black servant. Both of them were wearing white gloves and the fanciest black suits Caleb had ever seen. Zeke immediately unbuckled his gun belt and handed it over. When Caleb declined, the butler looked at Frissy, who glowered and then nodded curtly. The servant disappeared, and the Englishman led them into the house.

They crossed the polished marble floor, circling around a dark oak table with a vase big enough to take a bath in. That is, if it weren't filled with a field's worth of cut flowers. Above it hung a chandelier with gold branches extending out a half mile in every direction.

Zeke noticed him looking at it. "That thing come all the way from Boston," he whispered reverently. "I hear Paul Revere hisself made it."

Caleb recalled what Doc had said about Patterson's ambitions and his character. The affluence on display here went far beyond a person who would be content to live and work in Elkhorn. Unless he thought of the town and this house as his kingdom and his castle.

For the moment, though, Caleb needed to tuck those thoughts away and focus on why he was here.

Judge Patterson was waiting for them in his library. Half the books west of St. Louis were on shelves that covered almost every inch of wall space. Caleb had to admit, it was pretty damn impressive.

An ornate, marble fireplace filled a space between two alcoves of windows. A small fire warmed the room, though the hearth could easily hold a fire large enough to heat a Badlands bawdy house in a blizzard. A wide, dark-wood writing desk with a sloped top stood in a corner, near one of the alcoves, and an oak worktable with four chairs sat under a brass chandelier. Several clusters of heavy, comfortable-looking upholstered chairs were arranged around the room with small tables and lamps beside them.

The room was dominated by a large painting above the fireplace of Napoleon Bonaparte astride a handsome, rearing gray Arabian. The stallion's mane and tail looked like gold as they waved in the wind. The general's cape was a brilliant scarlet, and it billowed around him. Napoleon's arm was raised, and he was pointing at some mountain they needed to cross over.

"Marlowe, the sheriff tells me you were stabbed."

The judge stood to one side of the fireplace as they came through the door. He was dressed in a fancy, silk smoking jacket. To finish off his attire, he was wearing embroidered slippers and a matching Chinese cap with a tassel on top. The man definitely knew how to put on the dog.

"A scratch. A nuisance. That's all."

The blood stains on his trousers contradicted the statement, but he was standing on his own feet and had walked clear across town to get here.

"Have you had dinner?"

"Doc fed me."

"A drink, then."

The judge didn't wait for an answer. He walked to a cabinet in a corner and took out three tumblers. Upon filling them with brandy from an expensive-looking bottle, he carried all three back and handed two to Caleb and Zeke.

"So tell me." The judge waved his glass in the general direction of the window. "The assassin sent to do the killing at Doc's house. Will he live?"

Caleb looked at Zeke, waiting for him to answer.

"I believe so," the sheriff said. "Doc sewed him up good."

"Excellent. Move him to the jail tonight. I

want two men guarding that cell around the clock. Do you hear me?"

Zeke nodded, then took a gulp of the brandy. He glanced at the door and back at Caleb. The sheriff looked like he was wondering if he should go and do that right this minute.

"Marlowe, you're looking a bit peaked. Come and sit. You too, Sheriff."

They followed the judge to a trio of chairs by the fireplace. Caleb saw no point in being ornery. Sitting put pressure on the stitches on his side, but it was better than standing. Once settled, he took a drink and felt the liquid slide warm and smooth down his throat.

"You did well tonight, Marlowe. You seem to always be where you're needed. For me the other day. For Doc Burnett today. Of course, the best news tonight is that you didn't let the murderous scoundrel get away."

The best news was that Sheila and Doc weren't hurt.

Patterson was not a man to remain seated for long. He was immediately up and pacing by the fireplace. He stabbed at the blaze with a poker, sending some sparks crackling up the chimney.

"Did you talk to the villain?" he asked.

"Some."

"Did you get *any* information out of him?"

"I got a name."

Zeke sent Caleb a surprised look. "I didn't know you got him talking at all."

"When I run him down."

"I couldn't squeeze a word out of that snake."

Patterson hushed the sheriff. "Did he mention Goulden?"

Caleb put his glass down on the table beside him. "No. But have you ever heard of a fella named Elijah Starr?"

"I have, indeed." The judge's face lit up. "Damn me, Marlowe, but that's nearly as good."

Patterson began pacing again, unable to hide his excitement.

Caleb's gut twisted, and a sharp pain fired from his chest to his brain. Here was proof that the bastard was alive. Elijah Starr had never been punished for what he did to Caleb's mother. Never paid for the crime he committed.

But for all the turmoil churning within him, Caleb kept his mask of indifference on tight.

"This Starr fella works for Goulden?" Zeke asked.

"Not only works for him. He's his top

man in this whole region."

"What exactly does he do?" Caleb asked.

"I believe, on paper, he's an operations director for the company. Officially, he's one of the men who oversee the construction of the railroad lines. But in truth, he's no more than a henchman. He directs gangs of brutes to eliminate anyone who opposes the expansion of Goulden's rail empire. They will threaten, geld, or kill anything that slows them down or stands in their way. He terrorizes the workers and clears the land of any homesteader, rancher, and townsman who refuse to knuckle under."

Caleb thought about the kind of man who would succeed in such a position. He'd seen them serving as officers. They were men who followed orders without hesitation or question. They were men who, in turn, issued orders that caused indescribable pain and hardship — on their own soldiers and on people identified as the enemy.

Arrogant, ambitious, ruthless men. Men without souls.

Elijah Starr was exactly that kind of man. But to go from being a schoolmaster to this required rising from the ashes like some vile phoenix.

"Don't recall ever hearing that name afore, Judge," Zeke put in.

Patterson shrugged. "He's a company man, and that's well known. But he's one of only a few who direct the strong-arm work for Goulden."

The judge crossed the library to the cabinet, filled his glass, and returned with the bottle. He refilled Zeke's glass, but Caleb waved him off. Now, more than ever, he needed to keep a clear head.

"I should have guessed he'd have a hand in the attack on my life," Patterson continued. "He's the one who was sent to Elkhorn with an offer to buy out everything along the route Goulden has planned. The offer was a mere pittance."

So Elijah had come to Elkhorn. "When was that?"

"Last month. Let me see. He arrived in town a day or two after the last attack on the Wells Fargo stagecoach."

"I never heard nothing about it."

"You were out beyond Devil's Claw, tracking down those outlaws."

"Nobody said nothing about my land."

"Because I sent him packing. I've been securing the deeds for quite a bit of the property Goulden wants. Without my agreement here, they can't extend the line south."

There were legal issues about the rights-of-way, but Caleb couldn't care less about any of that now. Besides, the judge and Goulden were just two dogs fighting in an alley over a very juicy bone.

"This Starr fella couldn't talk you into line," Zeke put in. "So he sent some killers to put you under."

"His boss gets what he wants, and he doesn't care how." Patterson stared thoughtfully at the brandy tumbler in his hand. "But now that we have a confession, I can tie Goulden to the attack. That gives me leverage."

They had no confession, but Caleb wasn't going to come clean. He finished his drink. "Any idea where Elijah Starr is now?"

"Yes, I believe so. They've been running a rail spur up along the Roaring River from the mining country south of the Blue River. Their center of operations is in Bonedale, and Starr runs his gang out of there."

Caleb traveled through that area a couple of years ago. It was about two days' ride west of Elkhorn. Back then, the place had no name. It was just a tent city of prospectors moving north from Aspen in search of more gold. Perched on the river's edge, the future town was situated in what was the Ute tribe's shrinking territory.

"I believe I seen the place," he said. "But it wasn't much of anything then."

"Goulden started building fairly recently, after bringing in cheap labor to work on his railroad. I understand that they've got a town going now with enough gaming, drinking, and whoring operations to keep the miners and the men coming."

"And broke once they get there, I reckon," Zeke said.

"It's a wild and lawless place, from all accounts," the judge added.

Now that Caleb had a destination, nothing would stop him from going there.

"I'll go and fetch Elijah Starr for you," he offered.

Surprised, both men fixed their attention on him. Caleb knew that with the judge's new army of men, he'd be left out of going after Starr. There'd be no chance for revenge once Patterson brought him back to Elkhorn.

"You can do whatever you want with him once you got him under lock and key here," Caleb said.

The judge stared at him for a moment before answering. "Getting Starr won't be easy, but I admire the way you think. The way you see things through."

Patterson had no idea.

"When are you leaving?" the older man asked. "I want this business cleared up long before the eclipse."

They had more than five weeks. "I leave tomorrow."

"Take some of my men with you."

"I go alone."

Zeke started. "Marlowe, you just got stuck like a prize pig in winter. That's rugged going between here and there. How are you going to manage it?"

"I'll manage."

The sheriff stared at him and then shook his head admiringly. "You are the damnedest . . ."

The judge strode to the desk and sat down, immediately starting to write.

"It probably won't help if you get into trouble, but these papers call for Starr's arrest. And I want you wearing a badge when you go after him."

Caleb looked over at Zeke's outstretched hand. He was holding a tin star. He must have gotten it from the body of the murdered deputy.

"Are you well enough to take this on?" Patterson lifted his head from the documents he was signing.

Caleb took the badge from the sheriff and slipped it into his pocket.

"Never been better."

CHAPTER FIFTEEN

High puffs of clouds, gray and white, raced across a sky of the deepest blue. The air was crisp and washed clean by the rain. Except for the water running high in the river and the drops of rain glistening like diamonds on the meadow grass, the storm that blew through last night was only a fading memory.

Caleb watched his herd slowly moving across the green valley below the cabin, but he had other things on his mind. He was anxious to leave. His bag was packed. Pirate was fed, watered, and saddled. Bear lay by the cabin door, casting sulky glances at his master. He knew he wasn't going along.

It had been sometime after midnight when Caleb left Judge Patterson's house and fetched his horse from the livery stable. Because of all the trouble and revelry in town, Malachi Rogers had still been up, and Caleb had arranged for Gabe and Paddy come out to his ranch this morning.

He wouldn't go until he saw them. After the dustup with his neighbor, Frank Stubbs, he wasn't going anywhere until he had a talk with both boys.

Caleb wanted to hit the trail before the sun rose too high, even though he knew the urgency resided solely inside himself. Patterson told him there was no reason to think he wouldn't find Elijah Starr in Bonedale. The rail line through there was far from being completed, and the work had to progress while the weather was good. And Eric Goulden held his directors accountable for every foot of rail they did or didn't put down.

Caleb gingerly stretched his side. The stab wound hurt like hell, and he could feel the effects of it. It was as if he were carrying a heavy chunk of sponge in his gut, and it was pulling energy and strength out of his entire body.

He'd gotten an earful of advice from Doc that he needed a few days to rest and mend. It didn't matter what anyone said. He had to go after Elijah Starr. Every day the man was above ground was another day that the death of Caleb's mother remained unavenged.

He checked his gear for the fifth time. He'd donned his trail clothes this morning.

Plain, brown, woolen shirt. Elk-leather vest. Buckskin pants tucked into his boots. His bearskin bedding was rolled up and secured with his duster behind his saddle. He'd cleaned his Winchester '73 and his pair of Colt Frontiers, and he'd sharpened the great hunting knife that had been a gift from Old Jacob Bell.

Elijah Starr's knife was wrapped in a piece of buckskin and tucked into his other boot.

Caleb had no idea how this confrontation would take place or how it would turn out. He'd think about it during the two-day journey to Bonedale, when his mind was a little clearer.

He opened the saddlebag and looked once more at the leather pouch containing the arrest warrant signed by the judge. Even if Caleb chose to use the document, there was no way his father or the people working for the railroad company would submit to Judge Patterson's authority.

None of that mattered to Caleb, however. His business with Starr had nothing to do with the attempt on the judge's life. Their business was personal, and he planned to take care of it in Bonedale. He had a fairly good idea that only one of them would be standing when it was over.

Bear lifted his head and was on his feet

staring at a point beyond the river a full minute before the riders appeared. Caleb waited, surprised when not two but three horses appeared. Immediately, he knew who it was with Gabe and Paddy.

Sheila.

He was happy that she'd come. She'd worried about him last night, and he figured she was still fretting. That was why she was here. He was glad to see her, but he had someplace he needed to go right now. A man he needed to run to ground. While Elijah Starr was out in the world amongst the living, Caleb didn't want to think about anything but the killing he needed to do.

Bear, however, didn't share his sentiments. The yellow dog was off across the field, barking and dancing around the newcomers like they were the circus come to town. Before they even reached the cabin, that fool animal had raced back, grabbed a half-chewed wooden peg, and taken it back down to show the boys.

Caleb walked over to help Sheila down. But she was faster than he was, and her boots hit the ground before he could get there. Sheila received most of the dog's exuberant affection.

She was wearing her father's duster and her own wide-brimmed hat, which kept much of her face in shadow.

"I don't recall hiring you to look after my ranch."

"No need to hire me." After petting Bear, she took out a small, leather satchel out of her saddlebag. "The truth is, I'm here bearing gifts."

Caleb didn't open the bag she handed to him. "What did you bring?"

"Medical supplies from my father. You should keep the dressing dry and change it in a day or two."

"Nothing from you?" he teased.

Pink colored her cheeks. "Actually, you might find some sugar cookies in there. And there will be more waiting for you when you get back."

"In that case, I thank you kindly." He lifted the flap of one of his saddlebags and carefully nested the satchel in with his extra ammunition. "I'll be coming by collecting soon."

Her smile caused the corners of her eyes to crinkle. The eyes peering up at him were as blue as the Colorado sky above them.

"How many days will you be gone?"

"I don't know. A week?"

"Is it safe that you're going alone?"

"That's who I am. Happiest alone."

She put her hands on the swell of her hips

and looked away. Caleb guessed his words had stung.

"Traveling, that is. Fellas like Zeke get to smelling pretty bad after a few days on the road."

He looked at the boys. Gabe had led their horses where they could graze and was coming back. Paddy was already wrestling with the dog for the wooden piece, and Bear was growling happily.

"Gabe," Caleb said solemnly. "I don't need to tell you what needs to be done."

"I'll take care of things, Mr. Marlowe. Don't you worry at all."

"I ain't worried." Caleb turned toward the younger boy. "Paddy, Gabe is in charge, you hear? He'll tell you what to do, and you do it."

Paddy let the dog run away with the stick. "Yes, sir. I'll do it."

"And the two of you . . . I don't want you going nowhere near the eastern ridge. No fishing up in the creek there by Frank Stubbs's claim. It don't matter if you're on my land. I don't want him laying eyes on you."

Paddy's face became serious. "What if he comes down here with his cane like the other day? What if he has a hankering to tan our hides, whether we go up there or not?"

"What cane?" Sheila asked, flaring up. "Who is this man?"

"Day before yesterday," Gabe told her. "Mr. Frank Stubbs, the fella who lives over the ridge, came after us. He's a low-down dog, as mean as they come. But he was plenty surprised, let me tell you, when Mr. Marlowe gave him a right good thrashing and sent him on his way."

Sheila turned a questioning glance at Caleb, but he kept his gaze on the boys.

"If you two see him riding in this direction, you get on your horse and go straight to Elkhorn. Find the sheriff and tell him." Zeke knew about the problem with Stubbs. Caleb told him about the incident when he left the man's weapons with him. "Stubbs has no right and no reason for coming over here. So, you see him, you just git."

Both heads nodded.

This wasn't the first time Caleb was putting Gabe in charge of the daily chores on his ranch. The young man was competent and confident and, regardless of Paddy's playful distractions, did an outstanding job.

Frank Stubbs, however, was something of a worry.

Caleb gave Gabe money for him and Paddy with some extra for supplies. As the boys ran off to do their chores, Bear seemed torn between going with them or staying and keeping an eye on Caleb.

"Who is this horrible man?" Sheila had been biting her tongue, but she clearly couldn't hold it any longer. "Why was he threatening the boys?"

"Frank Stubbs has a mining concern over the ridge." He motioned toward the east. "I'd say he learned a lesson after his last visit. He won't be back."

"Do you want me to ride out here with the boys when they come back?"

Caleb shook his head. "They'll be fine. They're both smart young fellas. They know what to do. They'll look after each other."

"Seriously, it would be no trouble for me. Gabe said they'll be coming out early in the morning and be back in Elkhorn by noon."

"No. At their age, they're plenty able to do things on their own. Independent-like. And they're proud of their work. Especially Gabriel. I don't want him thinking he needs someone looking over his shoulder."

"I understand." She stared in the direction the two had gone. "There must be something I can take care of?"

She had that furrow in her forehead that said she wasn't giving up.

"You want to help me while I'm away?"

Her face brightened. "Yes. Absolutely."

"Take care of yourself."

"I do that. Every day. All the time."

Before he realized what he was doing, Caleb reached up and brushed an eyelash off her cheek with his thumb. Surprised by his own forwardness, he quickly backed away. He didn't want to cloud his thinking when he had a dangerous task ahead of him.

"I want you to mean it," he said gruffly. "But now I gotta go."

Before he could turn away, Sheila took hold of his vest, rose up on her toes, and brushed a kiss across his lips.

"Do the same, Marlowe. Take care of yourself. And come back soon."

CHAPTER SIXTEEN

Leaving his ranch behind, Caleb followed the river north until he saw the distinctive twin peaks that bordered the long mountain lake to the west of Elkhorn.

This was the headwaters of the shallow river flowing south through Caleb's land and continuing its course for a few hundred miles, always descending, always growing in size and strength. By the time it finally left Colorado's mountains far to the south, it was a river deserving of the name. There in the foothills, it would make a gradual turn to the east before meandering out onto the wide, flat plains of Kansas.

Once, while he and Jake Bell followed the banks of the tumbling, churning water on their way to Santa Fe, the old scout told Caleb that same river went all the way to the Mississippi. He claimed it was a mile wide at its mouth, with endless swamps on both sides. He said he saw gators twenty feet long there with jaws so wide, they were known to snatch full-grown cows off the riverbank.

Caleb's old mentor tended to exaggerate when he was filling a dark evening with a fireside story, but there was a kernel of truth in most of what Jake said. Still, it was hard to believe that the stream he crossed without so much as wetting his stirrups would eventually become something so impressive.

Caleb skirted the southern edge of the lake for most of the day, nudging Pirate through heavy brush and thick pine forests and catching occasional glimpses of the turquoise water.

It was slow going, and he saw no one. But he'd expected as much. The terrain was too rugged for any cart or wagon, and anyone traveling west from Denver would be more apt to take the much longer but less arduous way far to the north, past Ten Mile Peak and Bald Mountain before descending to the Eagle River valley. In the past year or so, even stagecoaches had begun to use that route.

By the time he'd climbed up through the twisting passes and finally reached the top of the ridges of gray rock, Caleb was exhausted from his wound. For the past few hours, he'd felt unable to fight off a numbing weariness that threatened to overwhelm him. A fog crowded the edges of his vision.

Resting himself and Pirate by a mountain spring, Caleb drank deeply and decided against stopping here for the night. He wanted to put in a few more hours on the trail. Caleb didn't want to make the two-day journey any longer. Below him, he could see the small spring-fed lake that disappeared into thick forest and the winding ravine. Somewhere to the west, he'd find Bonedale.

"All right, big fella," he said to his buckskin as he slowly pushed to his feet. "Let's put in a few more miles."

As Pirate picked his way downward through the chunks and shards of sharp rock, Caleb's head was getting increasingly heavier, and the ache in his side was sharper. The descending sun became a blinding glare of yellow gold.

At one point, while they were following a narrow trail above the white, frothing stream that roiled through an endless stretch of gray boulders, the color of the rock rising steeply to his right changed. As Caleb admired the layers of deep red, he realized he wasn't entirely alone.

On a ledge not fifty feet above him, half hidden by a sturdy pine that had pushed up through the rugged terrain, a mountain lion was eyeing him steadily. Tawny and sleek, she was close enough that Caleb could have hit her with a rock. She didn't have that poised, muscled look of a big cat about to pounce. Her tail twitched as they stared at each other.

She simply appeared to be curious, but he knew how quickly that could change. Watching carefully, Caleb slowly drew his Winchester from its scabbard.

"We're passing through, miss," he called out loudly. "We ain't looking to disturb you. So how about you just go about your business, and we'll go about ours."

The cougar watched him for another few seconds. Then she dipped her head and picked up a good-sized rabbit that was lying at her feet on the ledge. Taking one last look at Caleb, she turned and bounded effortlessly up the steep mountainside before disappearing above a treelined ridge.

Returning his rifle to its scabbard, Caleb nudged his mount on until the sun dropped behind a series of peaks.

In the growing gloom, he found a grassy, fairly level space a short distance from the creek and set up camp for the night. As he gathered wood for his fire, he inadvertently pressed a branch against the injury on his side. A sudden sweat washed through him, and he dropped to one knee until it passed. The constant ache was a nuisance.

After settling Pirate in for the night, Caleb sat by the fire and cooked up a pan of beans and dried beef and pulled a couple of biscuits out of his saddlebag. His appetite wasn't what it usually was, but he ate his fill and left the rest for the morning. He cleaned up in the stream and then sat on his bedding with his back against his saddle.

The coffee was strong and hot, the way he liked it, and he held the cup in his hands as he stared into the fire. He was bone-weary from the day's travels, and the damned knife wound wasn't helping at all. Still, he didn't think sleep would come easily. His mind was racing.

He couldn't help but think what it would be like when he came face-to-face with his father. Wild images from the past rushed through his mind. His father's hard face, white with rage as he swung the rod at Caleb or one of the Shawnee or Kickapoo students at the training school. The dark moments loomed up in front of him, and hot flashes of anger wracked his tired body.

He thought of the silent, gloomy rooms of the house where Elijah kept Caleb's mother virtually a prisoner. No one was allowed to come into the house and visit her when she showed the cuts and bruises she'd received at her husband's hand. And as Caleb got older, that was nearly all the time. He recalled trying to hide whenever he saw that look come into his father's face, for Caleb knew his old man would start on him just to provoke some anguished and protective maternal response. Elijah Starr used the son to get to the mother. He was a monster.

But monsters were *not* invincible.

Caleb winced as he stretched out. The stab wound throbbed painfully. His face and his eyes felt hot. Trying to clear his mind of the evil days of his past, he listened to the night sounds. A pair of wolves called to each other in the distance. An owl hooted in a tree not far away, no doubt hoping to get some small creature running. A family of foxes yipped and barked farther down the creek.

He looked up at the clusters of diamonds scattered across the black, velvet sky and thought of Sheila.

Their brief kiss. Her words before he'd walked away. *Take care of yourself. And come back soon.*

Before he knew it, the taut muscles of his face gradually softened, and the hard pumping of his heart slowed. By the time Caleb

210

felt himself dozing off, her face was written in the stars above.

The sun had already risen above the eastern ridges when he awoke. He sat up and took in a sharp breath of chill mountain air as pain cut through him. He felt like he was being trampled by a dozen razor-shod mules. He stayed where he was for a minute to wait it out, but he knew he was in rougher shape than he'd hoped to be this morning.

In his life, he'd been beaten, shot, and cut more than any other man of his acquaintance. He'd been frozen near solid in a Wyoming blizzard, and he'd been scorched by both fire and the Texas sun. He'd broken bones and dug himself out of a collapsed mine. His hide had taken more stitches than a Dutch quilt. So Caleb knew that the day or two after a mishap always felt worse. Common sense said to stay put for a day or two. But he didn't want to make this ride to Bonedale any longer than it needed to be.

"Toughen up, Marlowe," he chided himself.

Moving gingerly, he dropped some kindling and a few more branches on the embers of last night's fire, stirred it all into a flame, and then sat on his saddle for a moment to catch his breath and watch the morning light chase the darkness out of the ravine.

The breakfast of coffee, last night's beef, beans, and biscuits helped, and Caleb felt heartened about the journey ahead. He was moving a little easier, but he was far from right. Before packing up, he opened the bag containing medical supplies. He decided the dressing on his wound could wait till evening. But he ate all the cookies that Sheila put in the bag for him.

"I'm counting on you doing some of the work today, Pirate," Caleb said, once he hauled himself up into the saddle. "Thought I was gonna have to carry *you* last night when that sun started dropping low."

Caleb proceeded in a westerly direction, following the creek. The red bluffs often hemmed them in, but the sky was clear and mountain blue. He continued to descend steadily. Once, he needed to double back a ways when a waterfall provided no passable route for the horse and rider. Eventually, he found a steep path that allowed them to climb around the obstacle.

The sun was again sinking in the west, but they still had an hour or so of daylight when the steep-sided ravines they'd been passing through suddenly broadened into a thickly forested valley. The air was warmer here, and the light took on that golden hue Caleb had always been partial to.

For as far as he could see, groves of pine, spruce, cottonwood, and scrub oak covered the rugged terrain, and tall peaks and redstone ridges hemmed it all in, north and south.

Caleb directed Pirate toward a wide pool formed by a beaver dam forty yards or so downstream. Tall clumps of meadow grass ran down to the edge, and reddish boulders jutted up through both soil and running water. The boss beaver, fat and brown, was sitting on his haunches on top of the structure. He was keeping an eye on the newcomers and surveying the work of two other beavers going in and out of the water at the base of the dam.

Caleb should have been paying more attention to his own business, however. He didn't see the hole and, apparently, neither did Pirate.

The horse stepped into the depression and stumbled. The hole had been dug out by some hungry coyote, no doubt, burrowing after a rodent. The damn thing was concealed beneath a clump of matted grass.

When Pirate faltered and stopped short to right himself, Caleb plunged headfirst over the mount's neck. Before he knew it, he'd gone clear out of the saddle and was tumbling ass over teakettle. Somehow, he managed to hold on to the reins as he flipped through the air. Not that it mattered to Pirate — he wasn't going anywhere — but the reins gave Caleb something to keep him upright when he landed.

When he hit the ground, the outside of his left boot struck the edge of a rock, wrenching his whole body. Bullets of hot fire shot inward from the stab wound. He almost managed to stay on his feet, but his left leg gave out, and the momentum of the fall threw Caleb onto all fours in the stony dirt. When he tried to get up, he felt the pain in his ankle, and he cursed with enough violence to cause Pirate to back up a step.

He took a deep breath and let go of the reins. As he hobbled over to a flat boulder, his horse wandered over to the beaver pond and lowered his head to drink. Pirate showed no embarrassment or concern. He was clearly taking no responsibility for Caleb's fall.

Caleb sat down, pulled off his boot, and tucked the knife belonging to Elijah Starr into his vest. He felt his ankle through his woolen sock. He'd twisted it pretty well, but it wasn't broken. He rubbed the sprain for a few minutes, but he knew he'd need to get his boot back on before the joint swelled up.

He scowled at his horse, and Pirate flicked an ear and turned an eye toward him.

"You *do* realize that your job is to avoid holes like that and keep me in the saddle."

The horse went back to drinking, refusing to defend himself.

"And just the other day, I was telling Malachi Rogers you were as sure-footed as a mule. Guess I was talking you up a little too high."

Pirate shook his head and turned his attention to a nearby clump of grass.

Getting no satisfaction from his horse, Caleb stared at his ankle. He had to do something about it. He glanced at his saddlebags. There were the bandages Doc had sent along. He decided it would be best to wrap the injury now and then try to pull the boot back on.

Caleb pushed himself upright and limped toward Pirate, carrying his boot in his hand. He was eyeing the coyote hole his horse had stepped in when his foot brushed against another clump of grass.

There was no rattle to warn him. That is, it came only a split second before Caleb caught a glimpse of the deadly triangular head darting toward his unbooted leg.

He knew what was coming, but he had no time to react. The rattler flew at that woolen sock with the speed and snap of a Montana bullwhip and hit Caleb's calf with its jaws wide open.

CHAPTER SEVENTEEN

Caleb stopped dead, astonished by the suddenness of the strike. His instincts about impending danger seldom let him down, but this viper had taken advantage of his wounded state.

The snake was nearly the same color as the dusty, faded grass on the edges of the newer, greener clumps. The pattern of darker diamonds painted along its back and sides only added to the disguise.

Because Caleb was favoring that ankle, his foot was in midair when the rattler struck. The bite felt like a hornet's sting, but the snake wasn't done yet. In a flash, it had pulled its hooks out of the sock and was rearing back with a hiss. Its body was as thick as Caleb's arm but looked even bigger when it drew back into a coil. With its forked, black tongue flicking, it let go with a rattle that they probably heard in Elkhorn.

The damn thing was ready for another go.

That creature was a sinuous corkscrew of death, but before it could hurl itself at him again, Caleb flung his boot hard at the snake's head. The heel connected. The rattler, clearly having decided that it'd made its point, started speeding with its undulating body through the grass away from him.

The only problem was that the snake was heading straight toward Pirate, who had backed up and was looking on with wild, flashing eyes.

Caleb wasn't about to leave his horse to fight off this viper. Pirate probably could have handled the rattler on his own, but it made no sense to risk him being bitten as well. One of them needed to be able to walk.

The Colt was in Caleb's hand and spitting fire in an instant, and the serpent jumped into the air as two slugs tore into its body.

He scuffled over to the reptile, picked it up by the rattles, and flung the limp carcass as far as he could away from them. They say a snake can't die until sundown. Caleb knew that was just an old myth, but he was taking no chances.

He sat on the ground, shoved the sock down past his ankle, and inspected the wound. The thickening bruise on his injured ankle was now matched by a rising welt on his calf. One small pinprick stood out on the whitening skin. Blood oozed from the hole.

"Well, at least you couldn't get both of your damn hooks into me."

Somehow, in all his time on the trail, he had never given much thought to being bitten. He had seen a whole passel of rattlers over the years. He didn't like the critters much and stayed clear of them. But he'd seen two men die from bites. They were both tough fellas. One had been a young Ute warrior scouting for the army. It had been incredibly painful, and it wasn't pretty to watch. They'd both been dead inside of an hour. Both had wished it was quicker.

And now, here he was, taken down by a rattler.

It all seemed so unreal to him. He'd been bitten, but everything around him was incredibly peaceful. Only the lingering smell of gun smoke gave a hint that any violence had occurred at all. That and the hole in his leg.

Across the pond, a beaver slapped his tail on the water, drawing Caleb's attention. Two of them were swimming down by the dam, and they didn't seem to care much about working or about his plight. The boss beaver had disappeared.

Caleb's eye was drawn to the golden sun descending toward the mountain peaks and the various shades of green in the stretches of forest on either side of the valley. Above him, the sky was a wide-open field of pale blue, with just a few wisps of clouds that seemed to hang motionless up there. Two hawks sailed across a ridge and began circling lazily.

He shook his head, trying to focus. This might be a pretty place to die, but he wasn't ready to go yet. He had more living to do.

Caleb looked down at his leg and then dragged himself to the water's edge.

As he scrubbed at the snakebite with water and sand, Pirate clopped over to him and nosed his shoulder.

"Stay right there, big fella."

Grabbing hold of a stirrup, Caleb hauled himself upright and pulled Doc's medical supplies out of his saddlebag. His side was killing him, but he had other things to worry about.

He had to think of others who'd survived a rattlesnake bite. He knew some. One was a young soldier who'd suffered from some swelling of his leg and had spent a few days with a headache, puking, and fighting his way through a fever. But he made it through.

Leaning against Pirate's shoulder, Caleb

went through the bag to see what might be useful. He took out some rolled white bandage cloth and a bottle of something. Uncorking the bottle, he smelled it and decided it had vinegar in it.

Caleb eased himself back down. Once he was sitting again, he pulled out his hunting knife and cut a piece of bandage long enough to go around his leg twice, just below the knee. Twisting the cloth into a kind of rope, he tied it as tight as he could. He needed to slow the snake venom from traveling up his leg into his body.

The young soldier who'd survived had been treated by an old-timer who grew up in the mountains of Missouri. He'd seen it before and had his own idea about what to do. With four men holding the patient down, he cut out a chunk of flesh around the bite marks. While the young fella was passed out, they let him bleed some and then poured whiskey on the wound before wrapping it up.

Putting his knife sheath between his teeth as a bit, Caleb began to cut away both flesh and snakebite. The first incision was the worst, and he felt suddenly light-headed. Bearing down, he made the second cut, forming a canoe-shaped gash in his calf muscle. The excised piece of flesh dropped into the grass.

The blood flowed strongly now, running off his leg and dripping onto the red, sandy ground. He let the wound bleed. Then, bracing himself again, he poured the vinegary medicine directly into it.

The moment the liquid hit the cut, Caleb thought his head would explode. Yellow-gold lightning flashed in his brain, blinding him. His teeth nearly bit through the thick leather.

When he could breathe and see again, he wrapped a second bandage over the wound and tied it tight.

The rattler's attack had been swift and sudden. It came when a snakebite had been about the furthest thing from his mind. If this trouble didn't kill him, then it had to be a reminder, a lesson. He'd been too arrogant and unclear in his thinking. He'd been figuring he could simply ride to Bonedale and call his father out. Shoot Elijah Starr down in some fair-handed gunfight.

If he even got to his father, the man would be as swift and deadly as this snake. He'd never been one for fair play. Caleb had to be smarter. He had to be more alert and more prepared.

Slowly, deliberately, he pulled the sock up

over the bandages. He crawled to where his boot lay in the grass and tugged it on, then he slipped the knife into his other boot. After resting a few minutes, he stood up, whistled Pirate to him, and swung into the saddle.

Caleb realized that he wasn't sure where he was going, but he felt a need to put some distance between himself and that place. Riding toward the setting sun, he recalled that grizzled, old Missouri soldier saying that a man was better off resting after a snakebite. To Caleb's thinking, it did make sense that the more worked up he got, the deeper that rattler's poison would go.

True or not, he rode on, sticking to the easy ways wherever possible and not pushing Pirate at all.

Caleb wasn't feeling too chipper. His stomach was up in his throat. It felt like his leg was about to bust the seam of his boot. But what was worse, his eyes were playing tricks on him. When he wasn't seeing double of everything, his vision was blurred.

When he was able to blink the world clear for a moment or two, he was seeing snakes everywhere. One minute, there was a rattler coiled up at the edge of the trail. Or the next minute, he saw one slithering through the grass. And the next, he'd see one curled around the branch of a cottonwood.

"Get a grip on yourself," he muttered. "There ain't no snakes."

Caleb wasn't sure how far he'd ridden, but he was suddenly aware that the sun had set, and he hadn't even seen it go down. He was leaning forward, his chest resting on Pirate's neck. It was a miracle he hadn't fallen off somewhere.

He reined his mount in and sat up straight, fixing his gaze upon a tall pine tree that rose close to the trail. His heart was pounding, and he couldn't stop himself from swaying back and forth in the saddle. In the deep green of the bows, he saw the hard face of Elijah Starr sneering at him. Caleb drew his Colt, and the face disappeared.

Caleb blinked and looked again. The branches of the tree moved a little in the light breeze that had started up. It was just a tree. He let out a long breath.

He knew he needed to find a place to bed down for the night, but he couldn't think straight. Somewhere up ahead, his father was alive and pursuing a livelihood inflicting pain and death on others. Caleb drove his boot against Pirate's flank, riding forward past the tall pine.

The poison was into him. It was running

riot in his blood. Slithering through his veins like the snake that put it there.

He was losing strength. It was all he could do to stay in the saddle.

"Where can we get help, Pirate?"

His buckskin's ears angled back at him, but man and horse both knew it was hopeless.

When Caleb opened his eyes again, it was dark. They'd stopped, and he clung to the pommel with a death grip. Still, his body was swaying from side to side.

The smell of a fire clawed its way through the fog, registering in his brain. Not just a fire. Food.

"Go, Pirate," he mumbled.

He nudged his horse forward. Light flickered through the branches of scrub pine. The sound of voices. Getting closer. A clearing. The woodsmoke was strong now.

He went past a few mules tied on a line. There lay a camp beyond. People. Someone to help. He nudged Pirate into the clearing. Blankets stretched around the fire. Dishes lay about. But there was no one around. No one anywhere.

"Need . . . help . . . snake." He didn't know if he'd shouted or whispered the words. Or if he'd even said them out loud.

Caleb tried to dismount, but his fingers

refused to grip the hard leather of his saddle. He felt himself falling. And falling. A thick, soft darkness swirled around him. Down into some abyss he fell.

For minutes, hours, days, he dropped. And he never hit bottom.

CHAPTER EIGHTEEN

Bonedale, Colorado

Elijah Starr stood in the open second-floor window of his office and looked out across the stacks of timber, piles of iron rails, and crates of rail spikes. A few moments before, clouds along the horizon had devoured the setting sun, and only a few bloodred streaks above the distant mountains colored the darkening sky.

Sounds of revelry reached him from one of the infernal saloons down the one passable street that comprised Bonedale. The raucous laughter and shouts annoyed him, as they always did. But this evening, the addition of some fool playing on a harmonica only added to his irritation.

Elijah fixed his gaze on the dock he'd had built months ago beyond the storage area and the three new sets of tracks. Two guards with shotguns cradled in their arms stood smoking by a piling at the end of the structure, silhouetted by the fading western light reflected in the water. As they talked, one of them gestured toward the flatboat that had arrived late in the day. It was loaded with the final shipment of iron rails needed to complete the branch line to Aspen.

On the riverbank, wagons had already been moved into position for unloading. Naturally, the teamsters wouldn't be working in the morning, tomorrow being the Sabbath. They'd be observing the Lord's day as they usually did, drunkenly carousing in the saloons. His crew of Celestials, being heathens, would carry the rails off the flatboat and load them onto the wagons. They had their uses.

A chill breeze picked up, and Elijah closed the window. He crossed the room to his desk and lit a lamp. He looked around the space he'd been occupying for the past six months. He wouldn't be here much longer, not past September.

He'd been in worse places. Living in a tent and ramrodding construction crews was worse. Here, at least, he had a reasonably comfortable bed in the adjoining room.

His office was a large and airy room with three windows and paneled, unpainted walls. It was adequately equipped with a pot-bellied stove and two upholstered chairs, a large worktable, a high-sloped desk in the corner for his secretary, and a solid desk for himself. Two Rand McNally railroad maps hung on the far wall. One showed the entire continent; the other covered the central part of the country. A third, hand-drawn map of Colorado was spread out on the worktable along with piles of documents and charts.

The room's only drawback was the Dry Bottom Saloon, which occupied the first floor of the building.

Elijah carried the lamp to the maps on the wall and looked at the larger one. He needed to consider the future. He was certain his employer would be looking to add to his holdings. And he had a good idea Eric Goulden was looking toward the southwest to expand his railroad empire.

A knock on the door interrupted his thoughts.

The voice of one of his men came through from the hallway. "Mr. Starr?"

"Come in."

Muffled sounds from the saloon downstairs entered with him. "Got a fella here to see you. Says he's come from Elkhorn."

"Not Tuttle?"

His man shook his head. "Some dandy.

Won't give his name. Said he's been on the road for days."

Elijah frowned. "Disarm him and send him in."

"Already checked. This fella ain't no gunhawk." He handed over a Remington derringer with a black walnut handle. "But he did have this little toy."

Elijah took the firearm and put his nose to the two barrels. It hadn't been fired for some time. The visitor outside was definitely no gunman. If this derringer weren't fired and reloaded every day, it was more likely to misfire than do any damage. He slipped it into his pocket.

Dandy was a fairly accurate description of the caller. He entered and stood by the door, trying to look casual as his sharp eyes scanned the interior of the office.

Elijah was tall, over six feet, and this man was close to him in height. But whereas Elijah was broad across the shoulders, his visitor was thin as a flagpole. He had a long, lean face and cobalt eyes that were set too close together. A reddish, carefully waxed moustache perched beneath a long, beaklike nose. He was wearing a light-gray suit with a matching vest. The lamplight picked up a reflection from a gold watch fob decorated with a small pendant indicating his membership in a fraternity of some sort. The fellow removed his light-gray bowler, exhibiting thinning ginger hair, plastered flat across the top in an attempt to hide, unsuccessfully, a shiny, bald pate.

"Mr. Starr," he started. Considering his lean physique, his voice was unexpectedly deep and resonant, like that of a stage actor. "I have some news to convey to you. From Elkhorn."

"And you are . . . ?"

"Lassiter. Edmond Lassiter. Attorney-at-law. Traveling across the frontier of our fine state, dedicated to helping our brave pioneers find justice in Colorado's rude wildern—"

"Admirable, Mr. Lassiter. You say you have news you wish to convey?"

"Indeed." The lawyer gestured toward the pair of chairs by the unlit stove. "May I be so bold? I've traveled night and day to reach you."

Elijah nodded, and the man sat, laying his bowler in his lap and running his hand over his flat strands of hair. This fellow might have been hurrying to get here, but he wasn't in any hurry to speak his piece.

"Would you care for a drink, Mr. Lassiter?" It was Saturday evening, and Elijah was ready to indulge.

Not waiting until his visitor completed the long and eloquent reply in the affirmative, Elijah retreated to his desk and took out a bottle of whiskey and two glasses. He filled them and returned to his guest.

"What do you have to tell me?"

Lassiter savored the whiskey for a moment and complimented his host before finally getting around to the question. "I believe you already know that there was an assassination attempt on Judge Patterson in Elkhorn."

He knew the fools he'd hired had failed to kill the judge.

"Your man, Dud Tuttle, is presently languishing in the Elkhorn Jail. He murdered the last survivor in the gang of attackers. Cut the man's throat in a sickbed. I should say, *allegedly* cut his throat."

Elijah let that hang. In the event that Bat Davis and his men might fail, Tuttle's job was to lurk in the shadows and tie up any loose ends. No one could remain to testify as to who was behind the assassination attempt. He'd accomplished his task, but he failed by getting caught. It was a shame. Elijah had a measure of respect for Tuttle. Being inconspicuous and meticulous in the way he got things done made him something of an artist. Men like him were difficult to come by.

"What makes you think I have any interest in this, Mr. Lassiter?"

The attorney sipped his whiskey, obviously choosing his words carefully. "I'm here at the behest of . . . well, another friend of yours in Elkhorn. He suggested that you would be willing to compensate me for delivering a message to you."

Elijah ran a finger under the edge of his eye patch. His "friend" in Elkhorn was proving very useful.

"What is this message?"

"The judge has sent a deputy after you. They suspect *you* were behind the assassination attempt on his life."

Elijah shook his head, feeling disdain for Patterson crystallize within him. For the past few years, he'd dealt with other local power brokers who thought they could stand up to him and to Eric Goulden. The fools always ended up drowning in their own hubris.

"I rode like the wind to get here before he did, but I am still amazed that I reached Bonedale first. In any event, he has been given the job of arresting you and conducting you to Elkhorn. And I'm told to inform you that the deputy is a *very* capable man."

Elijah thought the judge was smarter.

Perhaps he was wrong about the man. It was madness to think some deputy could waltz into Bonedale and take him into custody.

"How many men are traveling with this deputy?"

"No one else. He comes alone."

Alone? This was becoming more ludicrous by the moment.

"Do you know who this man is?"

"His name is Marlowe. He is a former lawman and army scout. He was like a son to Old Jake Bell, by all accounts. He recently started ranching on a spread south of Elkhorn."

"I've never heard of him." With the large company of gunmen Elijah had in his employment in Bonedale, he could arrange to have Marlowe cut down before he climbed off his horse.

"Caleb Marlowe. He's quite famous up north."

Elijah reflected for a moment on the name Caleb. When his son was born, he'd graciously allowed his wife Eliza to name him that. Like his Biblical namesake, he'd be brave, she said. Faithful. Devoted.

In the end, his son had turned out to be a fraud, exactly like Caleb in the Book of Numbers. The way Elijah saw it, the Caleb of old had been nothing more than a self-serving opportunist sent by Moses to spy on the people living in the land of Canaan.

His own son had proved himself to be faithless and disloyal.

Elijah banished those thoughts. He couldn't dwell on the past now. He had more pressing matters in Elkhorn that needed his attention. He got up and went to his desk, then unlocked a cashbox he kept in a drawer and took out some money for Lassiter.

"I hope you will consider engaging me in the future, Mr. Starr. The expansion of the railroad is a noble task, sir, and not one to be obstructed by those too shortsighted to see its value."

The lawyer saluted Elijah with his empty glass and pocketed the cash without counting it. He clearly thought himself a clever man.

"In fact, sir, I believe you — and Mr. Goulden — would find a man with my skills and talent quite useful *working* in your organization. I'm aware that this is the first time we've met. But my credentials speak for themselves. I know the law, and I am — if I may be so bold — a writer of considerable talent, having written numerous speeches and manifestos for well-known politicians while on their campaign trails. Trusted in many circles, I have . . ."

The man droned on, but Elijah's thoughts had slipped elsewhere. He thought about his own entrance into Eric Goulden's company.

After Eliza's death and Caleb's betrayal, Elijah had no interest in continuing his training school in Indiana. He still had funds supplied by the trustees of the institution, and he saw himself at a crossroads. The West was opening up. Fortunes were there to be had.

And then came a letter of condolence from an old acquaintance he'd served with in the early stages of the war, before his injury sent him home. That note changed his life. John Moore was a supervisor in the Saratoga Railroad in New York, a company owned by Eric Goulden. A letter of introduction from his friend and a trip East sealed Elijah's future. The successful climb up through the ranks that ensued was due solely to his own industry, intelligence, and tenacity.

That and the supporting hand of the Almighty, of course, he thought.

"For I know the plans I have for you, saith the Lord," Elijah said aloud. "Plans to prosper you and not to harm you, plans to give you hope and a future."

"Thank you, Mr. Starr. Thank you," Lassiter broke out in excitement. "You'll never regret it. I promise you."

Elijah stared in surprise at the hand being thrust at him to shake. He'd been reflecting on his own life. But it didn't matter.

Lassiter cocked his head and lowered his voice as if they were conspiring to storm the Vanderbilt family vaults.

"Tomorrow morning, I shall be going back to Elkhorn. Is there anything more I can do for you, Mr. Starr?"

Elijah pondered that. The man was a pompous fool, but he could be useful.

"You said this Marlowe has a ranch near Elkhorn."

"That is precisely correct. Three miles south."

"Good. There is something you can do for me, Mr. Lassiter."

CHAPTER NINETEEN

In the darkness and the rain, Caleb scrambled for solid footing along the muddy riverbank. His enemy was everywhere, darting this way and that. Coming through the trees and brush. Rising and swaying and rearing back. Constantly looking for an opening to strike. The creature had the gleaming yellow eyes of a snake.

Caleb had been fighting for hours. His arms were so tired, he could barely lift them. He didn't know how much longer he could hold off his vile foe.

Behind him in the churning shallows, Sheila was holding Caleb's mother and struggling to stay upright. If she slipped, if the waters took them, they'd be gone forever. Both of them were shouting to him, but he couldn't hear their words above the piercing hiss of the creature.

He had to protect them. But his guns were gone, his knife was missing. He'd fight with his bare hands if he had to. Moonlight broke through the clouds for only a moment, but it was enough to reveal the monster. Half man, half snake, it had the face of his father with the eyes of a viper.

Caleb was soaked in sweat and shivering as the dream receded and awareness gradually seeped into his brain.

Slowly, he became more and more conscious of the real world. The snake creature's threatening sound gave way to the homely hiss and crackle of a fire. The swaying monster was a hanging pine bow. Soft, hushed voices surrounded him. He couldn't understand the words. He didn't know the language being spoken. But he heard the unmistakable note of concern in every utterance.

Keeping his eyes open took effort, but Caleb forced them to focus. Sparks curled and danced in their upward climb. The dark points of treetops framed the starry night sky.

He arched his back, trying to stretch, but every inch of his body was stiff. Still, Caleb decided he was more alive than dead. He had no idea how long he'd been lying here, except that it had to be a while. His stomach growled fiercely.

The voices went silent.

Out of the long habit of self-preservation, his fingers felt for his Colts, but his gun belt was gone. The last clear thought he recalled was riding into an encampment but finding no one around. Someone had heard him coming. They must have hidden in the trees and only come out when he'd fallen from Pirate's back.

But they hadn't killed him.

Caleb ran his palms over the coarse texture of the blanket he was lying on. Whoever had saved him had also decided not to bother tying him up.

At the sound of someone approaching, he opened his eyes again. A shadowed face appeared. A steady hand used a cloth to wipe the sweat from Caleb's face and neck. Cool, callused fingers touched his forehead and the side of his face. He heard whispers from a few feet away. The one leaning over him replied. The voice was quiet, but abrupt and commanding. He was giving an order. Footsteps retreated.

Caleb tried to lift his head. The world blurred dizzily around him. His head landed back on the blanket with a thump.

He struggled to focus on the face of the person kneeling over him. The fog thinned a little, and the man's features emerged. Gray beard, dark eyes deeply etched with wrinkles at the corners. He was wearing the familiar black cloth cap Caleb had seen Chinese laborers wearing as they worked laying railroad lines.

The fellows he'd come across spoke their own language. They didn't want to have much to do with the white workers or overseers. They stuck close to each other for safety. Caleb couldn't blame them. He had seen the harsh treatment the Chinese endured. If it didn't come from the other workers, the senseless violence was directed at them by the locals.

"Zhāng kāi zui."

Caleb stared, not comprehending what he was being told.

The elder man repeated the words. Understanding came quick when he pulled down on Caleb's chin.

"What are you giving me? Medicine?"

A bitter liquid was poured down his throat. He coughed and gagged but swallowed it. It warmed his throat all the way down.

Whatever was said to him next sounded like an order. He had no idea what he was being told to do, but because of what these people had done for him already, he trusted that it was for his own good. The man stood up nimbly and carried the bottle to a large bag by the fire.

Caleb lifted his head. Thankfully, the spinning sensation was gone.

The fellow tending to him was solid-looking and middle-aged or older, wearing an immaculately clean black coat with wide, full sleeves over a black vest. A white woolen shirt was fastened with cloth buttons all the way to his neck and extended out from the bottom of the vest and coat and ended just below the knees. Slits ran up the sides of the long shirt. Beneath wide, calf-length black trouser legs, he wore high-topped leather moccasins with Shoshone beadwork. He was unarmed, except for an ivory-handled knife sheathed in his right shoe.

He looked as healthy as a man half his age, and the dark eyes in his round, bearded face were as clear and alert as an eagle's. When he bent over the large bag by the fire, Caleb saw that his black braid draped halfway down his back.

Caleb tried to assess the situation. He'd sustained some damage over the past few days, and he knew he was lucky to be alive after that rattler took a bite out of him.

A blue-and-green striped blanket covered him from knee to waist. His left ankle and calf had been bandaged. They'd removed his vest and his shirt but draped a thinner blue cloth over his chest. He touched the stab wound in his side. The dressing was gone, and the stitching had been left open to the air. It was still tender but seemed to be mending. He spotted his boots and wool socks standing against a nearby rock. He knew that in removing them, they must have taken his knives.

He tried to flex his knee and his foot. The ankle hurt like the blazes, and his leg felt swollen and stiff. At least the sweating and shivering were easing up.

Over to his left, a fire crackled, holding off the chill of the night. Two large pots hung suspended over the flames, and tin plates with food on them were scattered about on the ground as well as on a number of woven mats.

The camp was neat and organized. The clearing was fairly level and ringed by scrub pine and cottonwood trees. The grass had been matted down by the travelers, and it had the same reddish rocks protruding here and there from the ground. Packs for the mules sat in a line by a grove of wavyleaf oaks on the far side of the clearing, and Caleb heard Pirate nicker from somewhere beyond the trees. Blanket rolls had been set out at the heads of the woven mats, along with walking sticks and neatly folded garments.

More awake now, Caleb had a clearer recollection of others leaning over him, helping the elder man. From the amount of gear he could see, there had to be half a dozen people lurking in the shadows beyond the edge of the clearing.

Two small, carved horses lay on their sides on one of the mats. He guessed that at least one of the travelers was a child.

His host came back, carrying Doc Burnett's bag, several clean white cloths, and a tin wash basin partly filled with water. He said something and pointed to the stab wound. When Caleb made no reply, the man knelt down and dipped a cloth into the basin.

"Thank you. You saved my life, I reckon."

The Chinese fella worked with the sure-handed, competent air of a professional medical man. The wound was washed with care and precision, just as Caleb had seen Doc treat his patients.

"Lucky to find your camp."

The traveler made no answer. He was looking closely at the stab wound and concentrating on his task.

"Where are your other people?" He motioned toward the dishes and the fire. "I won't cause you no harm."

Tired, aging eyes met his. "White man."

Caleb paused a moment and then nodded. He understood what the old man was saying. Life wasn't too easy in the West for people with skin that was different from his.

He supposed it was the same everywhere, but he'd seen it out here clear as water in a mountain lake. Frontier law meant keeping what a man thought was his own, even if he'd fought dirty to take it from someone else. Men could be pretty damn brutal about getting what they wanted. Land. Gold and silver. Power. That was at the heart of it all, as far as Caleb could see. It was what folks pushing west called "progress."

The US Army had been pushing the Sioux north and moving the Cheyenne and the Arapaho and others west into land that belonged to other tribes. There were plenty of Mexican and Black cowboys riding the range and driving cattle, but fellas like Malachi Rogers who wanted to settle in the growing frontier towns faced too many stiff-necked white men like Frank Stubbs.

And then there were the Chinese. Caleb had seen how they were being treated. The men were conscripted to build the railroads and then treated worse than dogs on the work crews. And the women? Caleb didn't like to think about some of the back-alley brothels where he'd seen their gaunt, empty faces.

Caleb watched the other man in silence for a moment. There was nothing he could say that would ease his mind. Of course he was going to be cautious. Caleb was a stranger. If their positions were reversed, if he were as vulnerable as they were, he'd do the same thing. He'd hide his family too.

But the fact that Caleb was alive said a great deal about these folks. They could have left him for dead, and no one would ever have been the wiser.

His host knelt back on his heels and extended a hand to him. Caleb shook it before realizing the man's intention. He was offering to help him sit up.

The pain in his side was now a dull ache and didn't bother him much when he sat. The older man ran the bandaging around Caleb's middle.

"Marlowe."

"Sing Lee."

"Thank you again."

A curt nod was his only answer.

Caleb ran a hand over his face. His mind wasn't completely clear. Days were running into one another. He'd planned to get to Bonedale in two days. But he didn't know if this was his second or third day on the trail. "How long have I been here?"

"Last night. One day." Sing Lee closed Doc's bag and put it closer to Caleb. "Doctor?"

"No. Not me. A friend of mine sent this with me. A rattler got me."

Sing Lee motioned to Caleb's leg. "Snakebite. Bad." He then gestured to the stab wound. "Better."

The sound of a coyote, barking in the distance, drew the attention of both men.

"Your people ain't all that safe out there. Dangerous animals could be hunting them woods. Coyotes. Cougars. Bears."

Sing Lee understood him, but the look on his face spoke volumes. He considered a white man more dangerous than any forest animal.

"I get it. I'll go."

Caleb pushed to his feet but paused, fighting off a moment of dizziness. He leaned over to pick up his boots, but he needed to grab for the rock to stop from going down.

"Not well, Marlowe."

"I'll camp downriver a ways."

Pirate's panicked roar and the terrified braying of mules cut Caleb off.

"Something's after the animals," he barked.

Sing Lee stared in the direction of the sound.

"It could be a cougar."

A woman's scream ripped through the night.

Without a moment's hesitation, the older man started running toward the sound.

Caleb could see no sign of his guns or his knives. As he limped after Sing Lee, he grabbed a burning brand from the fire.

In the darkness beyond the edge of the clearing, he came to the string of mules and Pirate. The mules were bucking and kicking and making a racket. His own mount was throwing his head around, and his eyes flashed in the light of Caleb's makeshift torch.

Just clear of the animals, a tall, young fellow — maybe fourteen or so — was flailing away with a stout branch at a half circle of wolves that clearly had their minds set on a dinner of horse or mule flesh. Right beside him was a woman, wielding a hatchet and clutching a little boy in her arms.

Sing Lee was only a few steps ahead of Caleb, and he dove into the fray, roaring out something fierce and brandishing a long knife.

Caleb took a stand beside the young man, making sure he stayed clear of the flying hooves. He would have thought that the added numbers might scare off the pack, but these hunters were not easily discouraged.

As he waved the burning wood at the gleaming yellow eyes and bared teeth, he realized the pack's plans had suddenly changed. It was as if some silent signal had been given. Two of the wolves dashed off into the dark and reappeared on the far side of them. The pack was trying to cut off any escape back to the camp.

They no longer wanted the mules or the horse. The burning brand in his hand had discouraged that. They were now going after the woman and the child.

The first time Caleb saw wolves hunting, he and Old Jake had been coming down out of the Bull Mountains in Montana. In the grassland north of the Yellowstone River, they'd come across a wolf pack scattering a small herd of pronghorns. There were about a dozen of these fast, gray hunters, all working together.

From a rise that gave them a clear view, the two men watched the wolves herd their prey down into a gulley with a shallow creek running through it. Jake was just pointing out a young doe that he'd wager they meant to have for dinner. It was clear they were working together to cull her out of the herd. But at that moment, a big, old buck went down in a patch of wet sand and stone. That was all she wrote. The pack changed direction in the blink of an eye and was on him like there was no tomorrow. Which was true for that pronghorn, at least.

One of the wolves made a try for the woman and the boy. With a shriek, she let go with a hard swing at the gray head. Her timing was perfect. She caught the animal in the ear, sending him rolling and yelping off to the side. Up on his feet in an instant, the wolf decided this wasn't the fight he'd signed up for. He turned and ran unsteadily off into the darkness, shaking his head and trailing blood.

But the others weren't backing down.

Another wolf immediately made a dash at them. Head low and teeth showing, he clearly meant business. Sing Lee was quick, though, and his blade caught the beast in the snout, drawing a cry as the snarling animal retreated to the others.

Caleb sidestepped by the tall boy, shoving him back toward the string of mules and Pirate. He threw himself in front, waving his torch at the pack. The wolves instantly became a constantly moving line. Suddenly, a smaller hunter feinted an attack as another streaked at the woman from the far side.

As Caleb turned and moved, his bad ankle gave out, and he stumbled slightly, dropping the stick as he went down on one knee. Then the attacking wolf was in the air, trying to leap right over him, but Caleb rose and got a handful of gray fur.

He was a powerful animal, but Caleb was not letting go. He had the wolf by the thick mane. Teeth snapped at his face, and the sharp nails of the front paws clawed away at him. Sing Lee was shouting over the snarls.

A gunshot cracked, exploding through the sounds of their struggle, and Caleb felt the wolf twist and jerk in his grasp.

CHAPTER TWENTY

The fearsome killer in Caleb's hands twitched and went limp. He was heavy enough when he was squirming and raking at him with all his formidable strength. Dead, he seemed even heavier.

Caleb dropped him on the ground and quickly rose to his feet as he picked up the burning brand. The other members of the pack were scattering and turning tail. They disappeared in an instant into the darkness.

More shots split the night, adding incentive to the wolves' flight.

The shooter, who appeared to be a few years younger than Sing Lee, stood with a small group of men close to the woman and child. He was holding a '60 Army Richards six-gun. The cartridges were spent, but he kept pulling the trigger and the empty cylinder clicked around. Caleb understood. The Chinese traveler's blood was fired up from the danger.

A shorter man, closer to Sing Lee's age, stood beside the shooter. In his shaking hand, he was holding a lantern up high. It was a battered mining lamp that must have been ancient years before they discovered gold at Sutter's mill. But it still did the job.

Caleb turned his attention to the woman and child. To be attacked by a pack of wolves was a harrowing thing. The baby must have looked like easy pickings. The thought of what could have happened just now sent a sickening jolt through him. He'd seen what a pack could do in moments, and it was too horrible to think about. But throughout the attack, she'd been a lioness. He figured she would have fought the beast with her bare hands if she had to.

Sing Lee put his arm around them. The teenager with the stick brushed past Caleb and stood at the older man's shoulder.

Caleb looked in the direction the wolves had disappeared. They meant business, and they could easily circle around and come back.

The woman said something to Sing Lee. Her expression was one of assuring him that she was fine. Her calm demeanor after what had almost happened showed more toughness and resilience than most men possessed. And the child was no milquetoast either. He hadn't uttered even a peep in the face of snarling wolves and gunshots.

Relieved that they were safe, Caleb glanced around at Pirate and the mules. They were still jumpy and wild-eyed in the light of his torch and the lamp, but they were also unharmed.

The other travelers, including the shooter, gathered around the woman and boy. They were all closer to Sing Lee's age and wearing clothing not too different from his, but two of them were coatless. The sleeves of their shirts billowed out like sails and took on a golden hue from the lamplight. Caleb counted six adults, the tall boy, and the toddler. They all wore Shoshone moccasins, and that told him they'd traveled through Indian territory far to the west.

Caleb tested his bad ankle and touched his side tentatively. Wrestling with that killer probably didn't help the mending any, but he reckoned he'd live.

Everyone started talking excitedly. He could hear the nervous energy in the tone and the pitch, even if he couldn't understand the words.

Sing Lee shot a look at him and then gave some directions to two of the men. As they started over toward the mules and Pirate, they stopped to look at the dead wolf. He was a handsome specimen, as large as they come, with a massive head and a gray coat beautifully marked — eyes and ears trimmed with black fur — and a white snout. They exchanged nods with Caleb but said nothing to him.

With a glance out into the darkness again, Caleb went over to the mules and Pirate, who was glad to see him.

"You're all right, fella." He stroked his muzzle and neck.

Sing Lee's voice called out to him. "Marlowe, come. They bring."

The two men approached and went to work untying the rope holding the animals.

Caleb could hear the voices of the others who had already moved back into the clearing, but Sing Lee waited for him. They walked together into the camp, where he found the travelers standing all together to one side of the fire. The little fellow was leaning against the young woman, his dark eyes flashing in the firelight.

Caleb knew what he had to do. It was because of him that they had been off hiding in the dark and putting themselves in danger. They'd saved his life, tended to his wounds. If he'd fallen from his horse a half mile away, he'd have been dinner for the pack. He couldn't have them endangering themselves for him. He needed to leave right away. He owed them at least that much.

He put a hand on Sing Lee's sleeve, detaining him for a moment. "It ain't a good thing, your people out there in the woods. I'll be going. Keep them close to the fire."

His host shook his head. "No. You stay. They stay."

Sing Lee turned on his heel and walked toward the group. He was clearly one of those men who were born to lead. The others jumped to their respective tasks once he gave directions. More wood was added to the fire. The tin plates were gathered up.

A moment or two later, the mules and Pirate were led into the clearing, and a line was secured to hold them within view of the light from the campfire. His horse nickered when he saw his master.

Caleb hobbled to his blanket and sat down. Donning his shirt and wool socks, he watched the activity of the others. Around the fire, they settled down in groups, conversing in low voices. From their animated gestures, he guessed they were talking about the incident with the wolves. The glances coming his way were neither hostile nor fearful. He'd done little enough, but it appeared that Caleb had earned something in the way of goodwill in their eyes.

Still, he needed to get back on the trail as soon as possible. He shifted his weight, and his throbbing ankle reminded him that the smart thing would be to stay the night and leave in the morning.

Caleb's guns and rifle were nowhere in sight, but he spotted his saddle and bags sitting by a gnarled oak at the edge of the clearing, away from the mule packs. He suspected that, out of caution, they'd put his weapons over with the saddle.

The four men huddled with Sing Lee were middle-aged. Except for their leader, they all wore black bowlers, and their braids hung long in the back. The woman, apparently the mother of the toddler, was young and busy refilling plates of food for the party. Sitting on a deer skin nearer to Caleb, the tall boy — who was around the same age as Gabriel — was keeping a close eye on the little one.

Caleb wondered vaguely what the connection was between these people, where they'd come from, and where they were headed. From their clothes and from Sing Lee's demeanor, he judged they hadn't escaped from some crew of rail workers.

The teenager got up to fetch a plate of food from the young woman.

The toddler sat cross-legged on the deer

skin with the carved toy horses in front of him. He was a cute thing. A black cap like Sing Lee's lay beside him, and his hair stood up straight as a bristle brush all over his perfectly shaped head. He wore a long, deerskin jersey over wide-legged trousers closed at the ankles with leather thongs. His moccasins looked Shoshone as well. The little boy showed no fear of Caleb but sat with his arms crossed over his chest, studying him with intense dark eyes.

Since leaving Indiana, Caleb had had little experience with children this young. He guessed the toddler was two or three years old. He gave a small wave. The thin eyebrows of the boy drew together, registering his distrust. In the seriousness of the expression, Caleb saw something of a miniature version of Sing Lee, minus the gray beard.

The teenage boy came back and sat next to the toddler again. With a tap on the shoulder, he started feeding the little one with chopsticks. The first time Caleb had seen anyone eating with the thin, wooden utensils was in camp of rail workers in Wyoming. He was so impressed by the way the food moved from the bowl to the lips that he realized he was openly gawking. He'd wanted to try using them, but there'd been no opportunity for it.

Watching the stewed meat going in that little mouth, Caleb felt his stomach rumble. His throat was as dry as a desert gulch in July. Whatever medicine Sing Lee had given him, it was now carving a hole in his gut. He had some food in his saddle, and he considered walking over there and fetching some beans and dried biscuits. Maybe they wouldn't object to him using their fire to rustle up some dinner. Or maybe he'd just eat the beans raw and drag himself down to the river and drown his thirst.

The toddler must have read Caleb's mind. He grabbed a fistful of meat off the plate and held it out to him.

Caleb wasn't the grinning sort, but he couldn't help himself in this situation. He smiled and shook his head. "No. Much obliged, but that's yours."

"Yours," the child repeated.

"No. You eat it."

"You."

The mother must have caught the demonstration of forced hospitality. She called out to the child. The boy smiled and stuffed the food into his own mouth.

Caleb was happily surprised when she approached a moment later with a tin plate and a cup. She knelt between him and the child and held out the food to him.

In the firelight, he had a better view of her. She was a pretty, small-boned woman with chiseled features and a serious, but not unfriendly, expression.

Her close-set eyes shone like polished black stone on either side of a straight nose. Her hair was black and sleek, and she wore the front locks pulled tightly to the sides from a part about an inch long. Another part formed a T across her scalp, and from there, the hair went straight back into a braid that hung past her rump when she was standing. Right now, it trailed on the ground like a fine rope.

For a moment, an image of Sheila and her thick braid appeared in his mind's eye. Sometime in recent weeks, he'd become partial to women who wore braids.

She wore a puffy black tunic over another shirt, and her long, black dress had slits on the sides that ended about the knee. When she knelt, he noticed black leggings tucked into high moccasins.

He'd already seen the deference everyone showed her when they spoke to her. She was important to all of them. Right now, she simply looked tired, and Caleb knew the wolf attack had to have taken a lot out of her.

"For you."

"Thank you."

Her face relaxed into a shy smile as he accepted the food. Caleb immediately took a swallow of the drink. Tea. The hot liquid slid down his throat, warming him.

"You prefer coffee?"

"No." He hadn't smelled any coffee, so he figured there wasn't any. "I'm just fine with the tea."

"Good. We have no coffee." The woman had a sense of humor. And she spoke English better than Sing Lee.

He looked down at the food. Stewed meet and greens, and it smelled damn good. It was all he could do not to plough his face into it. He was surprised when she took a spoon from her pocket and slid it onto the edge of the plate.

"Do you have any of them chopsticks, ma'am?"

"Instead of a spoon?"

"I ain't never tried it. But I'd like to."

"And more tea?"

"Much obliged."

She took his cup and went back to the fire. The tall boy and the toddler were watching Caleb's every move. He was too hungry to wait. He used the spoon and shoveled a bite of food into his mouth. It was even better than it smelled. The stewed rabbit was the best he'd ever tasted.

The child jumped up and plunked himself down in front of Caleb.

"Hullo there, little fella."

The teenager called out something to the woman before rising and going over to where the men were sitting in a circle and chatting.

The spoon was a definite source of fascination to the toddler. Caleb didn't put up a fuss when the child took the utensil out of his hand and dug into the stew with it. Immediately, it was heading for Caleb's mouth.

The little one planted a small hand on Caleb's shoulder. His aim was only off by a little. If he'd been hunting and that spoon was filled with buckshot, Caleb would have been dead. As it was, he took warm stew all down the front of his shirt. He couldn't help but laugh at the effort.

The mother was on the two of them quicker than the swish of a squirrel's tail. With a cloth in one hand and Caleb's tea and chopsticks in the other, she was all apologies and stern looks at the young one. As soon as her hands were free, she tried to pick the boy up and detach him from the spoon. But he wasn't willing to go without a fight. For his part, Caleb enjoyed the little rascal.

"Won't you sit, ma'am?"

She hesitated a moment, and Caleb was pleased when she knelt down a few feet away, slid over onto one hip, and pulled the toddler onto her lap. While the boy played with the spoon, she fed him with chopsticks.

Using the wooden utensils was a helluva lot more challenging that he'd thought it would be. His fingers were too big and too clumsy. Caleb watched the smooth, easy movements of her hand. He couldn't quite get them to hold anything. He wasn't about to give up trying and managed to get a morsel or two in.

Sing Lee walked up and stood over him. He was clearly amused as he watched Caleb's struggle. It was the first time he'd smiled. "Hungry?"

"Very."

"Like food?"

"It's very good."

"Ah Won built." He motioned to a man who was sitting and smoking with the others by the fire.

"Ah Won cooked," the young woman corrected.

The elder frowned and sat down on the blanket by Caleb. The baby immediately left his mother and crawled onto Sing Lee's lap.

"My grandson. My daughter. My son."

He motioned to the tall boy who'd been watching the baby.

"Caleb Marlowe, ma'am." He gave a polite nod to the daughter.

"Liang Lee. My son's name is Ho."

"Ho," the little boy repeated, pointing to his chest.

Caleb turned to the grandfather. "Thanks again for helping me. Yesterday was not a good day."

Sing Lee started to say something in English but decided against it and spoke to his daughter instead. Liang translated for him.

"My father says the cut in your side was taken care of by a doctor. But not yesterday."

"A fella put his knife in me three days ago." Caleb thought about licking the gravy off his empty plate but figured a show of manners might be more respectful. He put it down next to him. "My friend Doc Burnett stitched it up before I left Elkhorn."

"What is *Doc*? A name?" Sing Lee asked.

"Short for *doctor*. Doctor John Burnett."

"My father is a doctor too," Liang told him.

It made sense. Whatever he'd done about that snakebite, Caleb was still breathing. And he'd known how to handle his knife wound as well.

He nodded his gratitude to Sing Lee. "The bite from that rattler should have killed me."

She translated for the older man. He said something back.

"My father always carries medicines. He studied under a famous doctor in Qinglong. He was highly respected for his knowledge of herbs and medicines in his province of Fujian and more recently in San Francisco. He knows all about treating poison snake-bites."

San Francisco. That bit of information cleared up where this group was coming from. And maybe why they left.

Caleb recalled reading in the papers last summer about the two days of riots there. A lot of Chinese people were killed and a lot more were hurt. There had been thousands of dollars of damage. Apparently, the tension and the violence being directed at the immigrants didn't go away afterward either. He wondered where these folks were going if they were looking to escape all that.

Sing Lee said something else, and Liang translated, "My father believes you are a sheriff."

Caleb glanced at his vest lying beside his bedding. He must have seen the tin star in

265

the pocket. "Only a deputy. Occasional-like. I'm a rancher."

"So, you work as deputy to make money."

There was no way he was going to explain why he was on the road and who he was searching for. The best answer was the simplest one. "Yep."

"We have money."

Caleb was surprised by Sing Lee's words. "I ain't about to tell you your business. But I wouldn't go telling that around. You're in the mountains of Colorado, and there are all kinds of blackguards in these hills."

He turned to the daughter, making sure she was getting every word he was saying.

"I'm talking about some very bad men. Never mind robbing you of your money. If they got the upper hand on you, they'd take your guns. And then they'd rope the whole bunch of you together and sell you to other white men who'll force the menfolk to dig in their mines or lay track for their railroads. And you wouldn't fare any too well, either, ma'am." Caleb looked gravely from Liang to Sing Lee. "I reckon you know already . . . they'd hurt you for no reason at all."

The father waited until he heard everything. "I know all you say is true."

"My father is not in the habit of such openness," Liang said. "We understand the dangers all around us. We have seen it. That is why we are traveling through the mountain passes and not on the main roads."

Sing Lee put a hand on his daughter's arm, interrupting her. "We hire you. Pay you money, and you keep us safe. To Denver."

CHAPTER TWENTY-ONE

Denver. Why the blazes they were going there was beyond Caleb, but it wasn't for him to meddle.

There was a voice inside squawking at him to help. He owed them. But they were going in the opposite direction of where he was headed.

"I can't."

"Why?" Sing Lee protested. "Say how much. I pay."

If he were able to do it, he definitely wouldn't take their money. That's for damn sure.

Caleb shook his head. "You're going east. I have a job I have to do, and that takes me west."

The older man was clearly disappointed, and he barked a few things at his daughter. She replied, gesturing toward Caleb. He sensed she was explaining his situation. Finally, Liang turned to him again.

"He'd like you to reconsider. He will pay you more than your current job."

"I can't do it, Sing Lee," Caleb replied. "This job ain't something I can put off."

The older man's lips thinned, and his chin dropped. Caleb truly wished he could do something. He knew the journey from San Francisco must have been long and hard. They'd been truly fortunate to get this far. And even if they were able to find their way through these mountains, Sing Lee and his people could run into trouble anywhere between here and Denver. The dangers facing them could come in both two- and four-legged varieties.

With a curt nod of his head, the older man gently pushed Ho toward his mother, rose to his feet, and walked away.

Liang gathered the child in her lap. "My father no longer trusts white men. Nor do I. To be honest, I am surprised he asked you."

That didn't make Caleb feel any better about turning them down. In fact, it made him feel worse. Sing Lee didn't trust white men, but he still had saved him.

He thought of how similar this man was to Doc. They would save someone's life, regardless of who it was that needed their help. A person's worthiness, or lack of it, didn't matter a damn to either of them.

Once again, Caleb realized how he wasn't cut out for doctoring. For more years than he liked to count, his life had been shaped by the taking of a life. And he had never regretted it. He still believed that some men deserved to die.

"How long have you been on the road?"

"Nearly three months."

To set out from San Francisco on foot with a pair of mules was slow going. Even so, that was a long time to be traveling on foot with a toddler in tow.

Caleb's gaze fell on Ho. The child had fallen sleep in his mother's arms.

"A far more difficult journey than we thought," Liang said.

He could well imagine. From San Francisco, they would have needed to travel through the mountains and deserts of California and Nevada, across the dry salt plains of Utah before climbing into these Colorado mountains. Mormon country was not particularly hospitable to outsiders, and staying clear of the railroads meant they must have passed through rugged, untamed land. Caleb guessed that nowhere would they have been likely to receive a warm welcome.

"How'd you find your way without a

guide?" he asked.

"My father has a map he purchased in San Francisco. It has many blank spaces on it, but it shows some landmarks that have been useful."

It was in those blank spaces that a man, a woman, or a wagon train could wander around until the buzzards finally picked their bones clean.

His eyes gestured to the toddler's deerskin jersey and the moccasins they were wearing. "Are those Shoshone?"

"Yes." She ran her hand affectionately over her son's chest. "We had been traveling for over a month. One of the landmarks on our map was the Great Salt Lake. My father had heard that we'd be safer going south of it. We were crossing a wide valley when we came upon a tribe of Shoshone in a small village. They were farmers. And Mormons."

In his experience, people didn't talk much about the tribes in Utah, but Caleb had picked up a few things in his travels. He'd heard grim stories of native children purchased from white men who'd managed to steal them from their people. The Mormons justified their actions in their own minds by saying the "heathens" needed to be converted and civilized. The truth was that the young ones provided the settlers with a source of slave labor.

Caleb thought back to his childhood and the training school his father ran in Indiana. Elijah Starr was doing the exact same thing. Work them to death and save their souls. *Kill the Indian and save the man.* And in the meantime, profit from their labor.

Caleb was certain the farms Sing Lee and his people had come upon were church-owned. They allowed the Shoshone to settle on land they once lived on and hunted. And in return, the harvests belonged to the Mormons. Caleb had traveled through that area a few times over the years. He'd seen the guarded bitterness on the Indians' faces far more than he liked.

"I'm surprised they didn't drive you off."

"When we came upon the farms, we found some women and children working in the fields. One told us her people had been struggling with a very bad sickness. They'd already lost a child in their settlement. When she described it, Sing Lee knew it was what you call measles. There was no stopping him from going to give them aid. In return, they took us in and fed us."

If there was one thing Caleb knew about the Shoshone, no matter how badly they'd been treated, they saw it as a matter of honor to reciprocate kindness.

"We stayed with them for two weeks."

"That's where the shoes and your son's clothes came from."

She nodded. "We bartered and paid them cash. When we left, they sent a guide with us. He led us through their country into the foothills of the great mountains. At the Blue River, he left us. Sing Lee offered money to him, but he wouldn't go all the way to Denver."

"Why Denver?"

"My father has a friend who went there two years ago. When the troubles became very bad in San Francisco, he sent word for our family to come." She cast a glance at the others on the far side of the fire. "None of those men are farmers or ranchers, like you, Mr. Marlowe. They have professions that they can use in a city where there are people."

"What kind of professions?"

"You know my father is a doctor." She motioned to a man sitting and smoking at the edge of the fire. "Hing is a cigar maker. That one, seated beside him, is Ah. He is a very good cook and had his own restaurant. It was destroyed in the riots. Tong, with the gun over there, had a general store that was burned to the ground. Wing Chee, sitting by my father, is a fine tailor."

"The man you know in Denver, will he help you get settled?"

"He is a trustworthy man. And he told my father there are a few others there who came from Guangdong and Fujian, places all of these men came from." Little Ho fussed in his sleep, and the young mother stroked his back until he drifted off again. "It's safer if we find people like us."

Caleb agreed. And he hoped Denver was a safer city than San Francisco. They'd come a long way already, but there was still some hard travel ahead of them. He hoped it was not for nothing.

"You said your father don't trust white men. And you neither."

"We don't. And we have good reason."

The look in her eye was one of challenge, but Caleb felt no inclination to tangle with her. "I read some things in the papers about the riots in San Francisco."

"It was very different from what they printed. They only told the white man's side of things."

He believed her, but even the newspapers Caleb had seen could not hide the ugliness of what had occurred. Lives were lost. So many had been injured and killed. They estimated thousands of dollars' worth of damage had been done to property of the

Chinese immigrants.

"Tell me about it?"

"Do you know of the Burlingame-Seward Treaty?"

"I don't."

"It was a friendly agreement between your government and mine ten years ago. It expanded on another treaty signed ten years before that." Her chin was high, her cheeks flushed as she spoke. "My father brought our family over after the first treaty. I was born in China. My brother was born in San Francisco."

"What does the treaty do?"

"It encourages trade between the countries. And it also says that the Chinese people are free to immigrate and work and travel in America. Many came because the treaty promised protection. We thought we were welcomed."

Caleb already knew that was a lie on the part of the government. There was no protection. As bad as the trouble had been in San Francisco this past summer, the massacre of the Chinese in Los Angeles seven years ago was even worse.

"For my people, there has been no welcome. Only mistrust. And anger. And violence." Her hand rested protectively on her sleeping child. "The same politicians who signed those treaties now create hate. They stir a fire in the white people against us. They blame us for all bad things."

Caleb knew how politicians worked. They were always looking for scapegoats to take the blame for a lack of jobs or for businesses going belly-up. And all the while, they were constantly cooking up money-grabbing schemes. Hell, it seemed like there was a scandal uncovered every week while old U. S. Grant was running the show. And to turn attention away from themselves, governors and congressmen pointed their crooked fingers at Black people, the Chinese, and anyone else they could think of. Caleb believed they'd sell their wives and children to the devil to keep their own snouts deep in the public trough.

He kept his eyes on the young mother. A blind man could read the sadness in her expression. "You lost someone?"

Liang Lee paused and then nodded. "My husband. It was on the very first day of the riots, before they really started. He was an apothecary. He worked with my father. He was delivering medicine to an elderly woman on the edge of Chinatown. Two white men approached him and stabbed him to death. They didn't take his money. They left the medicine behind. They killed him for no reason. None."

She drew a deep breath, trying to keep her composure, but Caleb saw a tear escape and fall.

"We could not stay in San Francisco and wait until the next time. We could not see my brother die. My child die."

She leaned down and placed a kiss on her son's head. It was clear to Caleb that she was trying to hide her face.

Whatever it was that drove men to do these things was beyond Caleb's comprehension. To kill an innocent man was evil, regardless of the rage a person was feeling. He was not a religious man, but he'd read the Bible with his mother plenty when he was a sprout. It was pretty damn clear. *Do no wrong or violence to the foreigner, the fatherless, or the widow. Do not shed innocent blood.*

Caleb looked at the group by the fire. It wasn't right. So many lives torn out by the roots.

When he left his childhood home in Indiana, he was an outlaw. He got running so he wouldn't hang. He ran because he was scared and lost. In some ways, he imagined that these folks felt the same fear. They were running for their lives. The difference was that, as a white man, he could find a place in the world far more easily than they could.

"My father is tired." She swept a hand toward the others in the camp. "We all are tired."

She lifted her sleeping son into her arms. Ho buried his face into the crook of his mother's neck.

"Sing Lee asked you to help us because we have come far and have farther to go. But I don't think we can make it."

Caleb expelled a deep breath and looked around him. These people needed him. He'd received kindness at their hands. And he needed to return that kindness.

"I can't take you to Denver right now, Liang, but I have an idea."

CHAPTER TWENTY-TWO

The foul-smelling tent city that had been strung along the muddy banks of the Roaring River was gone. The place Caleb recalled from his travels through here a couple of years ago had been transformed. In those days, it was mostly just prospectors on their perpetual hunt for gold or silver. The possibility of instant, unfathomable wealth attracted an ever-changing population of dirty, ragtag dreamers. And, of course, the schemers who fed off them.

Bonedale was indeed transformed. And though, to Caleb's eye, the place didn't exactly display the beauty of a butterfly coming out of its cocoon, the town was looking like it could be on the map, at least.

As he rode in through the rolling valley, with its green fields and forests guarded by red stone ridges, he'd seen farms and cattle ranches that hadn't existed the last time he laid eyes on the place. Corn and potatoes seemed to be crops favored by the people who were carving homesteads out of what had very recently been Indian land.

Even before the unpainted siding on the farmhouses and the barns had time to fade completely to gray, it was clear that changes had overtaken them, as well. The mines down around Aspen were becoming company-held affairs, prospectors had — for the most part — moved farther into the mountains, and the railroad men had arrived. The whole area was taking on a feel of permanence. Once the tracks were laid, it was like some wizard had waved his magic wand over everything.

Caleb had seen it happen in other places. No matter what an area had been like before, once the iron horse arrived, life changed. For many, the presence of the railroad was a blessing. Telegraph lines came in right alongside the rails. The mail came faster, no longer needing stagecoaches to deliver sacks of letters. Travel became simpler and quicker. Caleb thought of Sing Lee and his fellow pilgrims. How much easier it would have been for them to buy a ticket at the station in San Francisco and get off the train in Denver.

It wouldn't be long before it happened. Of that, Caleb was sure.

But the business of building the railroad was not about making the lives of folks easier. It was about money and profit. And there was a crowd of greedy, brutal men — suitably referred to as robber barons — who were no longer scouring the marshes for smaller prey to devour. They were out in the open now, looking to take their share. And they had come to Bonedale.

Caleb's stomach was telling him that it was getting late in the day as he entered the town. There was no telling by looking at the sun, however, because it had been crowded and then smothered by thick, gray clouds not long past midday. Now, the sky was dark and heavy with rain, and it seemed low enough to touch.

Approaching from the southeast, he'd been following a string of high, round-shouldered hills that, from this point, continued on north of the town. Ripples and folds ran up the sides of the hills from the valley floor to the crest. It was as if some giant had haphazardly draped a heavy pine-green blanket over them.

The town itself was a single line of wooden structures that stood with their backs to the river. The railroad tracks following the riverbank from the south ran between the buildings and the water. One street was all they could muster, thus far, but it was crowded with laborers, miners, horses, mules, and wagons of all sizes. At both ends of the muddy thoroughfare, Caleb saw some shacks and lean-tos that he guessed were meant to house the rail crews.

Bonedale was definitely no butterfly; it lacked both delicacy and color. Caleb rode past three gray saloons chock-full of drinkers and gamblers, two gray brothels also doing a land office business, a hotel, a restaurant, and a general store that broke up the monotony with a large blue-and-white striped awning.

Near the far end of the street, a small building had been squeezed between the butcher and the barber. It featured one barred window facing the street and an open front door. Caleb figured this had to be the jail.

Not exactly caught up in the wonder that was Bonedale, he nevertheless rode on, passed a livery stable, and turned back when he reached the last building in town, where a line of fellas in various stages of undress were waiting their turn in front of the bath house. They all turned and stared at him.

Caleb rode back to the livery and boarded Pirate. He asked the stable man where he might find Elijah Starr but got only a shrug and a guarded look in reply. Caleb started along the street toward the jail, but as he walked, it occurred to him that he was glad he and Henry had decided on Elkhorn rather than a place like this. The air seemed grittier here, and even the carousing had a feeling of grimness to it.

Wherever Elijah Starr had situated himself, Caleb figured the town lawman would know. If news of the trouble in Elkhorn had already gotten back here, his only hope was that his father was still around.

He knocked on the open door and went in. The sheriff's office was barely more than a shack. The building was not over twenty feet square, and no attention had been given to making it anything more than functional. The walls were bare studs, and no one had even bothered to nail down the warped, mud-covered floorboards. Both the front and back doors stood open, and the only window faced the street.

A bench ran the length of one wall, with three iron rings bolted about shoulder height. Shackles dangled from the rings. The place had no cell. The rest of the furnishings consisted of a stove in one corner, a small crate with scraps of wood, a battered spittoon, four chairs, some shelves, and a rough, wooden table that served as a desk.

One of the chairs was behind the desk and empty. In another chair next to the desk, a burly, pock-faced fellow in a bright-green coat, black vest, and gray pants sat staring at Caleb. He was wearing a black bowler big enough to hide a small child in. He had a large nose that pointed west when he was facing north, small, suspicious mud-colored eyes, and a hard slash of a mouth mostly concealed under a drooping, tobacco-stained moustache.

He was sitting forward, his long legs pulled in next to the chair, giving him the appearance of a giant grasshopper ready to take off into the wind. He had his right hand resting on his holstered iron. A small knife sat on the corner of the table with a sharpening stone beside it.

"You the sheriff?"

The hopper continued to stare without offering a response. Finally, he spat a long stream of tobacco juice into the spittoon without removing his gaze from Caleb. "Who wants to know?"

"I do. You him or not?"

"Wearing a badge, ain't I?" he returned shortly, his voice a belligerent growl.

Caleb had dealt with enough sheriffs and deputies. He knew not to trust any of them right off.

In front of the empty chair, a polished black stone held down a few sheets of paper, and a pen and inkpot were positioned on the left side of the stack of papers. This fellow wore his pistol on the right. Whoever sat behind the desk wrote with his left hand and probably shot with it too. This lawman only shot with his right.

Caleb opened his coat and flashed the tin star on his vest. "I'm coming from Elkhorn. I need to see the sheriff. And you ain't him."

The deputy shrugged. "He's rode out west of the river with some of the boys, chasing after some rustlers."

"When will he be back?"

"Who knows?" The big grasshopper sat back in the chair. He kept his hand on his pistol. "You need the law here? I'm the man. So, you need my help or not?"

Caleb nodded, already knowing this fellow would be about as helpful as a three-legged mule. "I'm here to arrest someone."

"Hold on a damn minute!" the deputy barked. "Let's do this thing right. You got a name, Elkhorn?"

He hit the spittoon again, eyeing Caleb with a look of contempt in his muddy eyes.

"My name is Marlowe. Judge Patterson sent me." He held the other man's gaze and patted the pocket that held the papers. "I got a signed warrant to show to the sheriff if he needs it. Only stopped in here to be courteous-like. And to see if you'd be a help."

The deputy ran his hand across his moustache, thinking it over. He didn't ask to see the warrant, and Caleb figured he probably couldn't read.

"You say your name's Marlowe. You seem awful damn familiar to me. Do I know you?"

"Don't know." The day was fading fast. "Where do I find Elijah Starr?"

The deputy's eyes opened wider, and then the lids dropped. His gaze slid away from Caleb. "What's he wanted for?"

He almost said *murder* but caught himself. For all he knew, the law in this town could be under the thumb of the railroad company. Hell, that was more than likely. And he wasn't going to give his father a running start.

"I didn't say he was wanted. But I have to talk to him about some of his men. Outlaws. That's what the warrant's for."

The hopper scoffed. "So, you come all this way for that? I coulda saved you the ride. Mr. Starr don't hire no outlaws."

The deputy was going to be less than helpful.

"I'll pass on your good word about him.

Where can I find him?"

"Don't know that I'd tell you if I knew."

Caleb came a step closer, crowding the deputy a little. "You get in my way, and I'll drag *you* back to Elkhorn. The judge will be very happy to put another fella behind bars."

His lips lifted in a sneer. "For what?"

"For aiding and abetting."

"Fancy words, Marlowe." His right hand tightened on his six-gun. "But maybe you oughta be thinking hard afore threatening me in my own town."

Caleb's voice was cold and even. "I ain't got time for no pissing contest."

Before the deputy could move, Caleb cleared leather and pointed his Colt at the man's heart.

"Get your hand off that rod. It'd be a shame to ruin that handsome green coat." He waited as the man raised his hands. "I been trying to go at this easy, but you're interfering with the law. We've had some killings in Elkhorn, thanks to the fella I'm looking for. And Judge Patterson is mighty eager to put a rope around someone's neck. I think you'll do just fine."

The deputy's face paled. "I ain't interfering with nothing. But why didn't you say right off that you're after a killer?"

He lowered his hands slowly and pushed

to his feet. Standing, he was nearly as tall as Caleb.

"Tell you what. You set right here. I'll go and ask around for Mr. Starr. Someone should know where he is."

"I'll do my own asking. Tell me where to start."

"That ain't an easy question. We got a few saloons here in . . ."

Caleb planted his left hand in the man's chest and shoved him back down on to the chair. "I'm done with this. You're going back with me."

"Try the Dry Bottom. It's the saloon halfway down the street."

"Much obliged." Caleb backed toward the door. "Don't come after me. It wouldn't be too healthy for you."

Once he was on the street and certain the deputy wasn't trying to get the drop on him, he pouched his iron. A dusky gloom was settling in over the town, but there was no rain yet.

Caleb didn't for a minute think he'd find Elijah Starr spending a convivial evening at a place called the Dry Bottom Saloon. He couldn't recall his father ever drinking in a bar. And he didn't trust Deputy Grasshopper back there.

He went down the street, scanning every

face for a tall, broad man with an eye patch. No luck. He passed the hotel and looked in the door, wondering if Elijah Starr might have a room there. Just then, a bespectacled Black man carrying a lamp and a newspaper crossed the cramped lobby and went behind the counter. He didn't glance toward the door, but Caleb sensed that he saw him.

The town was beginning to wind itself up for a wild night, by the looks of things. Lamps were being lit in the saloons and brothels. A trio of rail workers who'd started early came weaving down the center of the street, arm in arm, shouting at others they knew. Even before Caleb reached the entrance to the Dry Bottom Saloon, he heard the sound of a harmonica and the loud, off-key voices of men singing:

Oh! give the stranger happy cheer,
When, o'er his cheek the teardrops start,
The balm that flows from one kind word
   May heal the wound in a broken heart.
Oh! Give the stranger . . .

Caleb stood by the open double doors, peering in. A dozen fellows in wooden chairs crowded around the harmonica player by the front window. He doubted Stephen Foster would have recognized the song as his own.

Lighted lamps hanging on the walls lit a score of card tables, mostly filled with laborers, cowpunchers, and a few miners. Others stood around watching the games. Almost everyone in the place wore a gun belt. A long bar ran along the left side of the saloon, where men stood two deep, talking and joking with each other. Waiters ferried drinks to tables, and a handful of women circulated, advertising their wares in colorful, low-cut dresses that were slit up the leg to the hip. The laughter was raucous and loud. Just the regular Sunday crowd, he figured.

Nowhere did he see Elijah Starr, but that didn't mean someone here couldn't tell him where the man was.

As Caleb entered and strode toward the bar, the harmonica player stopped in the middle of a verse. The singers trailed off, and a strange and awkward hush spread through the place. He received stares and a few curt nods from men he passed, who backed away from him like he had yellow fever.

On the wall by the end of the bar closest to the street, a display of posters drew his eye. He stopped in front of them as the talk and the harmonica player started up again.

Wells Fargo Overland stagecoach advertising. WANTED posters offering reward money for the capture of various men and women for murder, robbery, horse stealing, and cattle rustling. The rewards were generous and enticing. Two hundred dollars. Five hundred dollars. Dead or alive. A man could make a lucrative career for himself chasing after these desperados.

Caleb's thoughts flickered to Mrs. Fields, the leader of the gang of road agents who had operated between Elkhorn and Denver up until a month or so ago. He'd let her go free, and her secret would remain safe with him and Doc and Sheila. He wondered if she and her son were already settled in California. He hoped so. There was no way he wanted to see their names on one of these posters.

One notice in particular caught Caleb's attention:

MANY POSITIONS AVAILABLE
for EXPERIENCED MEN
Ex-Military. Ex-Pinkertons. Ex-Lawmen.
To aid in the PROTECTION of company property
and in the capture of TRAIN ROBBERS.
Inquire at Dry Bottom Saloon
Mr. Elijah Starr

Caleb stared at the name at the bottom and then reread every line. Every word.

His heart raced. His hand fisted. The image of his mother's bloody body on the floor flashed behind his eyelids. Memories rushed back of beating the man's face, again and again. He'd kill him this time.

He pulled the sheet off the wall and read the notice again. *Many Positions Available.* His father was raising his own army. And train robbers were not the reason for it. His men were hired to harass, to bully, to keep disgruntled workers in line. And to show up in towns like Elkhorn to murder whoever stood in the way of railroad expansion.

Caleb looked up and caught the flash of a bright-green coat and a large, black bowler going out a back door. The deputy had taken the back route to the saloon. He'd come to warn someone, and Caleb had a pretty good idea who it was.

At the far end of the bar, a group of six men had their heads together, and Caleb started toward them. He was about fifteen feet from them when they broke up and began to move far too casually away from one another, spreading out as they ambled across the saloon. One of the men, who'd been facing Caleb the whole time, remained by the bar and ordered another drink.

Caleb stopped, bellied up to the gleaming wood of the bar. There was a large looking glass behind the bottles lined up against the wall, and he watched the men disperse to their assigned places. He unobtrusively loosened the thongs on his twin Colts.

The one who'd remained by the bar was dressed in a charcoal-gray suit with a shiny, silver vest. His wide-brimmed black hat cast a shadow over his face, but Caleb could see his eyes tracking the progress of his friends. He was wearing a fine-looking brace of walnut-handled Remingtons. When the others came to a stop behind tables of card players, they angled their bodies so their holsters were shielded from view. They stood and pretended to be looking at the hands being played.

Caleb waited for the signal that he knew was coming. He had his back to five of them. The man at the bar, still looking in the mirror, nonchalantly stroked his moustache, reached for his glass with his left hand, and picked it up.

The others immediately drew their weapons.

The saloon exploded with the sound of gunfire. Caleb moved forward and to his right a step, and the looking glass behind him shattered. Men and women were diving for cover and tables were upended, with cards and cash going flying.

His Colts spit fire. The leader, whirling toward him at the bar, shot a rail worker standing in the way before taking a bullet himself in the eye. He was still falling when Caleb, moving, unleashed a barrage of shots at the others.

Bullets whizzed by his head, splintering what was left of the mirror and the bottles on the shelf and tearing up the bar to his right and left with splintering cracks. Smoke filled the air, and in seconds, it was over.

Caleb's eyes raked the saloon for more assailants, but no one made a move for their gun. No one moved at all. He counted the bodies.

Blood spattered the far walls, and the unseeing eyes of the dead stared into oblivion. Five gunmen were stretched out on the floor in a variety of positions, and one was sitting against an overturned table, clutching his throat as his life pulsed between his fingers. He coughed up blood, spraying onto his shirt and pants, shuddered, and slumped to the side.

Caleb straightened up and slid one of his pistols into its holster. He was still holding one of the Colts in his hand and watching the room when a woman's voice came from just inside the saloon door.

"Put that gun down nice and easy. Do it *now.*"

CHAPTER TWENTY-THREE

Red Annie.

"Don't you be giving me that stupid look, mister. I said put it down."

Caleb turned in time to see the bartender lower the coach gun that was pointed at his back. Near the door, the woman stood with her revolver cocked and ready. Looking at her hard, piercing eyes, no one could doubt that she was ready to kill. And she'd do it with no regret.

Caleb knew of seven other men for sure who had underestimated Red Annie's ability and willingness to put a hole in them. The bartender was not such a fool.

"Lay that blunderbuss on the bar and step back," she ordered.

He complied, raising his hands as he did so.

"Never mind that," she barked. She waved her Colt Peacemaker at all the broken glass. "Pour two drinks, for me and him, if'n you can find one of them bottles that ain't shot up."

The bartender hesitated, casting an uncertain glance at Caleb.

"You heard her," he ordered, sliding the man's coach gun down the bar.

Red Annie O'Neal was a tall woman, taller than most men, and as tough as buffalo hide. She kept her fiery red hair cropped short and covered with a wide-brimmed hat the color of night. Caleb guessed she'd once been fair-skinned, but sun and wind and cold had weathered her face to a tawny gold, and wrinkles spider-webbed from the corners of her gray eyes. When she smiled, deep creases formed at the corners of her mouth.

She could be intimidating as hell when she chose to be. When she was angry, those smile lines disappeared, and her eyes narrowed to slits. That's what he and the bartender were looking at now.

For as long as Caleb had known her — about five years — he'd never seen her in anything except men's clothes, with a brace of Colts strapped to her hips. Right now, she was wearing buckskin trousers tucked into her boots and a jacket of elk skin that would keep out all kinds of weather. More often than not, she was carrying a Winchester '73 as well. An important tool of her trade. She was known to knock back a few in a saloon now and again, but she could shoot a flea off a mule deer's ass at two hundred yards.

She turned her gray eyes on Caleb, and one of those creases formed at the corner of her mouth. "Good evening, Marlowe."

Caleb nodded. "Red Annie."

He turned to the bartender, who was wiping glistening shards off the bar before putting down two glasses. The man had a round face with all his features jammed into the center, above a waxed moustache that spread out like curled wings. He was bald as a baby's behind on top with a thin fringe of stringy brown hair around the sides. Over a brown wool vest, he wore a dingy apron and two garters up around his elbows to keep his sleeves from dragging. They were pale green with black lace along the edges, and Caleb decided he must have stolen them from one of the prostitutes working the bar.

"That ain't too hospitable, shooting a customer in the back."

The barkeep quickly poured out two brandies, avoiding Caleb's eyes. "I weren't going to shoot nobody in the back. Now why would I want to kill a stranger who —"

"Hearing lies always makes my gun go off on its own," Red Annie warned as she came to the bar. "I sincerely hope you don't end up with a bullet hole right in the center of your forehead."

"I ain't lying, ma'am!" The bartender's eyes widened as he looked down the barrel of her revolver. "I mean it, sir. I was ready to act on your side, if you needed it."

Caleb exchanged a glance with Red Annie. They both knew he was lying.

The bystander who'd been shot had passed out, but he was still alive. He groaned as he came to, clutching his bleeding shoulder.

"Watch this fella," Caleb said to her, gesturing to the barkeep.

As he crouched next to the wounded fellow, two friends of the man approached, watching Caleb and Red Annie warily.

"He ain't dead?" one asked.

"Don't appear to be." Caleb looked at the shoulder. The slug had passed through the meaty portion high on his right arm. "You got a doctor in this town?"

The men looked uneasily at each other before one answered. "There is a sawbones, but I don't know that I'd call him a doctor."

"Well, you better get your friend over to

have him take a look."

"Will he be able to drive his mules, ya think? This outfit don't allow fer no lolly-gagging, mister."

Caleb shrugged. "He appears to be a tough enough fella."

The men helped the wounded teamster to his feet and led him, groaning, out the door. The rest of the Dry Bottom's clientele were coming to life as well. Except for the dead men, who had become the center of attention for groups of gawkers.

Caleb noticed that the harmonica player and some of the patrons had slipped out. Many had stayed, however, and were beginning to right the tables and chairs and gather up the scattered money and cards off the floor. Others were dragging the carcasses of the dead out onto the street, where a crowd was forming.

Red Annie drank her brandy and slapped the glass onto the bar. She was glaring at the bartender. "You go out there and tell your assembled citizenry what happened. I'll be listening, so you be sure to tell them it was six against one."

As Caleb stood beside her, the barman nodded and scurried to the front door.

The first time he met Red Annie was at a stagecoach way station up in Wyoming.

He'd walked in on a fight between her and two fellas who apparently had taken exception to her wearing trousers and riding as a guard for Wells Fargo. She had no trouble handling both of them. Caleb had only stepped in when a third tried to get into the mix and jump her from behind.

Red Annie was one unique individual. She refused to be submissive to anyone, and she was not hesitant about putting people in their place when the moment called for it.

He'd seen her on occasion since then. About the time Caleb was wearing a star up in Greeley, she got herself a contract with the U.S. Post Office working as a star route carrier. As an independent contractor, she carried mail for them from town to town along established routes, using stagecoaches for the most part. But where there was no stagecoach service, she carried the mail by horseback.

She was a woman who liked her life the way she lived it and was damn good at what she did. Stagecoach drivers liked having her along for her marksmanship, and road agents gave her a wide berth if they knew she was coming through.

After their first meeting, she decided that Caleb was worth being friendly with. When one of her routes included Elkhorn, she even went so far as to look him up for a drink when she passed through.

Caleb watched the cleaning up going on and drank his brandy. "Of all places, I never expected to run into a friend in Bonedale."

"What can I say? It's your lucky day."

"I didn't see you when I came in."

She glanced around her. "I wasn't in here when the shooting started, but I've been known to drink in worse shitholes."

Red Annie said that loud enough for the bartender to hear. He'd come in from the street and was standing by the entrance, scratching his bald head and eyeing the destruction.

Caleb slapped his hand on the wood to get the proprietor's attention.

"Two more?" the man asked, slipping around behind the bar. Broken glass crunched beneath his feet.

Caleb ignored the question. "I saw the deputy sneaking out your back door. What did he want?"

"He was searching for Mr. Starr, but he settled for talking to that first fella you gunned."

"Is Starr around?"

The barkeep refilled the glasses. "I ain't seen the man all day."

"He comes in here often?"

"Mr. Starr ain't one to drink with his employees." He motioned to the job offer that lay in a whiskey spill on the bar. "He occasionally comes over to the bar and asks me, personal-like, if anyone's asked about his posting."

The man's eyes skimmed over the crowd left in the barroom, and Caleb sensed that Elijah Starr came in here more than the man was letting on.

"What's upstairs?"

The saloon keeper took a moment to answer. "Rooms to rent, sir. And each one comes with company." He motioned to one of the women waiting to deal to some men who were starting to reassemble. He quickly looked up at Red Annie. "Of course . . . unless . . . unless you two are . . ." His stuttering trailed off.

"Why in blazes would you be wanting to stay in this fancy-ass pigsty?" Red Annie asked Caleb, sending a killing look at the bartender. "I'd sooner get a room in Beelzebub's boardinghouse."

"You could try the hotel, ma'am."

"Don't you worry none about me," she snapped.

Caleb pointed at the job flyer. "I'd like to talk to the man about these jobs he's offering."

"Are you interested?"

"Maybe."

One of the saloon employees started spreading sawdust on the pools of blood on the floor.

Red Annie snorted mirthlessly. "Safe to say there's six more openings?"

The barman smiled weakly and ran a hand over the top of his head. "I'll be happy to tell Mr. Starr you're interested when he comes by." He poured two more drinks for them. "These are on me."

"So were the others," she said.

She raised her glass to her lips, but Caleb left his.

"Thanks, Red. Gotta go." Picking up the damp flyer, he nodded to her and started for the door.

"Where are you going?"

"I wanna check on that hotel and see if Starr is staying there."

She slid her glass across the bar. "I'll go with you. I do hate drinking in a place where I'm the only one with any balls."

The two of them went out onto the street. Six planks had been brought around, and the bodies of the dead were stretched out on them. There was some pointing and murmuring as Caleb passed by.

The deputy was standing over the black-suited corpse, scowling fiercely in his bright-green coat. When he spotted Caleb, he looked away and spat into the street.

Another time, another situation, Caleb would have taken it up with the sleazy back-stabber. But he had no time to be teaching anyone any lessons now.

They went up the street toward the hotel, Red Annie matching his long strides. The crowds he'd seen earlier had thinned out, congregating in front of the Dry Bottom Saloon.

"So, what does bring you to this Garden of Paradise, Red?"

She scoffed. "The railroad company just got Bonedale on the star route. But there seems to be some foot-dragging now that I'm here. Personally, I think it's 'cuz I'm a woman. These fools don't know me."

"Well, I'm much obliged to you for watching my back."

"Hell, what are friends for, amigo?" She tapped him on the shoulder. "But what was that all about you looking for a job? You giving up on ranching already?"

"No. This is something else. I'm looking for Elijah Starr."

The thought of finding a guide for the Chinese travelers occurred to him, but before he could mention it, the rain started to fall. They stopped under the blue-and-white striped awning of the general store, and he reloaded his Colts.

It was nearly dark, and Caleb watched the rains filling the ruts and tracks of Bonedale's only street. From here, the storm would move eastward, soaking the valley before climbing into the rugged mountain passes, drenching the terrain between here and Elkhorn, turning difficult trails into treacherous ones.

"Could you use some money?" he asked.

Her eyes widened a little and then narrowed to flinty slits. "Of course I can use some money, but . . . one, I ain't taking no handouts." She took the flyer out of Caleb's hand and slapped it disdainfully. "And two, I ain't doing no dirty work."

He really liked this woman. "How would you feel about taking a party of folks to Denver?"

She looked at him suspiciously. "What's wrong with them?"

"Nothing's wrong with them."

"Why can't they go on their own? The roads are reasonably good if you go north from here. Wagons travel that route all the time. Hell, two babies and a blind billy goat could find their way."

"They ain't got no wagons. They got two

mules, and they want to stay off any main road that might cause them trouble."

"Okay." She cocked an eyebrow and handed back the flyer. "You got my ear, Marlowe."

"They're Chinese immigrants. Six adults, a young boy, and a little one. And they're on foot. They've come all the way from San Francisco, and they're plumb tired. They're finding this last leg of the trip damned hard."

When he left Sing Lee and his people, Caleb had suggested they stay right where they were for a few extra days. He told them that he'd come back after he did what he'd set out to do. And if he wasn't going to make it back this way, he'd hire someone to take them to Denver. Someone he thought they could trust. And if everything went to pieces, and they didn't see anyone coming for them in five days at the most, they should just keep going.

Finding Red Annie here was a blessing. There was nobody more trustworthy.

"I'll pay you a hundred dollars to take them."

She stared at him, frowning as she considered it. "You got that kind of money to spare for some strangers?"

Between what Patterson paid him and the

reward from Wells Fargo, last month had been lucrative for him.

"Yep."

"Why? I never knowed you to get tangled up in somebody's business like that."

He shrugged. "They saved my life. So, what do you think? You willing?"

He figured that was a fair price for taking them. Zeke was getting fifty dollars a month to serve as Elkhorn's sheriff, and the deputies got a dollar a day.

"All fellas?"

"No."

"You said there's a child with them. I don't gotta change no nappies, do I?"

He shook his head. "There's one woman traveling with them. The child's mother. She'll take care of him. And she's a good one. You don't have to worry about her or the boy."

She pulled off her hat and raked her fingers through her short, red hair. Caleb hadn't noticed it before, but she had a small braid going down between her shoulder blades. She screwed her hat back on.

"So who pays me? You or them?"

"I pay you."

"Up front?"

"Up front."

"You trust me?"

Caleb scoffed. "You just saved my life in there. Of course I trust you."

The creases appeared at the corners of her mouth. "I dunno, Marlowe. You give me that much money, you might just end up chasing me all the way to California."

"Well, you won't be hard to find with that new pigtail you got going."

"Nice, ain't it?" Red Annie snorted. "All right. You're on. When do you want I should leave?"

"Soon as you can. I can give you directions to where they're at."

"I'll leave first thing in the . . ." She stopped and stared at a woman watching them from the shadows of the building next door.

Caleb had seen her steal toward them a moment earlier. A toddler rode on her hip, and two young boys huddled next to her.

"You want something?" Red Annie asked.

Realizing she was discovered, the woman took a quick look to her right and left and herded her children forward until they were under the awning. She was wearing a man's dark-blue wool coat over her mud-spattered dress. The boys had coats on that fit them better, and she'd wrapped the toddler in a heavy shawl.

"I've seen you and your kids yesterday and

again this morning," Red commented. "You got something you wanna say to me? You need something?"

"I want to talk to *him.*" She nodded her head toward Caleb.

Strains of harmonica music started up, and she sent a nervous glance back in the direction from which they came. Moving closer, she pulled her children into the deeper shadows by the wall of the general store.

"I heard you was asking about Elijah Starr back at the Dry Bottom."

"You work there?" Caleb hadn't seen her in the saloon, and she wasn't dressed like the other women working there.

"No. A fella that helps around the place used to be a friend of my husband, and he's been kind to us since . . ." Her eyes slid away. "We been going there about this time through the back door. He feeds me and my boys when he can."

"What's your name, Mrs. . . . ?" Caleb asked.

"Caswell. These three are mine."

"Where's your husband?"

"Murdered. Shot dead in cold blood by Elijah Starr hisself in front of my very eyes."

Hot anger suddenly spiked in Caleb, sharp and furious. If he'd done what he'd intended to do thirteen years ago, this woman's husband would still be alive.

"What for?" Red Annie asked. Her voice was softer.

"My husband refused to sell our land to the railroad. We're farmers. It was a good place. Passed down from his own folks. We'd planned to work it and raise our brood."

The baby began to fuss a little, and she gently hushed him.

"I can't be seen out here talking to you. That wouldn't go over none with *them.*" She cast another look back down the street.

The light spilling out of the saloon illuminated the green coat of the deputy, who was standing by the door and talking to someone inside. The six corpses still lay on boards in the street with a few men milling about them.

"They'll hurt me and the boys, sure as winter ice."

"What can I do for you, Mrs. Caswell?" Caleb asked. He reached into the pocket of his vest for some money.

"No. No. That ain't it." She held up her hand in refusal. "I don't want no money from you, mister. I want revenge. I want to pay *you.*"

He glanced at the boys' round eyes staring at the Colts strapped to his hips. "I ain't a hired gunslick."

"Didn't you gun down them dogs that meant to do you?" she blurted. "Wasn't you looking for Starr, who they worked for? Ain't you a pistoleer?"

Caleb let that hang for a moment as she struggled to get her feelings back in hand.

Red Annie broke the silence. "Can't imagine why him shooting down six men back there would give you that idea."

He sent a hard look at her, but Red pretended to ignore it.

"I can pay good," Mrs. Caswell said finally, her eyes flashing. "They made me take half what they were gonna pay my husband, but I'll give you whatever you ask. *An eye for an eye.* I want Starr dead."

Caleb knew what was driving her to feel such hate. The right thing to do would be for her to take her money and go someplace where she could start again. Forget everything that happened in Bonedale. But she'd never forget. What she'd seen, what these boys had witnessed, would gnaw at her insides for as long as Starr was alive.

"I ain't saying I can help you, ma'am, but do you got any idea where Starr is right now?"

A glimmer of hope lit in her eyes. "I know he left town with a group of men."

"How do you know?"

"I'm renting a room down by the livery. With my own two eyes, I saw that filthy, one-eyed dog go. And if I'd had my scatter gun, I'd have done him myself."

"When was that?"

"This morning."

"Any idea where they was headed?" Red Annie asked.

The woman nodded. "I heard two of his men talking. They're going to Elkhorn."

CHAPTER TWENTY-FOUR

"What in tarnation is a red heathen doing going in and outta stores like a decent white woman?"

The two louts spat almost in unison. They hadn't moved from the kegs outside Mr. Lewis's hardware store. When Imala and Sheila went in, the men had been sitting there doing nothing but chewing tobacco, passing a bottle between them, and scratching themselves. They were equally busy a half hour later when the two women came out onto the street.

"And what in hell is she wearing?"

Sheila didn't need to look at her friend to know what the worthless idler was referring to. Imala was wearing the clothing of her people, and she was doing it with style. Her fringed and beaded buckskin shirt fell from her straight shoulders to just below her knees. Under it, she wore a brown, woolen skirt that reached the tops of her elk-hide shoes. A thick belt of dark leather cinched her waist, and from it hung a beaded purse and a knife. Her jewelry was always the same — a string of elk teeth around her neck and silver earrings.

Her long hair was braided and almost blue-black in the sunlight, and she walked with the regal deportment that expensive schools in the East attempted to drill into their young female students. Imala's face was still and appeared calm, but Sheila knew there had to be a storm raging inside her.

The men continued to make comments as they turned down the sidewalk, and Sheila wished she were carrying one of Caleb's six-shooters right now, because she could cheerfully blast these two into a state of eternal silence.

It occurred to her that Colorado was having a remarkable influence on her perspective on so many things. She was no longer the well-mannered young woman who let herself be forced to go from one party to the next in New York City's finest mansions. And she never would be again.

Even though the men of Elkhorn were often rough and uncouth, Sheila was surprised when these two actually gave up their cherished seats and began to follow them down Main Street. Trailing a few steps behind, they continued to shower both of the women with the vilest comments. And they were directing the worst of it at Imala.

By the time they reached the corner opposite the jail, Sheila's blood was boiling. She took Imala's arm as they crossed the street, and she felt the taut muscles beneath the leather sleeve. Still, the troublemakers followed, and the insults were becoming louder and crueler.

"Let's go inside the sheriff's office and borrow a rifle."

"Don't listen to them." Imala's voice was calm and controlled. "These men are less than we are. They are snakes without fangs. They have only their forked tongues and noisy rattles to make them feel powerful. They're weak. They don't deserve our attention."

"Well, they're getting on my nerves. If you'll loan me your knife, I'll be happy to cut out their tongues."

"Only after I've cut off their rattles. Men value those far more."

Sheila smiled. There was much that she'd learned from the older woman in the short time that they'd known each other. Imala didn't ask for protection, but she welcomed friendship. Sheila had to keep reminding

316

herself of that.

Even so, she wished these boors would go their way.

The sign that read, MALACHI ROGERS LIVERY. HORSES BOUGHT, SOLD, AND BOARDED came into view just ahead, and Sheila was more than glad to see it.

The two behind them had slowed down a little, and she wondered if they'd finally given up trying to get a response. She glanced back in time to see a bottle hurtling end over end toward them. Pulling Imala toward her, she watched the bottle sail past and smash on the sidewalk. It just missed them.

Imala's hand immediately went to her knife, and Sheila decided she'd never again walk the streets of Elkhorn unarmed. The women turned together, facing their harassers.

"Spineless cowards," Sheila spat. "Attacking two women. Throwing a bottle at them from behind? What kind of vile, lowlife scum are you?"

Their attackers took another step forward and then stopped. Their eyes weren't on Sheila and Imala but fixed on something behind them. It turned out to be someone.

"Can I help you ladies?" a gruff voice asked.

Malachi Rogers was a dark-skinned Black man not much taller than Sheila, but with the massive arms and shoulders of someone who'd worked for years at his livery and blacksmithing trade. Sheila had heard from her father that he had also served as a buffalo soldier.

Right now, he stood only a few yards away, near the entrance to his livery, and his eyes flashed with anger. He looked ready to tear these men apart.

"Indeed, Mr. Rogers. We were on our way to see you," Sheila said.

Suddenly, the drunkards appeared to have lost their forked tongues. She glared as they swung around and lurched back in the direction they'd come. And there was not so much as the shake of a rattle as they slithered away.

The livery owner was wearing his customary gray wool coat, black waistcoat, and black cotton shirt. Having rushed to their rescue, he was hatless.

"Thank you, Mr. Rogers."

"Miss Imala, Miss Sheila, I don't rightly understand why some fellas behave as they do. Guess it's the way they was brought up."

Much as Sheila would have liked to blame the harassment on the rough, unvarnished frontier life, she realized she had to agree with the liveryman. She'd seen similarly worthless reprobates on the streets and in the polished salons of New York.

"But that's neither here nor there," Malachi continued with a shrug. "So, were you really coming to see me?"

"We were, indeed," Sheila replied.

"I would like to hire a wagon from you," Imala said. "I have purchased some lumber to build a smokehouse, but the delivery man hurt his back yesterday. He is unable to bring the boards out to my claim."

"My only rig for that work is rented out for today. But I can have Gabriel and Paddy pick up your lumber and take it out to your place later on in the week."

"That will do. How soon will they bring it?"

"Give me a minute, and let me talk it over with them. They're doing some work for Mr. Marlowe in the mornings."

He went in, calling for the boys, and Sheila and Imala waited just inside the door.

Sheila breathed in the smell of hay and horses and leather. There was something very calming about the familiar smells of the stable.

This livery was neat and well kept. The large, wood-plank barn had a good-sized loft space, still adequately filled with hay.

Under the beams of the loft, a small office space was walled off closest to the street, and beyond it sat a row of enclosures for oats storage. The back wall had stalls for horses, and on the right, doors opened out to a large, fenced corral. According to her father, everyone in Elkhorn knew that Malachi Rogers was a skilled blacksmith, and his forge and anvil under the wide eaves were in constant use.

Gabriel ran in from the corral, followed closely by Paddy. Sheila already knew the boys were going out to Caleb's place every morning to look after the dog and the cattle. As they walked through the stable toward them, Malachi was explaining to his son what needed to be done. After a short discussion about when the wagon was being returned, he turned to Imala.

"How about the day after tomorrow?"

"If it's all right with you, Miss Imala," Gabe said, "Paddy and I can load up the lumber when the rig comes back in, stop out by Mr. Marlowe's first thing that morning, and then bring the lumber out to your place directly."

"You don't mind going in the opposite direction?" Imala asked.

"Not at all," Gabe answered in the self-assured tone of a young man who had everything under control.

"Mind if I ride along?" Sheila asked. She'd been thinking of dropping off some cookies at the ranch before Marlowe got back. Also, going with them would give her a chance to visit with Imala. "That is, if it's acceptable to both of you."

"I can ride on top of the lumber, Miss Sheila," Paddy chirped happily.

"Of course, miss. I know Bear will be happy to see you too. And maybe with you there, I can get this knucklehead to do some work and stop playing with the dog all the time."

CHAPTER TWENTY-FIVE

Overnight, the rains faded to a gray dawn mist that had disappeared by midmorning. By then, Caleb and Red Annie had left Bonedale far behind. The river tumbling out of the higher ground was running muddy and fast. When the sun finally burned through the clouds, fresh, cool smells rose from the earth. It was the scent of things growing. The greening of the sage and the cottonwood and the wildflowers blooming on the range proved that the promise of summer wasn't an empty one.

The two riders were nearing the end of the valley, and he knew they'd soon climb into the rocky pass that would bring them to the spot where he'd left Sing Lee and the rest of the Denver-bound pilgrims.

As they climbed, the air took on that rare purity that he'd only seen in the mountains. The sky was as blue and deep as Sheila Burnett's eyes.

He and Red Annie talked only occasionally as they rode, catching up on each other's news. She'd heard about him taking down the Wells Fargo road agents up in the wilderness beyond Devil's Claw, and she wanted to hear all the details concerning the shootout with Elkhorn's former sheriff, Grat Horner. Caleb told her about the dangers that Doc Burnett had weathered, and he couldn't help but see the sidelong look Red gave him when he mentioned Sheila.

"Don't think I ever heard about Doc having a daughter," she commented.

"That right?"

"Pretty?"

Caleb tried to look as nonchalant as possible. "I suppose some might say she's pretty."

"Marrying age?"

"I suppose." She was.

"All fine and well-mannered and all?"

"She is." When she wanted to be.

"With dresses like them fancy East Coast women?"

"I ain't no expert on fancy dresses, Red." He was beginning to feel uncomfortable answering these questions. But the way Sheila looked, whether in trail clothes or a dinner dress, always stirred something in him that he wasn't about to discuss.

"She must be smart as a whip, her being Doc's daughter."

It wasn't a question, so he didn't answer. But she was.

Red was openly staring at him. "Holy hell. I ain't never seen that look on your face, Caleb Marlowe."

"What look?"

"Ha! If you ain't mooning over this gal."

"I ain't!"

"Oh, I've seen fellas mooning! And you *are* mooning."

Damn. This was the last thing he needed. Sure, Sheila was pretty and smart and as fine a woman as walked the earth, but that didn't change anything. His future could come to an end in the next few days, and she deserved better.

"Am I invited to the wedding?"

"You're crazy. I ain't the marrying sort!"

Annie's *hmmph* told him exactly what she thought. Thankfully, she let the subject of matrimony drop, but Caleb saw the grin on her face. And it faded very slowly.

They rode along in silence for a while, but he knew something else was weighing on his companion's mind. When they paused by a pool to let the horses drink, she finally let her thoughts out to air.

"That Caswell woman ain't looking at an easy time of it with the three young ones and no husband."

"Yup." Caleb had been thinking the same thing last night. Life on the frontier was hard. It could chew up anyone, man or woman.

"I was thinking, maybe, there was something that could be done for her." Her voice trailed off.

"I saw her later and talked to her."

"When?"

He picked up Pirate's reins and climbed into the saddle. "When I went down to the livery to gather my rifle and things before meeting you for dinner. I walked her to where she and the children were staying. Felt a little funny asking her what she planned to do since it was none of my business. But I did anyway."

"You're a surprise a minute, Marlowe. What did she say?"

"Said she had kin down by Aspen that she could go to, but she was thinking that the fella who works in the Dry Bottom — her husband's friend — had been hinting that maybe they'd get hitched and buy a place of their own to settle."

"Does she like the fella?"

"That wasn't none of my business to ask."

325

"What good are you?"

He stared at her. "Are you serious? She just lost her husband."

"And maybe her husband was an ass. Maybe she's been mooning over this guy for some time. Something romantic. Like you and Doc's missy."

"Romantic?" He shook his head. "You know, Red, for a star route rider and a stagecoach guard, you might just be the most sentimental and soft-hearted woman operating between here and San Francisco."

"And you, Marlowe, can go shit in your hat."

She continued to grumble for a while, but before long, her spirits rose again.

"Whatever happened to that partner of yours?" she asked finally. "That Henry Jordan fella."

"He's still cooling his heels in the jail up in Denver. He's supposed to be out soon, but I ain't holding my breath."

Red Annie and Henry had met up north, but they hadn't exactly hit it off. At the time, Henry had a woman on his lap while he was playing poker and drinking heavier than a range rider on payday. All at the same time. She took exception to his lack of attention to the cards apparently.

"Well, he ain't no damn good, anyway,"

she grouched. But there was something in the way Red said it that made Caleb think she might not entirely believe that.

It was late afternoon by the time they reached Sing Lee's camp. The smell of rabbit stew had drawn them directly to the place. This time, none of them hid as they rode in, and the welcome he received was warm.

The toddler jumped down from his mother's arm and ran toward him as soon as they dismounted.

Red Annie gave him the eye as he scooped Ho up.

"Are you the same Caleb Marlowe I know?"

He felt a grin tug at his lips as the little one pulled his wide-brimmed hat off and put it on his own head. Ho's entire face disappeared for a moment into the crown.

"You didn't tell me they're family," she added, looking at the travelers gathering around them.

He pushed the hat back from Ho's face, getting a smile for a reward. "These folks saved my life. I *want* you to treat them like they're my family."

There was much that Caleb knew about Red Annie and much that he didn't know. But he believed in her character. He'd seen how she treated Malachi Rogers and his wife and son. But people were complicated creatures. Some had strange ways about folks who were different. He knew white men who could deal with Indians but wouldn't have anything to do with Black fellas. And he knew others who had no problem doing business with a Black livery owner but chose to believe the widespread foolishness that put the Chinese in a poor light.

Back in Bonedale, he'd told her he trusted her, and he did. He'd brought Red Annie to these people's camp, and he was putting them in her capable hands, but he had to make sure.

"Can you, Red? Can you treat them as you would if they were *my* people?"

She scoffed and tickled the boy's ribs.

"Of course I can. Hell, I'll treat them right in *spite* of being your family." There was no hesitation in her words, and her honest gray eyes held his. "You hired me to do a job, and I'm more than happy to do it. These folks will get safe to Denver. Don't you fret about nothing."

That was enough for him. Sing Lee and his family and friends would be in good hands.

Once Red Annie was introduced to the

328

others, Liang Lee stepped up to take back her son.

"I think this little fella trusts me, Liang," Caleb said.

"Like his grandfather," she said quietly. "My father trusted that you would return. But I had my doubts."

"I always keep my word."

"I'm glad, Marlowe," she said. "You will make me reconsider whom I should trust."

He frowned. "I think it ain't a bad thing to be cautious with strangers."

"And what about her?" she asked as one of the men led Caleb and Red Annie's horses away.

Caleb introduced the two women and explained what he had in mind. Red Annie O'Neal exuded rawboned strength and towered over the other, but Liang Lee didn't flinch at all.

"On behalf of my father and the others, thank you for your offer to serve as our guide."

"Any friend of Marlowe's is a friend of mine," she replied.

"Yes, but do you know the route we need to take?" the young mother asked. "Are you familiar with these mountains?"

Red Annie's eyes narrowed. "Familiar enough that United States government pays me to do jobs for them. Familiar enough that people trust me with their mail and their valuables. And familiar enough that our mutual friend here is willing to leave you with me."

Their tones had become sharp and their gazes sharper. For a moment, the air between them crackled like a summer storm. One woman studied the other, and as far as Caleb could tell, neither one blinked.

From the worlds they came from, he guessed these two were different in every way. But having seen a friendship blossom so surprisingly between Sheila and Imala, he'd come to accept that he was barely a novice in understanding women's minds. And he didn't have the simplest notion about how they related to each other.

Right now, it looked like a toss-up whether these two were going to be fine with each other or if they were about to start throwing punches. As the seconds ticked by, he was getting ready to put his money on the punching.

Little Ho was born to be a diplomat, Caleb realized. The toddler reached out from his mother's arms, patted the taller woman's cheek, and laughed.

Red Annie smiled. So did Liang. And the tension melted away like a snowfall in May.

Caleb let out a breath of relief and looked over to find Sing Lee observing the exchange from a few steps away. Liang nodded her approval to the older man. It was clear Sing Lee had given his daughter the authority to accept or reject their new acquaintance.

When Red asked about Ho and Liang started to talk, Caleb went over to the doctor.

"I need to go see to my own business. Red Annie here will take you to Denver. She'll make certain you connect with your friends there before leaving you."

"Thank you. You come to Denver in future, Marlowe?"

"I might."

"Come and see us."

"I'll do that. In fact, maybe I'll bring my friend Doc Burnett with me."

By the time Caleb left Sing Lee and the others, Annie and Liang appeared to be working together to prepare for their journey.

Sometime later, Caleb rode past the pond where he'd run afoul of that rattler. The family of beavers was working on their dam, repairing a breach that last night's storm had caused.

"I ain't stopping here," he called out to

them as he nudged Pirate along. "We got another two hours of sun, and I'm hoping the moon sheds enough light to keep us going in the right direction. So good day to you."

The trail back was now familiar to Caleb, and he followed the river, climbing steadily into the mountains. He figured it was well past midnight when he reached the top of the pass.

The long mountain lake that fed his own river stretched out far below him. It looked like a huge, black blanket that had been dragged through the forest by some ancient giant and left there for posterity. It was hard to imagine that this same lake was so blue in the day. To the north, the high ridges and sharp peaks glowed in the light of the moon that was already dropping toward Bonedale. Above him, the sky was as black as the lake and covered with pinpricks of light.

Caleb couldn't tarry here, and he urged Pirate down the trail. Even if they could keep up this pace, he had another full day of travel and another night before he reached Elkhorn.

He'd bed down when exhaustion set in. Not before.

The thought of Elijah Starr drove him on. Whatever he and his band of killers planned to do once they arrived in town, it had to be tied to railroad business. With the men he was bringing, he clearly had no fear of any law Judge Patterson could throw at him.

If Starr was going after the judge himself, though, it would mean war in the streets of Elkhorn. Patterson may have hired an army of men for his protection, but Caleb had a good idea he was going to need every one. Starr and his employer, Eric Goulden, wouldn't be going in there outnumbered or outgunned.

From the east, the scream of a cougar pierced the night. Another answered the call, closer to Caleb. He patted Pirate on the neck and murmured to settle him. And then, taking his Winchester '73 from its scabbard, he laid it across his saddle in front of him.

Killers were abroad.

CHAPTER TWENTY-SIX

"Give us an hour, Miss Sheila, and we'll be ready to get on the road again."

"Take your time," she told Gabe as he and Paddy ran off to go and check on the livestock. Imala's lumber and her supplies from Mr. Lewis's store were loaded on the wagon, ready for delivery, and her friend wasn't expecting them until the afternoon.

As the wagon approached the ranch, Bear had run up to greet the boys, bouncing along beside the pair of mules and barking. Once Gabe and Paddy got busy with their work, however, the dog chose Sheila as a companion.

"I'm happy to see you too, boy. I enjoy coming here."

Bear jumped up and put his giant paws on Sheila shoulders. She had to brace her feet so he wouldn't knock her down. Grabbing the ruff of the excited animal, she used some baby talk on him before finally pushing him down.

"I'd come more often if your master showed even a fraction of your enthusiasm." She smiled, patting him on the head.

Stretching her back, she breathed in the fresh air and admired the view. The mountains and the forests that surrounded Elkhorn were truly majestic, and the land that Caleb's ranch sat on had a clean, glorious charm to it. So different from New York.

Manhattan lacked this sunshine and clean air. Here, there was no smoke from legions of factories and hearths to blot out the sky and the sun. The deep-blue sky above the valley was unblemished but for a few wisps of gray and white skirting the edges of the distant mountains far to the south.

She could see the boys running down through the high meadow grass toward the herd of cattle grazing along the sparkling river. On the far side of the water, the groves of cottonwood trees had burst into leaf, and the residue from the recent rains still caused the pines to shimmer in the sunlight.

The entire valley was contained by high, forest-covered ridges that ran southward toward New Mexico territory, a land that Sheila knew very little about.

She knew that the spirit of adventure was in her. In part, it was what brought her out here to Colorado. But as she turned and looked at Caleb's cabin, she felt other stirrings within her as well.

Reaching into the wagon, she picked up the packet of cookies and the shirt she'd bought for Caleb at Mr. Wilson's general store. The one he'd been wearing when he was attacked at their house last week was ruined, though she was certain he would have worn it — stitched hole, bloodstains, and all.

Bear tagged along as she headed toward the cabin.

Feeling the warm sun on her shoulders, she realized it would be very easy to get used to this. The more times she came here, the more time she spent with Caleb, the harder it became not to daydream about what might and might not be.

Sheila sensed that Caleb Marlowe was attracted to her, but he was not too adept when it came to courting. In New York, all it took was an afternoon walk in the park, followed by a conversation with the family. With Caleb, though, something held him back.

She wasn't the prying or the swooning sort. She'd tease but never confront, and she'd never beg for his attention or affection. Still, she thought about him too much when he was gone. She'd talked her father into playing chess with her in the evening, hoping to improve her skills. She was intent on challenging him to a game when he returned. Sheila had also been practicing her marksmanship, with the sheriff coaching her, though she was already better with a six-gun than Zeke was from any distance.

She knew that she was constantly searching for ways to impress Caleb. And she realized that had a lot to do with how he'd thought she acted irrationally when she first arrived in Elkhorn. Riding alone to his cabin after dark when her father had gone missing was reckless. She understood that now, but he wasn't willing to let that go. He'd told her she wasn't suited for the frontier life, but she'd made up her mind to prove him wrong.

And she would, for there had never been a man in her life that she was so taken with. But as much as that seemed romantic and missish in a person who'd never professed love to another, it worried her too. After all, she was content the way she was. No husband. No attachment. Finally, here in Colorado, she had her father's company, and her life was her own.

"I just don't know, Bear," she said to him. The deep-brown eyes in the black face looked up at her. "The more I think of your master, the more confused I get."

The massive dog grinned, mocking her.

The porch and entry still gave off the smell of new-sawn wood. She unlatched the door and pushed it open, letting Bear go in first.

She felt like an intruder, and a slight thrill ran down her spine. The first night she met Caleb — the night he shot all those rustlers trying to steal his cattle — she'd fetched a lantern for him from above the fireplace. Since then, he'd never invited her to come inside.

Looking around the interior as her eyes adjusted to the shuttered darkness, she now knew why. The cabin consisted of one very large room, but it was almost as unfinished now as it was then. The place was as stark and austere as a hermit's cell.

Nothing decorative on the walls. No curtains on the windows. No real furniture but a small, rough-hewn table with a bench and a three-legged stool as well as a wood platform of a bed with a mattress and a coarse blanket on top. A couple of shelves had been put up for a half dozen tin plates and cups, an iron frying pan, and a cooking pot. And a stove that must have been brought over on the Mayflower. That was it.

His clothes, the little that he had, were either hanging from a few pegs by the door or stacked neatly next to the bed. She'd heard Caleb tell her father that the plan was to build a second cabin when his partner was let out of jail.

But as she looked at the one-room house now, another thought occurred to her. The cabin looked like it belonged to a man who didn't know if he'd made up his mind to leave or stay and make a home out of it.

She'd heard that Caleb only came to Elkhorn and bought this property five months ago. He'd built this cabin by himself. Alone.

Thinking of that, Sheila felt a little better. It was actually very impressive, what he'd done. She pushed open the shutter of a window on the back wall and studied the interior more closely. She paced around the inside of the building, her fingers touching the walls. His craftsmanship showed. No daylight peeked through between the logs. The roof seemed to be tight and dry.

This was a rustic life, compared with what she'd known. With her mother deceased and her father a doctor for the Union army, Sheila had been placed in the care of her grandparents when she'd been only nine years old. Even as a child, she'd known that the affluent life in which she was being raised was not one that everyone shared. So often, she was embarrassed by how she lacked for nothing, no matter how big or small. The neighborhood where her grandparents' brownstone mansion stood — at the corner of Fifth Avenue and Twelfth Street in Manhattan — was a far cry from the areas just a few blocks away. In the Bowery and the Lower East Side, the poverty and the filth were heartrending.

But she didn't need to leave their house to see the vast difference in how people lived.

Sheila had every human comfort, while hungry, soot-covered boys were jammed into the chimneys for the monthly cleaning. The girls who served as helpers to the maids and other servants were no older than she was. And yet, they worked from before dawn until darkness fell.

From her earliest years, she watched and she listened. From her grandfather's carriage and even from her bedroom windows, she saw them. The streetwalkers who would appear at dusk by the wrought-iron gates of the parks. The ragged immigrants hawking their wares. Children selling flowers and newspapers and pies and trinkets.

And what had she done to deserve the comfortable life she'd been given? As the years passed, New York society became more and more of a nightmare. Her father assumed she was safe there, well cared for, secure. But in the end, she had to escape from it.

The final push came when her grandfather, J. T. Spencer, told her flatly that she should accept the offer of marriage from his financial partner. Rudd Hughes was a man in his fifties with daughters older than Sheila.

She left without even telling her father that she was coming. And she managed to make her way to Colorado.

Sheila blinked back the past and stared happily at the emptiness of Caleb's cabin. She found Bear lying on his master's bed, and she smiled.

"There's a lot I can do with this place, you know. But do you think I'll get the chance?"

The dog flopped onto his side, offering no reply.

"He has to ask. I won't be throwing myself at any man. Even Caleb Marlowe. I have more to offer than . . ."

The sound of running footsteps coming toward the cabin stopped her.

"Miss Sheila!"

She went out the open door and onto the

341

porch, but the yellow dog was off the bed and there before her.

Paddy was racing toward her from the unfinished barn as fast as his legs would carry him.

"Riders," he cried out, pointing toward the river. "Gabe said to tell you. Someone's coming."

Sheila raised her hand to her eyes to block the sun and peered across the wide meadow to where he was pointing.

"Could it be Marlowe's neighbor?"

"No." Paddy shook his head. "Mr. Stubbs comes from that other way."

"Where's Gabe?"

Before he could answer, Gabriel came running up too. This was another difference between life in New York and here in the Rockies. Back East, visitors came to call and simply sent up their cards. Here, when someone appeared, folks expected trouble. Often they were right.

"I counted eight of them," he said. "Far as I can tell, they're strangers."

Bear was looking toward the river and already growling. Sheila turned to Paddy.

"Tie Bear up, will you?" she directed.

"What for?"

"We don't want to frighten any visitors." Much more importantly, Sheila thought, she didn't want some idiot shooting the dog.

With a shrug, Paddy ran off to fetch a rope from the barn area.

Sheila wondered what she could do. The wagon was their only means of transportation. They'd left the mules hitched, but they couldn't outrun anyone with that load of lumber. She cast another glance in the direction of the visitors, and an uneasy feeling formed in the pit of her stomach. There were too many of them.

She put a hand on Gabe's arm. "I want you to get to the woods and hide."

"But I —"

"There's no time to argue. When you get to the woods, wait and watch. These men might mean us no harm, and they'll move on. But if you think there's something wrong, you need to run as fast as you can to Elkhorn and bring help."

"Who's going to protect you, miss?"

She placed a gentle hand on his shoulder. "You will, by bringing help. The three of us can't handle them if they mean trouble."

Gabe stared at her a moment, then nodded and ran back past the barn and across the meadow toward the line of trees.

Because they would be traveling up the Denver road to Imala's place, Sheila had taken her father's shotgun with her. She went to the wagon and retrieved it now. By the time she returned to the cabin, Paddy had the dog tied to a post on the porch. Bear continued to growl menacingly in the direction of the riders.

As the men forded the river and rode toward the cabin, her uneasiness grew. They were coming too fast. Sheila quickly explained her plan, such as it was, to the younger boy.

"No matter what," she said to him, "stay by me and go along with whatever story I come up with."

"All right, Miss Sheila. But don't you worry none, I'll protect you."

First Gabe, now him. The chivalry of these boys was precious. She looked down at the ginger-haired urchin and replied earnestly, "Thank you, Paddy."

It took only a few minutes for the riders to cross the meadow. When they disappeared for a few moments in a dip before climbing the rise to the cabin, Sheila cocked both barrels of the Greener.

They came into view, and she counted them. Gabe had been correct. Eight men on horseback, all in dark-colored dusters, fanned out across the meadow like angels of death. The worry in her stomach seethed, hot and poisonous. All of Caleb's warnings about the outlaws who occasionally passed through these hills came back to her.

Slightly ahead of the others, a grim-visaged man, wearing a black stovepipe hat and a patch over one eye, rode a fine chestnut stallion. He raised his hand, and the others followed his signal, reining in about ten feet from the porch.

Bear was barking and straining at the rope that held him.

"Quiet, boy," she ordered, and to her surprise, the dog calmed down but continued to growl ominously, his teeth showing.

"Ma'am." Eye Patch nodded curtly and touched the brim of his hat.

He sat tall in the saddle and appeared to be broader in the shoulders than most of his men. He ran a gloved hand over his moustache, gazing steadily at her. He shrugged out of his duster and laid it across the saddle in front of him. His clothes were finely tailored and stylish enough that he would not have looked odd among Manhattan's elite. His suit was blue, but it was as dark as the midnight sky and had subtle gray stripes running vertically in the material. His vest was silk brocade of a deep maroon, and his tie a blue that matched his coat and pants.

With the exception of the gun belt he

wore, he might have been a banker or a lawyer, out for a lunchtime ride along the cobbled streets surrounding Washington Square. When he turned his face slightly to look at the dog, however, the fearsome scarring on the side of his face startled her.

"What can I do for you, gentlemen?" she asked, keeping her voice steady.

"For one thing, ma'am," Eye Patch said, "you might lower your weapon."

"I will when I have reason to." All of the riders were wearing pistols, and their saddle holsters held rifles.

He thought about that a moment and then nodded. "Very sensible."

"What do you want?" she asked.

"Does this ranch belong to Caleb Marlowe?"

"Who is asking?"

"My name is Elijah Starr. These fellows work for me."

However nervous she'd been before, she felt a thousand times worse now. This man sent the assassins to shoot the judge. He also sent the killer who cut the throat of an injured prisoner in their house, the same one who attacked Caleb with his knife.

Caleb had gone to Bonedale to bring Elijah Starr back to face justice.

"I must assume you are his wife. Is this

his son?"

"We're not." She gestured to the wagon. "We only stopped to make a delivery from the hardware store. So if you don't mind, we'll be on our way."

Starr was the first one to dismount. The rest of them followed suit, and they spread out, blocking the way to the wagon. The dog barked and pulled at his rope.

"Quiet, Bear!" Paddy cried out, running and putting an arm around him.

Starr gazed at the boy and the dog for a moment and then looked back at Sheila. "Lying doesn't become you, Mrs. Marlowe."

"Think what you will, Mr. Starr. But you're wrong."

"Dogs are loyal creatures. And unlike people, they don't know how to lie."

Sheila hoped Gabriel was already running for Elkhorn.

"Step aside, sir. People are waiting for us elsewhere."

"You're going nowhere."

She felt the blood catch fire in her veins. "We're leaving."

Sheila edged over toward Paddy, and the eight men spread out a little more. There was no way they could make a run of it. They were trapped.

"That doesn't suit me," Starr said. He ran

a gloved finger under the edge of his eye patch and started toward her. "So you might as well put that cannon down and —"

The shotgun blast dug a circle of dirt four inches wide on the ground between Sheila and the intruder, freezing them all for an instant. The muzzle of the Greener was pointing at Starr again before any of the men could react, but it didn't stop them all from drawing their irons a moment later. All except Starr, who raised a hand.

"Pouch those weapons, men," he ordered without taking his eye off of her. They followed directions. "You and I have a few things to discuss, ma'am."

"We have nothing to discuss. Stand aside." She kept her gun pointed directly at Starr's chest.

"You have one more shot in that gun. You can't kill us all."

"I only have to kill you. And don't think I won't."

"Then what?"

Sheila felt her heart pounding in her temples. Her mouth was dry, and her throat was threatening to close.

"Boys, if she kills me, you know what to do."

She ignored the threat. "Paddy, get yourself into the wagon." She should have sent him off with Gabriel.

The boy didn't move. The men had cut off his path.

"Get out of the way."

"We have a few things to clarify before you leave us, ma'am," Starr said coolly.

"What is it? Speak your piece."

"How can I when you have that thing pointed at my chest? You're being awfully inhospitable, Mrs. Marlowe."

What if she played their game? Stayed and let them believe she was who they thought her to be. She could even make up answers to whatever questions they asked. She just had to buy enough time until Gabe got help.

Paddy had a mind of his own, however. He started to run. Sheila lifted the gun, pointing it at the leader's face.

"Let him go. I'll stay."

As Paddy passed between the men, one of them reached out and grabbed him by the collar, dragging him against his body as he pressed his six-gun to the boy's temple.

Sheila instinctively swung the muzzle of the Greener toward them, realizing her mistake too late.

"No woman tells me what to do."

Starr closed the distance in an instant, grabbing the gun barrel. In a single motion, he jerked it upward and struck her hard across the face with a gloved hand. Sheila staggered to the side as sharp pains lit up her brain.

By the time her vision cleared, Starr had tossed the shotgun to one of his men.

"*No one* holds a gun on me. Least of all, a woman."

Sheila felt her stomach drop as two men strode toward her.

"Tie them up," Starr barked. "We've got company coming, and she will prove *very* useful."

CHAPTER TWENTY-SEVEN

Caleb swung down from his saddle and let Pirate amble over to the lake to drink. He'd been going hard since leaving Red Annie with Sing Lee and his people.

"You're a good fella," he told his horse. "We got no more than eight, ten miles to Elkhorn. Once we're done with our business there, you can graze to your heart's content out at our place."

He'd stopped at the edge of a wide, grassy meadow that ended at the water's edge. Groves of aspen and pine bordered the rising grassland and lined the curving shore of the turquoise lake. For as far as he could see, only a few breaks of rock-studded meadowland broke up the woodland across the way. Above the lake to the north, a line of high, gray stone peaks, dotted with patches of evergreen, nearly pierced the heavens. The sky itself was fading into the lighter blue of midday, and the only clouds were behind him, far to the south.

Caleb had been pushing Pirate and himself, and both of them were tired. His side was still sore but appeared to be mending, and the last time he looked — which was in the dim predawn light this morning — the swelling around the snakebite and his ankle was going down.

But it wouldn't matter if the hole in his side opened up wide or if his damn leg fell off. He had things to do that couldn't wait.

Caleb stretched his back and thought about what he had ahead of him in Elkhorn. Killing. Pure and simple.

It made no difference what Judge Patterson wanted. Putting Elijah Starr on trial was an impossibility. Caleb had already decided what no judge or jury would be called on to consider. His father needed to be stopped, and he wasn't going to give him another chance to escape justice.

Starr's crimes probably went back to before Caleb was even born. The beatings and the eventual murder of his mother. The cruelties he had inflicted on the children he'd been entrusted with when he was headmaster of the training school. The cold-blooded killing of Mrs. Caswell's husband. How many other crimes had he committed? How many others had been carried out on

352

his orders?

His father could not continue committing such atrocities. His days were numbered. If all went well, Caleb thought grimly, Elijah Starr wouldn't live to see another sun rise.

Behind him, the forest was cool and dark. The brush was heavy and the going was slow, but he'd be in Elkhorn soon.

As he stood by the edge of the water, an osprey that had been circling suddenly dove close to the shoreline, not a hundred yards to the west of where Caleb was standing. With the white undersides of its wide, brown wings flashing, it hit the water with tremendous speed, snatching a swimming fish in its deadly claws. It lay on the surface for a moment, wings spread wide, as the fish struggled beneath it. Finally, with a show of awesome power, the bird lifted up off the water and skimmed along carrying a writhing trout that probably matched it in weight. When the osprey was nearly opposite Caleb, it was so close that he could see the golden-yellow eye of the bird. Then, the predator climbed in a curving motion until it was high enough to disappear over the tops of the pines.

That was the way to hunt, Caleb thought.

While Pirate sauntered off to graze on the meadow grass, Caleb knelt at the edge of the water and submerged his head into the lake. Scrubbing the miles from his face and hands and neck, he told himself he needed to be sharp when he reached Elkhorn.

The prickling feeling rose on his neck too late.

"Keep your hands where I can see them, Marlowe."

Sharper than he was right now, Caleb thought.

Frank Stubbs.

How he ever let the likes of Stubbs get the drop on him was a bitter testament to how exhausted he must be.

"I could shoot you right there, and no one would ever know what came of yer sorry-ass carcass."

"But I guess you ain't gonna, since a low-down dog like you woulda already done it," he replied.

"I wouldn't be so all-fired sure." Silence followed, but Caleb could hear his neighbor coming closer.

Caleb ran a tired hand down his wet face and pushed up to his feet. He'd been so focused on what he needed to be doing in Elkhorn that he'd forgotten to pay attention to where he was now. He looked around. Stubbs came to a stop ten yards away, pointing his Henry repeating rifle at him.

"Now, that wouldn't be too neighborly, would it? Shooting me in the back?"

"I ain't looking at your back."

Caleb measured up the man. Even with the muzzle of the rifle pointed at him, he knew he could sidestep, draw, and punch a hole in Stubbs before his neighbor could pull the trigger.

Stubbs had the look of a man who'd been filling up his time in the saddle nursing a bottle of brandy. He wasn't a fella who was too concerned with the time of day to be doing his drinking either. Caleb had a sense that he was rarely sober from one end of the week to the other.

All in all, Stubbs's appearance wasn't all that different from when he'd driven the man off his property when he came to beat Gabe and Paddy. The same lean face and long, brown mustache. The same small, dark eyes and greasy hair that hung to his shoulders. He was wearing the same dark-brown coat and black vest, but he'd exchanged his bowler for a wide-brimmed black hat that threw his face in shadow.

Behind him, a hundred yards along the edge of the meadow, his chestnut gelding was tied to a tree.

"How's your gut?" Caleb asked.

"I didn't eat for three goddamn days and

still can't take a full goddamn breath. And you ain't too smart to be bringing that up right now."

"You got your guns back, didn't you?"

"My guns got nothing to do with nothing. You humiliated me in front of those no-good little sons of bitches. And I —"

"I'm thinking we got off on the wrong foot," Caleb said, interrupting the man before he got too wound up feeling sorry for himself. "But I talked to them boys. They know they've got to respect your property. They'll never be fishing anywhere near your claim. And I'll make sure of it."

The rifle was still pointed in the general direction of Caleb's chest while the man fussed over whether to shoot him or not.

"Now, I got to be going, Stubbs," he said. Another thought occurred to him. "What are you doing out here? Looking for a new place to set up a claim?"

A guarded look clouded the grizzled face. "Don't know why you'd say that."

"You know, about three hours west of here, there's a stream that comes out of that mountain there." He pointed it out. "I got no interest in prospecting, but I'd swear there was color in the gravel bed."

Stubbs's eyes lit up. "You don't say?"

"Might be worth a look."

The cautious look returned, but Stubbs couldn't help but glance back toward the place Caleb indicated.

"Are we done here?"

"I s'pose so." Stubbs lowered his weapon and then hesitated. "Listen, Marlowe, if you're selling your land, why not sell it to me? Or lease them mineral rights. I could work that ridge for silver and split it with you."

Caleb could think of few things less attractive than being in business with this hound. "I ain't selling."

"You ain't selling to them railroad people?"

"What are you talking about?"

"I saw them in Elkhorn last month, putting up posters, saying they pay cash for land in the way of their tracks. After they left, Judge Patterson had all of them taken down."

Eric Goulden's people.

"The ranch ain't all mine to sell. I got a partner. But even if it were all mine, I wouldn't be selling it to them."

"Then why was a bunch of them heading toward your ranch today?"

"When?"

"This morning."

A cold feeling formed in Caleb's gut. "Do

you recall how many?"

"Dunno. Maybe eight. There was a big fella with one eye leading the way. Difficult to miss with the patch and the scars on the side of his face. It was the same fella that come through Elkhorn last month."

CHAPTER TWENTY-EIGHT

About a mile south of Elkhorn, the road that led past Marlowe's ranch became little more than a muddy track, winding through the groves of pine, spruce, and cottonwood. The high peaks were receding behind them, but the forested ridges running north and south on either side were increasing in height the farther Judge Patterson and his men rode.

By the time they'd worked their way to the river — lined with sage and aspen — Patterson knew they'd soon be riding into the valley where the ranch was located. He'd never been there. And he'd never thought an occasion like this would be the reason. The afternoon sun was dropping, and through occasional breaks in the trees, he caught glimpses of rolling grass-covered hills dotted with sage and evergreen.

He had to give it to Marlowe. He'd been smart to buy this land for ranching. With the town growing as it was, the close proximity was an advantage, and the market for local beef would only grow stronger.

The judge thought about other land in the region he could put to use for the same purpose. Hell, maybe he could squeeze Marlowe a little and take this property. He had no interest in living way out here; his own house in Elkhorn suited him just fine, but he could pay some fools to run the ranch for him and make a good profit.

All of these thoughts were paltry in the scope of his larger plans, especially now. His problems were going to finally be handled, taken care of. Now, Patterson could set his sights far beyond the provincial boundaries of Elkhorn. Denver and Washington, DC, lay ahead for him. Maybe even the White House.

The thought was still with him when an eagle sailed by him from behind, not twenty feet overhead. The judge held his breath as the golden bird swooped, carving a serpentine path between evergreen branches before rising out of sight between the trees.

That was something he hadn't seen much of lately. It seemed he spent more time in his office than he did anywhere else. And when he did leave the place, he had the henchmen of that damned Eric Goulden shooting at him. No more.

Seeing that beautiful bird was surely an omen of good things to come.

The judge breathed in the smells of the trees and the ground and the fine steed he was riding. Today was well worth the ride out here. Having two of his armed men ahead and two more behind, he had more protection than he needed. But a man in his position had to be always cautious.

He turned to Frissy Fredericks, surly and silent as a mountain at his side. "Tell me again what Elijah Starr wants. Tell it to me *exactly* as you heard it."

Frissy turned his black buttons for eyes toward him. "He wants all charges against him dropped. He wants to walk free."

"And what is it *exactly* that he says he'll give me in return?"

"His boss. Eric Goulden."

For that, he'd make Starr the emperor of Xanadu.

"How easily men sell their souls," he said under his breath.

"He can't do any selling if Goulden's men get to him first," Frissy responded.

"We're almost there. Aren't we?"

"Not far."

Patterson understood that not every item of business could be handled in his office.

Still, this arrangement was peculiar.

"What has he got *specifically* that I can use against Goulden?"

Frissy's massive shoulders lifted and dropped. "I don't know nothing about no specifics, Judge. I'm only telling you what Zeke told me."

It was little more than an hour ago that he'd learned of this. His buffoon of a bodyguard hadn't thought it important enough to interrupt a far less important meeting.

"I still cannot believe you didn't come into my office to let me know. It would have been far better if I'd spoken to the sheriff myself."

Frissy spit a stream of tobacco juice out the opposite side of the trail and then turned his attention back to the judge.

"I know. I woulda let you know. But you was in that meeting with the ladies of the reception committee for the solar eclipse celebration. You told me I was not to interrupt you, even if the town caught fire."

The judge had said exactly those words to impress the ladies. But he still didn't like the arrangement Zeke and Marlowe had come up with.

Why take Starr to the ranch? Why not put him in the Elkhorn jail? Or somewhere else?

They could have put him in a hotel room in town with a handful of deputies to watch for anyone coming to kill him.

He had faith in those two men, though. Particularly Marlowe. So he had to trust that this plan they came up with had to be based on sound reasoning.

He turned to Frissy. "And the sheriff came back out here?"

"That's what he told me he was doing. 'You bring the judge to Marlowe's ranch. We'll be waiting,' was his exact words."

The judge took a handkerchief from his coat pocket, removed his bowler, and wiped the sweat on his brow. It was getting warmer these days.

"Start again. From the beginning."

"Judge, we're almost there. That sonovabitch's ranch is right along that bend. In ten minutes, you won't need me to remember nothing. That murdering bastard Starr can tell you himself."

"I know we're almost there. But I want you to go through everything from the beginning."

"But Judge —"

"Start. From. The. Beginning." He drawled every word. Sometimes, that was the only way this hulking meathead could understand directions.

Frissy spat again and then let a deep breath slowly escape his barrel-like chest.

"Marlowe arrested Starr in Bonedale. They was coming back to Elkhorn. But they got wind of Starr's railroad men biting at their heels. So instead of going straight into town, he took to the forest and lost them. Then they go to his ranch. Then Zeke meets them there. Starr tells them he wants a deal. He gives up his boss if you let him go free. So then Zeke —"

"Wait. Hold on." Patterson reined in his horse, and their entire group halted like a line of cavalry. He turned to Frissy. "How did the sheriff know that Marlowe had returned?"

Frissy shrugged and shook his head.

"Why is Starr suddenly so ready to make a deal?"

Again, the mindless shrug.

"Marlowe and Zeke could have stashed that arrogant bastard anywhere and then come in and talked to me themselves."

Frissy was looking at him blankly, but his piggish face looked paler than ever.

Invisible fingers twisted Patterson's gut. Something wasn't right. All of a sudden, everything was too quiet. "Why the push to get me out of Elkhorn?"

A shot rang out, causing Patterson to duck

his head and clutch at the neck of his mount. But the bullet wasn't directed at him, and one of his forward guards went down.

"Ambush," he whispered, more to himself than anyone.

More shots cracked, and the air was filled with smoke and blood. The other man in front barely had time to draw his weapon before he was cut down. The two horses bolted in panic, and in a moment only the judge, Frissy, and the two bodyguards riding in the rear were left on the trail.

Patterson yanked at his reins, trying to get out of there. But before he could go anywhere, Frissy reached out and grabbed the bridle, stopping him.

"What the hell are you doing?" the judge yelled at him. "Let's go!"

The truth dawned on him as the ox hung on tight and said nothing. Realization of the betrayal came quick and cut as sharp as a knife blade. The two men behind him had made no attempt to draw.

Patterson reached for the short-barreled Colt holstered under his arm, but Frissy grabbed his wrist and shook the pistol loose.

Five riders emerged from the trees with smoking pistols in their hands, surrounding him.

Patterson turned to Frissy. "Where's Marlowe?"

"Bonedale."

"Zeke?"

"On his way to Denver on that errand you sent him on."

"I sent him on no errand."

Elijah Starr rode up to them, and the hulking bodyguard turned to the one-eyed son of a bitch.

Patterson looked from one man to the other and read the silent communication that passed between them.

It was all perfectly clear. He'd been betrayed and double-crossed. He didn't know how long it had been going on, but Frissy was now working for Elijah Starr.

CHAPTER TWENTY-NINE

Caleb heard the branches by the trail shake and had his Colt in his hand before the figure of a boy jumped in front of Pirate. He quickly reined in his mount and holstered his revolver, recognizing who it was standing breathlessly in front of him.

Gabe had been up to his knees in mud. Pine needles and last year's cottonwood leaves clung to his coat and trousers.

Frank Stubbs had warned him that Elijah Starr and his men were heading for his ranch. Caleb had hoped that by the time they got there, the boys would have already finished their chores and gone.

From the look in Gabe's face, though, Caleb feared the worst. He swung down from his horse and was at the boy's side in an instant.

"Are you hurt, Gabe?"

The teenager shook his head.

"What happened? Where is Paddy?"

"He's at the ranch," he said, still breathing hard. "So's Miss Sheila. She came with us today."

Damn. Caleb cursed himself for not coming earlier. Riding all night if he had to.

"We've got some lumber to take out to Miss Imala, but we stopped at your place first. While we were there, this gang arrived. They came in so fast, we didn't have time to do anything. But Miss Sheila told me to run for the trees before they saw me. She said to go to Elkhorn for help."

"You done right, Gabe."

Caleb went to Pirate and pulled his Winchester from the scabbard. He was close enough to the ranch that he'd do better on foot. Less chance of being discovered before he got near enough to figure out a plan. Besides, Gabe and Pirate had another job to do.

"You going after them alone, Mr. Marlowe?"

"How many of them are there?"

"Eight, including a one-eyed man who's giving orders. I waited around first to make sure they weren't rough-handling Miss Sheila or Paddy."

His father had a penchant for "rough-handling," as Gabe called it. Particularly when it came to his treatment of women and children. If Elijah Starr laid a finger on Sheila or Paddy, Caleb would tear him limb from limb.

"Did he hurt them?"

Gabe's eyes slid away. "I saw him slap her once when he took her rifle away."

Caleb felt the blood begin to roar in his head. Fighting his fury, he forced himself to stand and get any other information Gabe had. "What else did you see?"

"They tied her and Paddy up and shoved them inside your cabin."

"Anything else?"

"The one-eyed man and a few of the others mounted up and rode this way. I was getting ready to run, but I was afraid they'd catch me if they were going to town. I didn't know what to do, so I waited. I was thinking maybe I could bust them out of there."

Gabe looked back in the direction he'd come.

"What happened?" Caleb asked. "Did they come back?"

That would improve his chances of getting to Sheila and Paddy.

Gabe nodded. "I heard some shooting from out this way. It was close. Then, just a few minutes later, Judge Patterson and Mr. Fredericks and two other men came in with them. And from the way they were being escorted, it looked like the judge was their prisoner."

"Fredericks too?"

"No, that was the strangest thing. He looked like he was on the side of the one-eyed man. The two fellas that came with him looked like they were too."

So Frissy had turned on Patterson. Caleb recalled the shooting in Elkhorn last week. Pig Face wasn't as fast as he should have been in trying to protect his employer. He wondered how many of the other body-guards who were supposed to be protecting the judge were actually working for the railroad people.

"You heard gunshots?"

"From that way, I think." Gabe motioned down the trail in the direction of the ranch. "I reckon it was when they ran into the judge."

Eight men, including his father. Frissy and the two hired bodyguards. Caleb had to take down eleven men to save Sheila and Paddy and the judge.

They'd tried to kill the judge already, and it was possible he was already dead.

The image of Sheila's face flashed in his mind's eye. He didn't want to be thinking about Starr and his men doing any killing.

"Gabe, I need you to take Pirate and ride

straight to Elkhorn. Go to your father first, and then go to the sheriff. Tell them everything. Get them out here. If you can't find the sheriff, get Doc Burnett. He'll know what to do."

Gabriel was up in the saddle in an instant and was off in the direction of Elkhorn.

Caleb set out on foot as fast as his injured ankle and leg would take him.

He hadn't gone far before he came upon two bodies lying in the brush by the trail. They were still warm, the blood on the ground fresh. He didn't know them, but he had no doubt they'd been the judge's hired guards. So all of them hadn't been double-crossers.

When he was getting close to the spot where the forest opened up into the valley, he left the wide trail and cut through the pines until he reached the river. Finding a shallow enough place to ford, he wrapped his gun belt around his rifle, held them high over his head, and waded in. The water was cold, and the current tried to pull him downstream, but he managed to keep his footing and get across.

On the far bank, he strapped on his twin Colts and started for the cabin.

CHAPTER THIRTY

Sheila looked around her for some way to escape. The cabin windows were too small to climb through, but that hardly mattered. Their hands and feet were bound, and they were tied to each other, back to back. Somehow, she needed to free herself and Paddy of their bonds first.

The numbness was gone from the swollen left side of her face, and as she craned her neck, her cheek and the corner of her mouth stung. Her lips felt puffy.

That bastard Elijah Starr struck her.

Fiery anger and waves of frustration continued to race through her veins.

Standing there in front of the cabin, even before they grabbed Paddy, she'd realized she couldn't shoot this horror of a man. There was no point in it. She and the boy had no chance of escaping the other seven who'd have been left. They were trapped.

The more she thought about it, the angrier

Sheila became with herself for the way she'd dealt with them. She'd gone about it all wrong from the very start. She was outnumbered, and they had more weapons.

Maybe she should have greeted the blackguards and welcomed them like guests. Perhaps she should have pretended to be oblivious to the danger they presented. Rather than confronting them, she could have stalled and bought herself enough time for help to arrive.

There was no use in doubting herself. Elijah Starr would not have been fooled. And even if Gabe had run for Elkhorn the moment she sent him into the trees, no help would have arrived for a couple of hours, at least.

And now she knew they'd had other plans in place.

"I let you down, miss," Paddy said in a small voice, breaking into her thoughts. His thin shoulders were sharp and tense against Sheila's back.

"You did no such thing. You were brave, and I'm proud of you."

"I shouldna run so close to them."

"I told you to go."

She glanced at the cabin door. Before throwing them in here, Starr's men had carried out the table and bench and the stool.

They'd left the door ajar, and she could see the corner of the table. But she could see very little of what was going on beyond that.

Still, she had no doubt they were waiting for someone. The ranch was a meeting place.

Some time ago, a few of the men had ridden out while the others remained, sitting away from the cabin. She could hear their voices, but she couldn't make out what they were saying.

When the sound of distant gunfire reached them less than a quarter of an hour ago, the men outside had hardly stirred. She prayed Gabriel had gotten away.

"Whaddya think they're gonna do to us?"

Nothing good, she thought. "We'll be saved, Paddy. Gabe went for help. I'm certain the sheriff is already on the way."

The boy was silent for a moment. "I hope they don't do nothing to Bear."

"They haven't yet," she said hopefully. Paddy had tied Caleb's dog with a short rope, and except for an occasional growl, it appeared that Bear had settled down at the end of the porch.

"I wish Mr. Marlowe was here."

"So do I," she murmured.

A moment later, the pockmarked face of one of Starr's men appeared in the doorway, and his disgusting leer was enough to turn her stomach.

"Howdy, sweetheart. Everything all right in here?"

She glared in disgust.

"Stay away from my mother," Paddy snapped at him with his high-pitched voice. "If'n you know what's good for you!"

She pressed her back against the youngster, hoping he understood how much she appreciated the gesture.

"That right, sonny?"

The vile creature started to come in, but the sound of approaching horses in front of the cabin stopped him. He backed out and disappeared.

"Do you think it's Gabe with the sheriff?" Paddy asked.

"I don't know."

She wished it were, but he hadn't had enough time to get to town, gather help, and return.

"Paddy, let's try to move a little so I can see out the door."

Working together, they inched over until Sheila had a better view of the porch and the area beyond.

She was surprised to see a pale, angry-looking Judge Patterson and his mammoth bodyguard among those riding in. What shocked her, though, was seeing Frissy riding beside Elijah Starr and talking with him. And she could see he was still wearing his gun belt and pistols beneath his open coat.

"Don't Mr. Frederick work for the judge?" Paddy asked.

"He *was* working for him. But I'd say he's found a more lucrative source of employment."

The men dismounted, and Frissy rudely shoved the judge up onto the porch.

"Sit down," Starr ordered from somewhere off the porch.

"I refuse to do anything you say. Who do you think you are to treat me — ?"

"*Make* him sit."

Frissy took his former employer by the collar and slammed him onto the bench by the table.

"You'll be hanged for this, Starr. You and your whole filthy lot. You can't kidnap a judge —"

"Shut up," Frissy ordered, slapping the bowler off Patterson's head.

"Enough."

Elijah Starr appeared for an instant as he passed into and out of Sheila's view. He had a leather document folder in his hands. Through the narrow opening of the door, she could see the judge glowering up at him.

376

"Pay attention."

"The hell I will! I'll have you horse-whipped. I'll feed you to the wolves personally. I'll gut you like a trout from —"

Sheila saw Starr's gloved hand bang down on the table, silencing the judge. "A learned man of law like you surely must know the Bible. *Let every man be swift to hear, slow to speak, slow to wrath.* Good advice for you right now."

Patterson crossed his arms over his chest, cursing audibly.

"You don't seem to understand," Starr continued smoothly. "I'm going to give you a chance to walk out of here alive."

"Ha! You bought the allegiance of dogs I mistakenly trusted. Dragged me here against my will. And now you think you'll take me for a fool."

"Not a fool. A rich man. And I'm going to make you even richer."

"I'd rather die starving in the gutter than take one penny of Goulden's filthy blood money."

Starr laughed, but Sheila heard no mirth in the sound. "But you have no choice, Judge. You will either sign these papers, take his money, and retire to wherever your conniving heart desires — albeit, somewhere far from Elkhorn — or my directions are to

377

kill you."

"You can't make me do this. Whatever these documents are, I'll *never* sign them."

"I have no qualms about killing you. You're standing in the way of progress. This is our destiny."

The judge scoffed. "Is that what you call it? Are you such a hypocrite that you can't call greed by its name?"

"You understand that this is only a courtesy."

"A bald-faced lie," Patterson spat out. "What's to stop you from killing me once I sign?" He shook his head. "Only a week ago, your henchmen were trying to gun me down in the streets. You can burn in hell!"

"One of us will."

Sheila wondered what had changed from then until now.

"This is no courtesy. Suddenly, you need me." The judge stopped abruptly. A long, deadly silence ensued.

Sheila could hear Paddy breathing behind her. She was afraid to move for fear of drawing the attention of those outside. But she was wondering if something had happened on the porch that she couldn't see.

Judge Patterson whirled on the bench and pointed a finger accusingly at someone behind him. "You, Frissy! You are the Judas.

And not just a traitor. A spy! When I found you in my office, that's what you were doing. The map with the route for the rail line. The one with all the properties marked."

"That's right, Judge," Starr replied, drawing Patterson's eye back to himself. "We know that you've been busy securing options on all those properties. It wasn't good enough that you controlled the area in the center of Elkhorn, you wanted it all. You planned to cut Mr. Goulden out entirely."

"And I will, if he refuses to concede majority control to me," Patterson sneered. "I already have investors lined up. I tell you this now, Goulden will *never* own me or my town or any railroad line running through it."

"You are quite mistaken." Starr paused. "And you know what the Bible says about the prideful."

Sheila heard the cold note of danger in the blackguard's voice. The judge, however, appeared to be oblivious to it.

"You know — and Goulden knows — that without my signature, he has nothing. Not one foot of track that profits him will be going anywhere near Elkhorn."

Before he even stopped speaking, cold dread washed through Sheila as she saw a flash of a knife in Starr's hand.

"Let me explain to you, Judge Patterson, exactly what is going to happen . . ."

Sheila stopped listening. However Starr was going to coerce Judge Patterson into going along with their demands — and she was certain it was about to become bloody — the situation didn't bode well for her and Paddy. They were unwanted witnesses. They would never be allowed to live.

And if, by some miracle, the sheriff and his deputies showed up, a confrontation would result between Starr's killers and whomever Zeke was able to roust at a moment's notice.

The two of them would be used as hostages. She recalled how Dodger Clanton had tried to use her as a shield out beyond the Devil's Claw. He'd been beaten, but Zeke was no Caleb. She shuddered at the thought of everything that could go wrong.

The scream from the judge ripped through the air, and Paddy's back pressed harder against hers.

"You stabbed me."

"I secured your left hand to the table. Reasonable, don't you think? *The left hand doesn't know what the right hand is doing.* Pick up the pen."

The judge's groans and curses continued, but a sound outside the open window on the back wall of the cabin drew Sheila's attention. A footfall. A tap?

"Someone's outside," Paddy whispered.

The shutter on the window had been closed, but Sheila had opened it when she brought Caleb's shirt and cookies in earlier. That was about a hundred years ago.

The judge continued to put up a loud verbal battle against Elijah Starr, in spite of his hand being pinned to the table.

She gasped quietly when Caleb's face appeared in the window. The relief rushing through her at that moment was like nothing she'd ever experienced. For the first time since Starr and his men arrived, she took a full breath.

"Mr. Marlowe," Paddy whispered louder than he should have.

She hushed him and glanced nervously at the partially open door. They were too involved in their confrontation. She turned to Caleb. The window was far too small for him to crawl through. In fact, she was certain it was too small for either her or Paddy to get out through, even if they were free.

Caleb put a hand in and pointed to one of the wide boards beneath the window.

"Root cellar," he whispered. "Room for you both. Stay there."

She stared at the floorboard and realized it wasn't nailed down like the others. She looked up and nodded, twisting her body and showing him the ropes that were binding them.

Caleb reached in and carefully tossed a knife toward them. With a soft thud, it landed harmlessly not far from her thigh.

Sheila and Paddy rolled until she could reach it. It took only a minute or so before she managed to cut through the first rope. After that, they were free in a moment.

With a glance at the door where the argument still raged, she crept to the floorboard Caleb had indicated. Slipping the knife blade into the seam where it joined the one next to it, she pried the board, and it came up easily. Quietly, she herded Paddy into the dark, empty space and climbed in after him.

Sheila looked up at Caleb.

"You two stay there," he whispered. "Don't come out until I come for you."

Taking a deep breath, she lowered the wide board into place above them.

CHAPTER THIRTY-ONE

When Caleb peered through the window, what he could see was limited. He'd heard enough to know a knife had been driven through Patterson's hand, pinning him to the table. Painful as it must be for the judge, the battle of wills was a good distraction, and Caleb had to use it to his advantage.

At the very edge of his field of vision, he spotted Bear standing and wagging his tail as he stared toward the rear of the cabin, where Caleb was situated.

"Don't give me away, big fella," he murmured to himself.

Before crossing quickly through the high meadow grass to the rear of the cabin, he'd been able to get a good look at what he'd be facing. Just as Gabe had counted, there were seven men plus Starr. Added to that were Frissy and the two bodyguards who joined him in double-crossing the judge. If he was going to keep Sheila, Paddy, and

Patterson alive, he had ten gunhawks to kill. And his father.

Everyone was spread out in the front of his place, some standing in groups of two or three, and a few standing alone.

Caleb considered the situation. If he went right at them — coming around the building with his Colts blazing — he'd probably get half of them before one of them managed to plug him. That wouldn't get the job done. He had to be smarter.

He looked around him. The cabin sat on a grassy rise that had a few stands of cottonwood, scrub pine, and puffs of sage brush scattered here and there. In the field, there were some good-sized boulders sticking out of the ground, but retreating to one of them would put him out of range for his pistols. He could do some damage with his rifle, but he still wouldn't get them all before the rest took cover behind the cabin or inside of it. Then he'd have successfully gotten himself pinned down.

Behind him, the new corral he'd put in was full of Starr's horses. Crossing from the forest, he'd been able to use them as a blind. To his left, to the east of the corral and the cabin, there was a wagon, a stack of lumber, ten or twelve cottonwood logs ready to be hoisted into place, and the unfinished barn itself.

Clearly, that side would give him his best shooting position. The sun was beginning to drop into the west, but it would be a few hours before the sharp angles of sunlight made it difficult to see his targets.

From his enemies' vantage point, there wasn't a lot of cover in front of the cabin. But he'd still need to get them all before they could move.

He needed to figure a way to take some out before the bullets started flying.

Before he could move from behind the cabin, Bear solved that problem for him.

Two men that Caleb recognized as part of the judge's team of bodyguards were standing by themselves off to the side. One of them noticed the dog staring toward the back corner of the cabin. Nudging his pal in the ribs, he nodded and gestured toward the back. He started first, and then the other followed, a few steps behind. They swung wide of Bear before Caleb lost sight of them. But they were heading straight for him.

Quietly, he leaned his Winchester up against the cabin wall and pulled his long hunting knife from his boot. The smooth, wooden handle fit into his fist like it had been made for him.

The razor-sharp, ten-inch blade was straight, not curved, and came to a lethal point. A fella down in New Mexico territory once said it was very similar to the knife Jim Bowie used in his famous Sandbar Fight down in Louisiana. The one that disappeared after Bowie died at the Alamo. Old Jake had nothing to say on that subject, surprisingly, only commenting that the knife had brought him luck for over thirty years.

Wherever the knife came from, Caleb needed its luck today.

He could hear the loud voice of the judge and the cold responses of Elijah Starr coming from the front of the cabin. The sound of his father's voice set the chills of recollection hard against the flames of Caleb's anger. Years bled away in an instant, but Caleb knew he couldn't let that distract him right now. He forced those thoughts from his mind. He needed to focus on the two men coming toward him.

Pressing his back up against the curved timbers, he waited until the first one turned the corner.

The man's gray eyes widened as Caleb reached for him. Grabbing him by the collar of his coat, Caleb drove the blade up into the soft organs of the belly. Without pausing, he turned and slammed the man's face into the log wall before he could utter a cry. The momentum carried the sagging body to the ground along the cabin wall.

Caleb had just released the twitching body and righted himself when the second man appeared. He was looking beyond the cabin toward the horses in the corral as he turned the corner. He began to say something to his crony when he stumbled on a protruding rock. As he staggered, Caleb spun toward him, his knife flashing upward.

The blade grazed the blackguard's throat before cutting through his chin and slicing a groove into his brain. Caleb felt the tip punch through the top of his skull as the knife went in to the hilt. The man's knees buckled, and flecks of blood mixed with tobacco juice spilled out onto his chin, speckling Caleb's wrist. He grabbed at the shoulder of the man's coat and dragged him away from the corner before laying him down.

He yanked out the embedded knife and drew one of his Colts, listening. The argument was continuing. There was no shout of warning. Nothing.

Two down. Nine to go. The odds were improving slightly.

Caleb pouched his iron, sheathed his knife, and picked up his Winchester. He

387

peered back through the window at his adversaries. No one seemed to miss these two.

Staying low, he moved straight back from the cabin, not stopping until he reached the far side of the corral. The horses were a little spooked, and as he passed by them, Caleb murmured in quiet tones to settle them, with mixed success. No doubt they could smell the spilled blood.

As Caleb made his way around the corral, the men in front of the cabin began to come into his line of sight. No one was paying the least attention to the horses or anything else beyond the spectacle on the porch. Some of them were grinning, clearly entertained by what they were seeing. But Caleb was too far away to hear what was being said by his father. Only the judge's curses and incensed shouts about torture and Elijah's lack of humanity came through loud enough.

Suddenly, Patterson screamed, a nasty sound coming from a man so bullishly confident about his place near the top of the Great Chain of Being.

Caleb ran for the corner of the barn, watching Starr's men as he went. He reached the corner of the unfinished structure, crouched low, and continued around it.

It was a good angle to be shooting from. When the building was done, there would be two large stables and a wide, roofed space to connect them. So far, he'd put only the foundation course of logs in place for the second stable. But the walls of this one were above five feet high.

At its closest point, the barn stood about forty yards from the cabin. The building was about seven yards square. At fifty yards, Caleb could take the left wing off a baby fly with his Winchester. But he'd be equally accurate — and a lot faster — with his Colts, if he got a little closer.

He'd laid out the entire barn to stand at roughly a right angle to the cabin, with the stable doors facing each other. He figured it would make going in and out a great deal easier come winter. Getting inside the building would bring him plenty close enough, but the position of the door presented a problem. If they spotted him going in, the element of surprise would be lost.

Deciding it was worth the risk, he took one quick look around the corner.

The men had all edged forward toward the porch a little, forming a half circle around it. They didn't want to miss anything, apparently. The judge was seated at the table, and Frissy was behind him, holding tight to Patterson's left wrist. The hand itself was still pinned to the table with a knife. Another man was holding the judge's right arm.

Elijah Starr stood straight and tall, imposing in his black suit, his back to Caleb. His broad shoulders had not lost anything in terms of size. A stovepipe hat sat on a discarded duster beside Elijah. One side of his coat was pulled back, draped behind a holstered pistol.

It took all of Caleb's willpower not to gun him down then and there.

"But today's the day, I swear," he growled. "For Mama."

Hugging the wall, he moved toward the gap that would be the stable door. He'd barely taken a step, though, when one of Starr's men caught a glimpse of him.

In the wink of an eye, the gunslick's revolver was out, spitting fire. Bullets thudded into the log, sending splinters of wood showering over him.

Caleb dropped his Winchester, and his rods cleared leather in an instant. Beyond the man who'd spotted him, there was no time for choosing targets.

That man was the first to drop when the Colt's .44-.40 slug caught him right below the edge of his wide-brimmed hat. On either side of him, two more went down as Caleb put a bullet in the center of one chest and the chin of the other.

Frissy and the blackguard who had been holding the judge on the porch both released the older man at the same time. Frissy straightened up, confusion showing in his face. The other one was drawing a short-barreled revolver out of its holster. The muzzle on that gun might as well have been three feet from the hammer, though, because he never got a shot off. The judge yanked that knife out of his hand and plunged it backhand into the hound's ribs just as Caleb hit him directly between the eyes. A puff of red mist exploded behind his head, and as he toppled over, his pistol bounced under the table.

Clouds of smoke were hanging low in the afternoon sunlight. The judge tried to rise from the bench, pushing off of the tabletop. Suddenly, he jerked forward as a bullet ripped through his shoulder from behind, knocking him and the table off the porch and scattering papers everywhere. Frissy had his black eyes and gun fixed on his former employer.

The cracks of pistol shots matched the *whiz* and *thup* of bullets passing by Caleb's head, burying themselves in the log wall or sailing off into the distance. Two more of Starr's men were moving away from the cabin, running to Caleb's left and shooting on a dead run.

If they were trying to reach a small boulder nestled in some brush where the land started to drop away, it was a bad decision. Their last bad decision. Caleb leaned back, and the Colts barked. The men pitched forward at the same time and went sprawling in the dirt, their time on earth complete.

A third man was racing for the far side of the cabin, clearly panicked and unable to get his gun out. He, too, made a mistake. In his haste, he ran too close to a large, yellow dog with a black face who, tethered to a post or not, was more than ready to help his owner out. The rogue went down with Bear's teeth in his arm and his six-gun still stuck in his holster.

Caleb felt the bullet burn across his right cheekbone before he heard the report from the gun. The shot spun him backward, and he saw lightning flashes in front of him as he hit the side of the building.

He rolled and tried to blink away the lights as he heard a squeaky shout of elation. Frissy.

Out of his left eye, Caleb saw the ox-sized bodyguard lumbering to the end of the porch, peering toward Caleb before moving into the open to finish him if necessary.

From a sitting position, Caleb raised his pistol, unsure if his aim would be true with only his left eye. Frissy raised his gun as well.

Before either of them could squeeze the trigger, a shot rang out, and Frissy took a step forward, lowering his weapon a few inches. A questioning look formed on his blotchy pig face.

It didn't last long, for his forehead exploded from a bullet that entered the back of his skull and exited directly above his left eye, leaving a jagged hole of gray and crimson. Slowly, Frissy dropped to his knees and fell onto his ruined face.

Behind him, Judge Patterson sank down against the cabin wall, holding the smoking pistol and clutching his wounded shoulder.

Caleb pushed to his feet. His right eye was starting to work again. Blood was running down his cheek and jaw, dripping off his chin.

His Colts were nearly empty. He hadn't wasted any rounds. Before he could reload, however, a horse left the corral to his right.

The hatless rider dug his heels into the flanks of the mount. Bloody tears in the man's shirt showed the damage Bear had done. A second later, horse and rider disappeared from view on the far side of the cabin.

If there weren't a chance that this fool would run into Gabe or Doc or whoever might be coming from Elkhorn right now, Caleb might have let him go. But he wasn't going to take that chance. Picking up his Winchester, he sighted along the barrel, his right eye still blurry.

When the rider reappeared, Caleb fired, and the last man went down.

But he wasn't the last man.

Elijah Starr was nowhere to be seen.

CHAPTER THIRTY-TWO

"I don't hear nothing. Do you?"

Paddy's strained whisper came through the damp darkness. Sheila stared up at the paper-thin line of pale light between the floorboards.

She squeezed his hand. "The shooting has stopped."

"Think it's over? Think Mr. Marlowe done them all?"

She certainly hoped so.

Ever since they'd climbed down here, two claws had been gripping Sheila's insides. One clutched her stomach; the other, her heart.

What if he were injured? What if Caleb lay bleeding out there? Dying?

She forced herself to breathe.

He was one man against so many. What if he were dead?

Anger and grief struggled for dominance inside her. She wanted to move, to push the floorboard aside and go to him. To help him.

He'd told them to stay where they were. For Paddy's sake, they'd stay here until help from Elkhorn arrived.

Frustration washed through her. What if these wasted minutes of waiting *mattered*? One of these gunmen could be pointing a pistol at Caleb's head right now, ready to shoot him.

Sheila had to do something. She reached a hand up to the board above them and stopped.

"Hear it?" Paddy whispered excitedly. "He's in the cabin. He's coming for us."

She heard the footsteps too. Whoever it was, they were inside the cabin. The heavy tread of bootheels crossed the floor. He was almost directly over them.

A sick feeling curdled in her stomach. Sheila placed her fingers over the boy's lips.

Caleb knew where they were. If he'd already succeeded in stopping this devil Elijah Starr and the other demons in his employ, he'd call out to them. He would pull up the floorboard and let them out.

The thread of light filtered over Paddy's hand as he tried to push their way out. She grabbed it in hers, stopping him.

The footsteps moved slowly across the cabin. Whoever it was, he was searching for them. Though the area inside the building was fairly large, the room was sparsely furnished, and the ceiling was open to the rafters. Once he determined that they hadn't gone out the small window, there was only one place for them to go.

Something heavy tapped on the floor near where they were hidden. Sheila tried to picture what it was. A tap came again, closer. The sound had the metallic feel to it, like the muzzle of a pistol.

The knife Caleb had tossed to her earlier, the one she used to cut the ropes that bound them, lay on her lap. Sheila picked it up, trying to decide the most effective use for it, if she needed to strike. She wrapped her fingers tightly around the handle. The tip pointed upward, sharp and deadly.

If the board was pulled up and it wasn't Caleb, she'd launch herself at whomever it was and drive the knife straight into his heart or into whatever vital organ presented itself.

She waited, poised and ready to strike.

Another tap. Even closer. Sheila held her breath.

There was a long pause. The sound of the boots moved away. A few more taps. She tried to imagine where he was. By the stove, maybe. More taps. Where the table had been, perhaps.

Silence.

Paddy leaned closer and started to murmur something, but Sheila sent a warning look at him. He sat back, and she felt his cool hand on her forearm.

The pale stream of light between the boards ran across her arm and his hand. As she looked at it, a break appeared in the line.

Suddenly, the wooden plank lifted. The first thing she saw was the devil's eye patch.

Sheila pushed upward, thrusting with the knife at the same time.

The point never reached its target. Holding the floorboard in one hand, he swept his other across, striking her wrist sharply and knocking the knife back down into the hole.

Then, with the reflexes and strength of a cougar, he took hold of her hair and dragged her bodily from the hole. Jerking her clear of it, he shoved the plank back into place, shutting Paddy in.

CHAPTER THIRTY-THREE

The judge's face was locked in a grimace of pain, but Caleb had no time for him.

Holding the Winchester in his hands, he didn't slow down or break stride as he stepped up onto the porch. With his boot, he busted the door open wide, reducing the planks to kindling.

And then, on the threshold, he stopped dead.

Elijah Starr stood by the window on the back wall, holding Sheila by the hair and pointing his Remington at her temple.

As they faced each other, a light of recognition and surprise lit the older man's face.

"Well, after all these years. I've been waiting for this a long time. The day my son comes home."

Caleb stared at the man, feeling all the burning hate of a lifetime come flooding back. His insides were scorched with liquid fire that coursed through his veins, flowing into every corner of his being. This man was *not* his father. He was the raging demon who had beaten Caleb's mother until the light within her had finally flickered out.

But Eliza Starr was dead long before that afternoon when Caleb found Starr finishing her off. She died trying to protect her child from a monster.

He stared at the man who haunted his dreams. They were nearly the same size, the father as tall and as broad as the son. From his childhood, Caleb recalled the patch that covered the missing eye. The huge fists that wielded a stick with horrendous cruelty. The hard, taunting voice that twisted scripture to his own purposes. Caleb guessed that the scars on his face were from their last meeting.

"Lose the rifle. And those fancy six-guns while you're at it."

Caleb felt nothing but hate. As he stood looking at the man, the heat in his veins dissipated in an instant. His head cleared, and his blood turned to ice. Elijah Starr was going to die.

Without hesitation, he leaned his rifle against the wall and unbuckled his gun belt, dropping it out the door behind him.

He had no fear of being gunned down. He knew how his father's twisted mind worked. Why kill someone when you could watch them suffer first?

Sheila's eyes met his. There was so much about him that she didn't know. His parentage. The things he'd done. The horrendous guilt he carried.

The expression on her face showed that she had tremendous courage, regardless of the danger she was in. Paddy's muffled voice came to him from under the floor, crying to be let out. But Starr was standing on the floorboard.

"How long has it been, Caleb?"

"Thirteen years."

Back then, Caleb was still growing. He didn't have the height or strength of his father. He had always thought that Elijah was ten feet tall. His fists were hammers. The cane was a weapon no mortal being could shield against.

Now they faced each other. One last time. Caleb was most likely stronger, but his father still held the advantage. He had Sheila.

"When I rode out here, I didn't know it was you I was coming for." The tone was scornful. Accusing. "You changed your name."

"I had to wipe your ugly stain off me somehow."

"You were hiding. Running away," Elijah scoffed. "I'd say the truth is that you changed your name to escape justice. To avoid the gallows."

"Maybe both of those things. I was young." He shook his head grimly. "I tried to kill you. But I reckon I was wrong. 'Cuz here you are, standing right in front of me."

"It wasn't me you killed. It was your mother."

Every muscle in Caleb's body strained to rush forward and break this man in two.

"That's a lie!" he spat out. "You and I know who killed her. You did. By beating her. Over and over. She was lying at your feet by the time I got there that day. Already dead. Her face near unrecognizable. Her blood on your fists. *You're* the one I went after. And I thought I killed you. I was glad of it."

"But you didn't. You were sixteen years old. Weak. A coward." He sneered at Caleb. "Do you know how easy it was to blame the fire on you? Everyone believed it."

"What fire?"

"The fire that burned my house to the ground. The fire you started, burning your mother to death in her sleep." The recollection seemed to ignite Elijah Starr's face. "I waited and watched everything go up in smoke until nothing was left but ashes."

"I did no such thing. No one could have believed that."

"The stories I came up with about your temper, your bad friends, worked brilliantly. Even if you'd crawled back with your story, who would the law listen to? You? A scared runaway with blood on your clothes. Or me? A respected veteran. A revered schoolmaster?"

So many times over the years, Caleb had wanted to know who buried his mother. He'd wanted to go back there, see her grave. Say goodbye.

"I knew you were gone. I knew that place would never see any sign of you again." Elijah laughed without mirth. "So I let the rumors fly, but I told the town marshal what I wanted him to believe. That fire must have started *accidentally*. My beloved wife died *tragically* in her sleep. I *tried* to save her. And he believed me. The law never went looking for you."

"Am I supposed to be grateful?" Caleb snapped. "You killed her! You burned her to hide it."

"I told those tales because I intended to find you myself. Punish you myself. And I always knew it would only be a matter of time. I'd settle my own score."

Starr tugged hard on Sheila's hair, as if he'd just remembered that he had her. Her blue eyes were wide, and Caleb saw the fight still in them.

"The judge's bodyguard says she's not your wife, but this ferocious little chit has set her cap at you. And you're showing equal interest. How very nice! I get to do this again. I get to hurt someone who matters to you. And you have to watch it. I can't tell you how much pleasure it will give me to hear you beg for her life."

Caleb had done plenty of begging for his mother's life when he'd been a young boy. The words never mattered a damn. They wouldn't now.

Paddy started pounding on the floorboard Starr was standing on again. Crying out.

Caleb glanced down at the entry to the root cellar, and his father followed his gaze.

"Someone else you care about?"

Without taking his eyes off Caleb, he quickly aimed the pistol downward and fired once into the floor.

Sheila screamed and grabbed for the smoking gun as Caleb launched himself at Starr's throat.

Caleb's left fist traced an arc over Sheila's head and caught Elijah above the eye patch, snapping his head back and loosening his hold on her.

As he pulled Sheila away from his father, Caleb hammered the man with a right hook, staggering him and driving him back against the wall.

Elijah followed. The older man was not done. The knife appeared, and Caleb saw the gleaming blade coming at him, low and deadly. His left hand shot downward, grabbing Elijah's wrist even as he drove his right fist into his father's bloodied face. Caleb slammed the man's arm against the log wall, and the knife clattered to the floor.

Turning, Caleb slung his ancient foe across the room, going after him. They were on the floor. His iron fists were doing damage. After that, everything began to blur.

It all poured out of him. All the pent-up rage. All the desire for revenge. For his mother. For himself. For the children at the training school.

Caleb was on top of the man, pounding away at his face. Pounding relentlessly. Without any thought except hammering that face, making him pay for the painful history.

Suddenly, Sheila was on her knees beside him, clutching his shoulder. Her voice penetrated the bloody fog that filled his brain. He stopped, his fist still suspended in the air.

He looked at her. Her lips were moving.

"Stop. Please stop."

Her voice reached him from the end of a dark tunnel. Something clicked inside of him. He felt it in his head, in his chest. His fist opened.

In spite of it all, Elijah Starr could not stop. His face had the look of newly butchered meat. The eye patch was gone, and the empty socket was filled with blood. But still, his swollen lips lifted in a mocking sneer. "So weak! You still can't finish it. You're too much like her. You'll never be the man I am."

The desire to kill was there, edging back in. But Caleb stared down at the man's damaged face and knew the reason for his father's taunts. Elijah Starr had failed. In everything.

The shadow of the gallows hung over him. And if, by some miraculous event, he escaped that punishment, he had the lethal wrath of Eric Goulden to contend with. It was easier for him to die here.

Sheila's voice was there, pushing back the last of the darkness. "You are not him, Caleb. You're better than him. You are a *far* better man."

He looked into her calm, assured face and stood up.

Elijah Starr lay there, and Caleb wondered if he saw his fate ahead of him. He wondered if one shred of guilt or remorse existed in the man.

"You're *not* better than me," Starr rasped. "My eternal reward awaits."

"You're wrong." Caleb frowned down on him. "There are no sinners in heaven. No forgiveness in hell."

Paddy stood beside Sheila, unharmed by the bullet that had buried itself in the dirt next to him in the root cellar. She had her arm around him, and they both watched as Caleb half lifted, half dragged Elijah Starr out onto the porch.

Leaving him there, Caleb strapped on his gun belt. The judge sat slouched against the wall at the end of the porch. His eyes were closed.

Bear began to bark, pulling at the rope that bound him. Riders were coming across the meadow. Caleb drew his knife and cut the dog free. Bear immediately went to stand by Sheila and Paddy in the doorway.

Caleb retrieved the table and the bench and set them on the porch. He hauled Starr upright and plunked him on the seat. His battered head sank onto the table, landing in the exact spot where Judge Patterson's blood was staining the wood.

A moment later, horses thundered up to the cabin, and the rise was crowded with riders. Caleb moved off the porch to greet them.

Gabe jumped down from Pirate's back and ran to him, eyeing the dead bodies lying everywhere. "You done them all, Mr. Marlowe. You didn't need help."

"You done real good, Gabe. I'm proud of you."

Doc Burnett went directly to his daughter and held her in his arms for a moment before going over to tend to the judge. Malachi Rogers strode up, and the boys and the dog went off together, their mouths running.

Caleb directed one of the deputies to see to it that Elijah Starr was bound securely and readied for the ride into town.

"A dark day," Malachi said grimly. "But it could have been darker."

Caleb nodded. The men from town began dragging the bodies of the dead toward the cabin and laying them out in a line near the end of the porch. It wasn't a pretty sight.

Malachi filled him in on what had transpired in town. Apparently, Frissy had given

Zeke an order that supposedly came from the judge, directing him to go to the governor's office in Denver. When Gabe arrived, however, and told them what was happening at the ranch, Malachi and Doc managed to collar two of the sheriff's deputies and crib together a dozen men.

Caleb and Malachi walked over to where Doc was looking at the judge's shoulder and hand.

"Doc says I should live," Patterson said, a look of grim satisfaction on his face. "Well done, Marlowe. You kept the son of a bitch alive. Pardon the language, Miss Burnett."

Elijah Starr, bound and guarded, seemed to have withdrawn into himself. The fact that he was still breathing was only due to Sheila. Caleb studied his father for a moment and realized that the anger and guilt that had been weighing him down for years seemed to be less of a burden now. But it was still there. His mother was dead. Nothing would ever change that. He wondered if he'd ever be free of that weight.

There was an old saying about vengeance being a double-edged sword. Caleb didn't know what the future would bring or how he'd meet his own end. But he knew one thing: today he laid down the sword he'd been carrying for a long time.

Patterson broke into his thoughts. "I won't forget what you did, Marlowe. And you can be assured, Starr is going to hang. For all his crimes."

Caleb said nothing, wondering how much Patterson had heard of the words that were exchanged inside. This was a man he would never trust, no matter how much sweet-talking he did now. He knew there could easily come a time when the judge would want something from him. And he would use Caleb's past against him, sure as hell. If he knew it.

So Elijah Starr would hang. But his blood flowed in Caleb's veins. *The sins of the father . . .*

Whatever bond connected them had been severed because of the abuse this man had used to destroy Caleb's mother. And he recalled another line from his youth, one that he'd paid little attention to in the past decade. *Nor shall children be put to death because of their fathers.*

Still, as he glanced at Sheila, now standing behind Doc, the words gave him little comfort.

Her eyes were fixed on the bodies of the men he'd killed. Her face was pale, one hand pressed against her lips as if to quiet a cry.

He recalled the night he met her. Shock and anger had burst from her when she saw the rustlers lying dead and dying in his meadow not fifty yards from this spot. She'd shown more courage than common sense, and she'd lectured him about the senselessness of the killing. She didn't care who was at fault or who'd instigated the fight. Her upbringing, her naiveté, made her value life. Even worthless life.

He remembered thinking that night that it must have been the first time she'd ever seen men gunned down and dead. This time, there was no darkness to hide the carnage. Here, in plain sight, was death beneath a bright Colorado sky.

Caleb stared at the bodies, trying to see them through Sheila's eyes.

Next to Frissy, with his mangled face, lay men who had felt the cold blade of his knife and the scorching heat of his bullets as they tore through their flesh. Men whose names he would never know. Men who had histories and families. Like Bat Davis — who'd grown up in the same town as Caleb — they had childhoods. Hopes. Dreams. Now they had only endless darkness. Blood, slowly seeping into the soil, marked the places where they'd fallen.

Blood he had spilled.

He gazed at Sheila's face. She hadn't moved, but he saw tears welling in her eyes.

You are not him. You're better than him. You are a far better man.

How much better? Caleb thought. For whatever reason, these men were still dead. Like his mother. Still dead.

Would he kill again? Caleb knew that he would. Some men deserved to die. These men deserved to die. This was the world he lived in. But not the world Sheila Burnett was accustomed to.

He moved closer to her. He took her hand in his. Her palm was cold as ice, and he felt the tremors in her flesh. She didn't close her fingers over his.

He had so much he wanted to say to her. About his past. About the uncertainty of his future. And about the killer instinct that resided in him, that kept him on the shadowy fringe of decent society.

He had to explain that regardless of how they'd acted toward each other before, he didn't deserve her. Never would.

EPILOGUE

Six weeks later

The newspapers were making a mess of everything, as far as Caleb was concerned.

For weeks, every rag from St. Louis to Santa Fe had been touting the eclipse like it was the Second Coming. In fact, more than a few traveling preachers were doing just that, proclaiming at the top of their lungs with all the fire and brimstone they could muster that the end was near.

The *Denver Post* was the worst, promoting the exact time and date of the eclipse and crowing that the phenomenon would not be visible in its totality in any other established state except for Colorado. The Rocky Mountains and its crystal-clear skies would provide the finest vantage point in the world. And the judge was doing his damnedest to draw people to Elkhorn, where they could "view the once-in-a-lifetime spectacle in absolute safety and

413

comfort."

No one seemed to recall that it rained in the summer.

Apparently, word had spread to the rest of the country. According to a bunch of egg-heads at some university back East, this would be the first time in history that an eclipse would be observed at such a high altitude. Caleb couldn't help but wonder how the Arapaho and the Cheyenne felt about that claim.

In any case, Congress saw an opportunity to appropriate thousands of dollars to fund official observations in Colorado. Now, with the money carefully funneled into a few deep pockets, everything was set.

Judge Patterson was banking that the celebration would be the making of him. He figured that a successful eclipse would heap fame and fortune on him and further his political aspirations. Newsmen with their pads of paper and those big boxes with legs for taking photographs would be on hand to record the blessed event, and politicians from the nation's capital were expected to be in attendance.

The hotels and businesses in Elkhorn waited with bated breath, however. Despite all the planning and hoopla, no one really knew if people would actually come.

Caleb ignored the whole business. After the bodies of Starr's men were carted away, he went about fixing up the damage to his ranch. And aside from his everyday chores, he had construction projects that needed his attention. He wanted to be ready for the herd of young longhorns being driven up from Texas to add to his cattle.

Elijah Starr's trial was put off until after the eclipse. From what Zeke told him, the prisoner was unwilling to confess to anything that would implicate his employer. And not a word had been whispered about his relationship with Caleb. He just sat in his cell, unpleasant when he wasn't morose. Starr was apparently willing to accept his fate and hang for his crimes. Caleb didn't waste any time thinking about him. His father was dead to him. And that was going to be his answer if anyone, at any time, tried to push the past into his face.

News of the gunfight and Starr's arrest had traveled, though. Eric Goulden's plans had suddenly changed. He couldn't come to Elkhorn for the eclipse after all. In fact, his plans for putting a railroad through the region were on hold . . . indefinitely.

The eclipse was to take place on Monday, the twenty-ninth of July, and to everyone's collective relief, something glorious hap-

415

pened. A week before the sun was scheduled to disappear, a thousand prayers were answered.

Folks started arriving.

Stagecoaches. Riders. Wagons. People poured in every day, and Elkhorn filled up worse than before. As soon as the hotels and inns were jammed to capacity, enterprising local citizens began taking in borders, even housing enthusiastic sunwatchers in their barns. Zeke told Caleb that the saloon keepers were putting together card tables for use as rentable sleeping accommodations.

Elkhorn wasn't the only place cashing in on the boon. The newspaper reported that wealthy residents from all over the country were visiting some new "resort hotels" at some place called Colorado Springs and bringing plenty of cash to spend. All kinds of high-spirited mischief was going on, apparently, including the importation of musical orchestras to entertain the masses.

Judge Patterson, not to be outdone, was hosting an outdoor event in Elkhorn's Main Street. It was to take place on Sunday afternoon — to the chagrin of the local religious set — the day before the eclipse. He'd sent a personal invitation for Caleb to attend and had received a one-word answer. *No.*

Hours of political speechifying, followed by a reception where he'd have to mingle with strangers, just wasn't all that appealing. Zeke riding out and begging him to come was a waste of the burly little sheriff's time. He wasn't going.

Somehow, the judge must have gotten to Doc Burnett too. One night two weeks ago, while they were playing chess on his friend's porch, Doc slyly brought it up. Caleb told him the same thing. No.

There was a reason why he'd settled outside of Elkhorn. He wanted no part of this madness.

With the celebrations only a few days off, Caleb thought he was safe. He wasn't. Gabe and Paddy showed up with a letter from Sheila.

This was the first he'd heard from her since the shooting at his ranch. Even the night of playing chess with Doc, he was told she'd gone to bed early. Caleb figured she had some thinking to do; so did he.

He understood that what she'd witnessed, what Caleb had done, was troubling for her. She liked him. And he liked her more than he would ever put into words. But they were two different people. And right now he needed to keep his head screwed on tight and not let it go off on flights of fancy about

417

things he could never have.

Then Gabe and Paddy brought the letter from her. In it, she asked if he would kindly accompany her to a shooting competition that was taking place on the same Sunday afternoon.

She was competing.

He sent a message back with the boys.

He'd be there.

For six weeks, they hadn't seen each other, but he'd been hearing news of her from Gabe and Paddy and Doc and Zeke and everyone else he ran into in Elkhorn. Everyone just assumed he'd be interested in knowing what she was up to. Not that he would admit it to any damn one of them, but he was.

The stories he'd been hearing all ran about the same. Sheila seemed unable to say no to requests for help on the various civic projects taking place, and there were plenty of them in Elkhorn because of the big event. He was glad she was staying busy, glad she was finding a place among the townspeople.

Doc mentioned that she'd also been taking shooting lessons from Zeke. Caleb was amused, but he pretended to be mildly insulted that she hadn't asked him.

So on that Sunday afternoon, Caleb rode

along Main Street, trying not to growl at the hundreds of people packing the thoroughfare. He shook his head in disbelief at the folks who were already positioning themselves on their rented chairs, staring at the sky.

"There's a whole damn day left," he muttered, nudging Pirate along.

At least the fine weather was holding.

At the bustling livery stable, he exchanged a quick hello with Malachi and the boys before walking over to the Burnett house. Looking back up Main Street, he could see ropes with colorful ribbons were being strung across the road in front of Patterson's court building for the reception. He wasn't sorry to be missing that foolishness.

The sight on the porch that greeted him as he approached the house was the prettiest thing he'd seen in a while.

Miss Sheila Burnett was dressed in one of what he'd come to call her "New York outfits."

When she spotted him, she immediately stood up. The long-waisted, cream-colored dress fit her form like a glove, and he couldn't avoid noticing the many attributes of her womanly figure. The attraction of the wide-brimmed hat and the fancy hair was lost on him, however. In the little time they'd known each other, he'd become quite fond of the wayward curls and the long, thick braid of golden-brown hair. Her blue eyes put even the azure sky above to shame.

He pushed aside such poetic notions. What mattered most was that she looked healthy and happy. There was none of the confusion and fear he'd seen in her face with all those dead bodies lying around on his ranch.

And there was an uncharacteristic shyness in her look and the way she came down the stairs to greet him.

"Thank goodness you're here, Marlowe. We have to go."

There were things that he thought should be said before they went anywhere. "I reckon I have some explaining to do."

"About what?"

"About what you heard between me and Elijah Starr."

She gazed down at the tips of her shoes for a few seconds before looking up. "No, you don't."

"No one in Elkhorn knows my business with him as much as you. I'll answer any questions you have."

"I know enough . . . . for now. Maybe someday I'll ask more. And I meant what I said to you that day. You are not him." Her fingers rested for a brief moment on his arm. "We should go."

He was tempted to lean down and kiss her lips. He wanted to hold her. But he did neither.

"Are you planning to shoot, dressed like that?"

"Of course not! The competition was yesterday."

"Yesterday?" Caleb frowned. He was certain he'd gotten the message correctly. "But your letter said —"

"I didn't want you there. What if I embarrassed myself?"

He glared at her. "So you actually dragged me here for Judge Patterson's shindig."

She smiled and ignored the question. "Aren't you even going to ask how I did in the shooting competition?"

This was the way he liked their relationship. Safe. She all happy, and he all grumbly. But Caleb still tended to lose the direction of his thoughts when Sheila batted her eyes at him. Like she was doing now. Clearly, she was pretty proud of herself.

"How did you do?"

"I made it past the first round. Thank you for asking. The second round, we had to shoot nine-inch china plates from a hundred feet."

"How did you do?" he asked again. He was trainable.

"I broke three out of fifteen. Not nearly good enough. But I'll be practicing for next year."

"Far as I know, there ain't any eclipses next year."

"I believe they're already planning the event for Independence Day."

"So, then, you gonna keep taking lessons from that old boar hog of a sheriff?"

"I'd prefer to take them from you."

Hell, yeah.

She grabbed his hand, forcing him to walk with her. "We should be going, Marlowe."

"Your father was crowing that you're getting to be quite the chess player."

"I'm much better at chess than shooting. I'm looking forward to playing a game with you."

He knew she was taking him to Patterson's event, but he no longer cared. At least he'd be there with Sheila.

"Come on. I was given only one job today, and that was to get you to show up on time."

It took only a few minutes to reach the stands that had been set up for the invited luminaries. Crowds had already gathered for the speeches, and she led him directly to where Doc and Zeke were standing. Both were dressed in their finest clothes.

And neither of them seemed surprised to see him.

A moment later, Judge Patterson himself left a group he was talking to. He'd only this week left off wearing the sling that kept his shoulder immobile.

"Marlowe, you made it. Very glad. Very!"

"Judge." Caleb accepted the man's handshake and watched as Zeke and Doc wandered away with Sheila. "But I don't know why I'm here. You've got your hands full." He glanced around to see if they had an audience. No one seemed to be paying attention.

"You've done well by me, Marlowe. But I don't like to owe people favors. So here we go. A favor returned. As promised."

Patterson was pointing at a tall man who was speaking with Doc and Sheila. The man laughed at something she said.

There was no one south of the Badlands with a laugh like that. Beneath his wide-brimmed black hat, the man was wearing a brown leather vest and tan wool pants outside of his boots. The newcomer was a little shorter than Caleb, and his thick, brown hair hung nearly to his shoulders.

"It took some doing, after all, Marlowe. In fact, I'd say now you owe me."

"Think what you like, Judge. I say we're square."

Upon turning his back, Caleb strode over and put a hand on the man's shoulder. "Henry."

"Caleb."

The two looked at each other and nodded as Doc and Sheila moved off to the refreshment stand.

"Glad to see me?"

"Thought I was gonna have to build that whole damn ranch on my own."

"Make our fortune yet in silver?"

Caleb scoffed.

"Well," Henry replied, casting an appreciative glance at Sheila, "looks like you've been busy in other ways."

"It ain't what you think."

"Glad to hear it. That's good for me."

Caleb felt his hackles rise, but Henry just laughed and slapped him on the shoulder.

"So, my friend, tell me about this ranch of ours."

The two of them walked off to the side a little. Caleb and his partner had plenty to talk about.

■ ■ ■ ■

GET A SNEAK PEEK OF
CALEB MARLOWE'S NEXT
ACTION-PACKED
ADVENTURE IN
Silver Trail
Christmas

■ ■ ■ ■

CHAPTER ONE

Elkhorn, Colorado, September 1878

The hackles rose on Caleb Marlowe's neck, and a chill prickled his scalp. In his fist, the hammer hung poised, ready to strike the nail home. He rolled his broad shoulders and raised his eyes from the barn roof he was about a day from finishing.

This was the way with him. Caleb sensed trouble before it barreled through the door. The instinct had kept him alive more times than he could count.

Near the edge of the rise where the ranch buildings were taking shape, Bear was on his feet and looking to the southeast. The large, yellow dog had smelled something on the crisp, midmorning breeze.

The speck of a distant rider appeared at the crest of a far-off hill and then disappeared. A moment later, he came into view again. He was coming hard.

Caleb knew instantly who it was. He'd

know Henry Jordan in a dust storm a mile away. His partner had gone off this morning to round up two stray steers that wandered downriver. And the only time he'd ever seen Henry push a horse this hard, the fellow had a Cheyenne war party pounding along behind him.

Caleb stared out beyond the approaching rider, but he could see no one on his tail.

Henry was one of those people trouble trailed after like a hungry wolf. He didn't have to go out looking for it. He'd just turn around, and there it was. Once that happened, Henry's fierce temper blazed to the surface, and his customary good nature went up in smoke as quick as dry prairie grass in a lightning storm. He was strong and fast and deadly as a rattler once he got started. All kinds of mayhem generally broke out then.

Surprisingly, nobody died in the fight he'd won in a Denver saloon this past winter, but the damn thing had cost him six months in jail. And Caleb had to deal with the devil himself to get Henry out.

Caleb glanced over at the bucket holding his gun belt and twin Colt Frontiers. After laying down his hammer, Caleb worked his way over. Keeping his eyes on the far end of the valley — as far as he can see, anyway —

he strapped on his guns and started for the ladder. Whatever was bringing Henry back without those steers, he had a good idea the roof was going to have to wait.

He picked up his Winchester '73 from against the barn wall and stalked over toward the corral. As he reached the gate, Henry roared in like an Express rider bringing bad news from the battlefield.

"We got trouble, partner," he shouted breathlessly as he reined in. Henry pointed at the line of forested bluffs that formed the eastern border of their property. "Up there near the waterfall."

"What kind of trouble?"

"There's fellas up there working our land." He pulled his black, wide-brimmed hat off and ran a hand through the long, brown hair that hung nearly to his shoulders. "At least, I think it's our land."

"This side of the ridge?"

Henry nodded.

"It's our land." Caleb peered at the black cattle grazing along the river in the valley below them. "You think they're after the herd?"

"They're prospecting."

Even after months of trying to carve a ranch out of this valley, Caleb had not quite settled into the idea that owning a piece of

God's country meant you had to protect it. But he was learning. A while back, when six rustlers decided that they could just take his cattle, he'd suggested otherwise. That little incident didn't turn out quite the way those boys reckoned. They were now residing on Elkhorn's Boot Hill.

"On our land?"

"How many times I got to say it, Marlowe?"

As Caleb considered it, he knew that the last thing they wanted was to have prospectors find anything out here. When they discovered gold on Sutter's land in California, the poor bastard lost everything. Trying to keep 49ers off his land was like trying to keep fleas off an old dog.

"How many?"

"Four that I saw."

"Recognize any of 'em?"

"Nope."

"Talk to 'em?"

Henry shook his head. "I was thinking about running 'em off. But then I recalled what you been saying about me staying clear of law problems. So I came back for you."

"Well, that was damn thoughtful, partner." Caleb pulled his saddle off the fence and swung it up onto Pirate's back. The buckskin had been watching and listening, and

Caleb was certain he already knew they were heading out. "Glad you were able to keep in mind that this ranch will require the both of us."

Caleb and Henry rode south across the grass-covered valley for over an hour then turned east and moved up into forested foothills. Ahead of them, the long, rugged ridge rose above the tall pines, forming the boundary between the ranch and land belonging to Frank Stubbs, their neighbor.

Beyond the ridgeline, the Stubbs claim consisted of large areas of forest and open range, but their neighbor was only interested in the precious minerals that could be carved from the earth. Caleb had already had a few brushes with Frank Stubbs and knew him to be a tough, grasping, miserable bastard — a hard drinker with a penchant for bullying anyone he saw as somehow beneath him. The property border was clear, however, and good ridgelines made good neighbors. More or less.

When the two partners reached a ravine that led roughly southwest, they followed a creek that twisted and tumbled toward the valley lowland.

Caleb's plan was to approach the trespassers from above.

He knew the terrain. He'd been hunting here since he'd picked up the papers at the land office in Elkhorn back in January. He knew where the groves of cottonwood and aspen had fought to establish their space amongst the pines and other evergreens. He knew every ravine and wash and gulley, every mountain spring and creek. The ponds and small lakes formed by the lay of the land and the industry of beavers. The rocky bluffs and ledges where cougars and bears found shelter. The grassy meadows dotted with wildflowers in spring, now yellow as autumn encroached. Soon, it would all be covered by the deep snows of the long mountain winter.

"We're getting close," Henry told him when they reined in at the edge of the creek. The stream here was wide and shallow, with round, gleaming stones protruding from the surface of the rippling water. "I saw 'em where the gulley broadens out by the pond just before it drops over the waterfall."

Caleb nodded. Sure as hell, these fellas had to be panning for gold. Not three miles north of their ranch, miners were busily digging silver out of the hills that ringed Elkhorn, but he'd heard some talk of gold occasionally showing up as well.

He looked back at the ridge and then

gestured downward at the muddy edge of the creek. Hoofprints.

"Guess those would be our boys," Henry said.

"Yep. From the looks of things, these fellas came down onto our land from the ridge."

"From Frank Stubbs's land."

"They are fortunate men. If Stubbs spotted these knotheads on his side, he'd already have their carcasses nailed to his barn door."

Henry grinned. "If'n you ever finish that barn, we'd have a door to nail 'em up on."

Giving him a look, Caleb nudged his buckskin forward. But they hadn't even crossed the stream when two gunshots rang out.

Immediately, Henry had his rifle out of its scabbard and looked around.

"A revolver. A quarter mile that way," Caleb said.

"Maybe our trespassers decided to shoot one another. That'd save us some work."

"Too much to hope for."

The two men dismounted on the other side of the creek, tied their animals, and approached on foot.

The forest floor was a carpet of pine needles, and they moved through the forest silently. The land began to drop off, and it wasn't long before the sound of voices reached them, along with the smells of a dying campfire and burnt coffee.

When they reached a ridge at the top of the wide gulley, Caleb signaled to his partner. They moved past a grove of cotton-wood trees until they reached a small rise that afforded a good view. They were eighty yards from the edge of a wide pond below. In front of them, the terrain dropped off steeply. The sun was still high overhead. Between their vantage point and the creek, the grassy hillside was dotted with boulders and brush.

Lying on their bellies, they peered down into the gulley.

Below them, in a clearing on the near side of the wide creek, a slovenly camp had been thrown together. A few tarps had been hung over lines stretched between yellow-leafed cottonwood trees. Saddles and bedrolls lay beneath them. Smoke from a smoldering fire hung like a cloud over the camp.

Henry nudged him and held up four fingers. Caleb nodded.

Three tough-looking fellows were working with pans in the shallows. Shovels were stuck into the gravel at the edge of the pond. The fourth, stripped down to his breeches but wearing a pair of Remington six-shooters strapped to his hips, was busily butchering one of Caleb and Henry's stray steers by the edge of the camp, grunting as he cut into the belly hide. It must have been the steer that took the two slugs they heard being fired.

"Not too neighborly," Caleb said under his breath.

Saddlebags and gear lay in heaps by the fire, and Caleb spotted a pair of Winchester '73s, a Henry Yellow Boy, and a seven-shot Spencer carbine. Two more braces of Remingtons and a pair of short-barreled Colts lay in bundled coils close to the shoreline. In a wide, grassy spot just to the south of the camp, four horses grazed contentedly by as many saddles. Good horses, from the look of them.

Caleb only needed a glance to know these fellas were not typical prospectors. The pans and shovels they were using were still shiny, undented, and new. These chuckleheads weren't greenhorns, though. In fact, from the shooting irons they were packing, he'd bet his last dollar they were road agents laying low and hoping to strike it rich while they were doing it. Their one mistake was trying to do it on his and Henry's land.

One of them, big and burly and filthy as a hog, stood up, stretched his back, and threw his pan on the bank with disgust, cursing and eying his partners with disdain.

"Damn me but if that one ain't trouble," Henry whispered.

"They all are."

The big man's wide-brimmed hat was battered and had an ornate, beaded band at the base of the crown. He took it off and squinted at the sun. In spite of the cool bite to the air, sweat glistened off his not-so-recently shaved scalp. Stomping out of the shallows, he threw himself down in the gravel next to the Colts, propping himself up on one elbow.

The other two in the water noticed him and straightened up.

"You lazy shit, Dog," one of them scoffed. He was the shortest of the bunch, stocky and grizzled, with a ratty wisp of beard. "Not even one full day we been at this, and you're already quitting."

"Weren't this *your* idea?" the other huffed. He was tall and lanky, and his moustache drooped over this mouth, rendering his lips practically invisible.

"That's right," Rat Beard groused. "If you ain't kilt that lawman up north, we wouldn't even be here in Colorado."

Henry and Caleb exchanged a look.

Dog drew one of the short-barreled Colts

from its holster and sat up, cocking the hammer and pointing it first at one of his partners and then at the other. The two men stiffened, edging backward into deeper water, and Caleb saw the fellow butchering the steer had moved one hand cautiously to the grip of his Remington revolver.

Dog's Colt barked twice, and water splashed up between the men, who dove to the side, away from the line of fire. The gunhawk guffawed and slid the Colt back into its holster.

The men came to their feet, soaked through, cursing under their breaths and sending evil looks at the shooter.

"Whad'ja do that fer?" Moustache shouted angrily, wiping water from his long, thin face.

"Reckoned you needed a bath," Dog sneered.

"You had no call fer drawing on us."

Dog stood, strapping on his gun belt, silencing the men. "Who's the chief of this here outfit, Humboldt?"

The gaunt-faced man stared a moment, then averted his eyes. "You, Mad Dog."

"That's right." Dog swiveled his gaze to the stocky little man. "Unless you think you're boss man, Rivers."

Henry had edged away to his right, where

a tuft of grass made a good rest for the muzzle of his rifle. He knew how to position himself for a fight. The cottonwoods and pine and a jumbled stack of boulders behind them offered added protection.

Rivers shook his head.

"That's right," Dog crowed. "Then, do you no-account shit-for-brains got anything else you wanna say?"

The men stood still as rocks, and Caleb could practically see their frustrated anger — and fear — rippling across the surface of the water.

After a moment, the one called Rivers found his tongue, grumbling, "Just meant that this'll be easier once we get a long-tom set up, so's we can sluice this gravel."

"If you know so damn much about prospecting, you little shit, how come you ain't rich already?"

"Knowing how to do it ain't the same as being lucky."

"Well, you better hope your luck overall ain't running out."

Rivers scowled but said nothing. As he retrieved his pan from the shallows, Caleb saw him glance up at his gun belt a few feet away.

If that fella's fool enough to go for his gun, Caleb thought, he's a dead man.

Mad Dog saw the look too. "Two things, John Rivers. One, anytime you think you can take me, you'd best remember I can out-draw you any day of the week. And two, I got eyes in the back of my head, so if you think you can plug me in the back, think again."

The names suddenly rang a bell. Caleb knew them. John Rivers. Gustav Humboldt. And Mad Dog McCord. That would make the fellow butchering his steer either Lenny Smith or Slim Basher.

He'd heard of them when he was wearing a tin star up north. That was over two years ago. He'd found himself roped into serving as a lawman in Greeley after making a name for himself scouting and hunting with Old Jake Bell and leading folks across the western frontier from the Bighorn Mountains to the Calabasas. This gang never ventured into his town, though. And after the army conscripted him to work for them as a scout for a year, he didn't figure he'd ever cross gun barrels with the likes of Mad Dog and Rivers.

They were tough hombres. They'd made a name for themselves hitting rail depots, Wells Fargo stagecoaches, and the occasional solitary homesteader wagon making its way through the Black Hills of

Wyoming. Stone-cold killers, every one of them.

Caleb nudged his partner, whispering, "Stay here. Watch the butcher in particular."

Henry nodded, eased back the hammer on his Winchester, and swiveled the barrel of the rifle in that direction. Caleb saw he'd have a clear shot.

Below them, closer to the creek, a pair of cottonwoods cast their shade over the trunk of a fallen tree. Caleb decided that was as good a place as any to call out to these blackguards. He could use the fallen trunk for cover if he needed it.

Getting there unseen would take some doing, though. The steep, grassy slope was mostly wide open, though it was dotted with boulders and clumps of scrub pine. In addition to the cottonwoods, several groves of aspen had established themselves on the hillside farther from the creek.

Leaving Henry, Caleb backtracked along the ridge. When he reached one of the aspen groves, he moved stealthily down the hill to the cottonwoods.

When he tossed that tin badge on the table in Greeley, Caleb told himself he was done with it. Never again did he want to spend his time gunning down outlaws in the streets of a town where the exploits of low-down vermin like these fellas made them heroes to schoolboys and merchants alike. It was true that he could find an albino mountain goat in a winter storm and track a water moccasin across a rushing river, but he had no interest in going after lawbreakers for the bounty money either. A man might as well shoot rats in a slaughterhouse for a living.

Right now, Caleb was not looking to shed blood. He just wanted these villains off his land.

As he reached the fallen cottonwood, he scanned the scene below him. The butcher had gone back to his work, and the two working the shallows had come up by the shore to shovel more gravel into their pans.

The sun was slightly behind Caleb, and he took his position in the shade beneath the spreading branches of the cottonwoods. The outlaws were in full sun, a good forty yards from him. Only the butcher had any chance of getting to the cover of the trees, but Henry would take care of him. Considering they'd only have their pistols, these boys would need to get off a good shot even to wing him. They'd never come close. Not with him and Henry raining lead down from the hill.

Caleb unhooked the thongs over the hammers of his Colts. Cocking his Winchester, he raised the rifle nearly to his shoulder.

"Listen up, fellas," he called out sharply. "And keep your paws clear of them irons."

Four surprised sets of eyes swung toward him.

"No need to get riled. But you're gonna pack your things and clear out. Got me?"

Mad Dog's hand drifted toward a short-barreled Colt, and the movement was not lost on Caleb. His Winchester barked, and the slug buried itself in the gravel two feet in front of McCord, spraying stones and sand at the big man, who flinched and raised his hands. The sound of the shot echoed off the woods and along the valley, louder and more authoritative than the pistol shots that had alerted Caleb and Henry earlier.

Caleb swiveled his rifle toward the butcher, who stood with his hands raised, a bloody knife in one of them. There appeared to be no interest in getting into it from that quarter. He swung the barrel back to the others.

"What do you want?" Mad Dog growled. "We ain't making no trouble here."

"That depends on what you call trouble. You're prospecting on my land and fixing to eat one of my steers. That sounds like trouble to me."

"That all?" The outlaw visibly relaxed, lowering his hands a little. "Well, hell, we're sure sorry about that. Ain't we, boys?"

"We sure are, mister," John Rivers agreed, jerking his bearded chin toward the butcher, who was nodding adamantly. "We found that steer a-wandering. It's an honest mistake, friend."

Mistake. Caleb eyed them coolly. He knew these four would happily put a bullet or two in him, mistake or no.

"Well, then, you can just leave that critter where he lies, put your gear on them horses, and get moving. Now."

"That ain't too Christian, fella," Mad Dog said, lowering his hands a little more. "We only reckoned we'd —"

"Don't test me, pilgrim," Caleb replied. "Or you'll be explaining to your Maker how Christian a fella you been. Now get moving."

The two outlaws behind him were edging closer to their gun belts. Caleb felt his hackles rising again. Some boys absolutely didn't know when to fold their hand and walk away.

"How about if'n we pay you for that meat?" Mad Dog suggested with all the charm of a fat, mealy worm. "And the use of your creek here for a few days? A week or so, at most. We ain't fixing to be bad neighbors."

He shook his head. "No deal. You got nothing I want. Now, get moving, or the wolves will be dining on your mangy carcasses tonight."

Mad Dog's eyes narrowed, and his face darkened. Caleb could see he was calculating whether he could muster enough accuracy with those short-barreled Colts to drop him at this distance.

Before the killer could decide whether to throw down or live to fight another day, the bark on the cottonwood trunk exploded next to Caleb's head, showering him with splintered wood.

ACKNOWLEDGMENTS

We want to start with Christa Désir, whose encouragement, invaluable advice, and sense of humor sent us on this exciting journey with Caleb Marlowe.

Many thanks to our publisher Sourcebooks for their support and energy and working endlessly to get everything right: Jess, Christa, Rachel, Stef, Heather, Dawn, Kelly, and everyone else on our fabulous team.

ABOUT THE AUTHOR

Nik James is a pseudonym for award-winning, *USA Today* bestselling authors Nikoo and Jim McGoldrick. They are the writing team behind over four dozen conflict-filled historical and contemporary novels and two works of nonfiction under various pseudonyms. They make their home in California.

The employees of Thorndike Press hope you have enjoyed this Large Print book. All our Thorndike, Wheeler, and Kennebec Large Print titles are designed for easy reading, and all our books are made to last. Other Thorndike Press Large Print books are available at your library, through selected bookstores, or directly from us.

For information about titles, please call:
(800) 223-1244

or visit our website at:
gale.com/thorndike

To share your comments, please write:

Publisher
Thorndike Press
10 Water St., Suite 310
Waterville, ME 04901